PLAY FOR ME

TAM DERUDDER JACKSON

Editor: Nikki Busch Editing
Cover Design: Steamy Designs
Formatting: Damonza
Distribution and POD: IngramSpark

Print ISBN number 9781736469514
Ebook ISBN number 9781736469521

Jack

When I made my deal with the devil, I thought I was on my way to my rock 'n' roll dream. Too bad I didn't read the fine print. Having it all meant giving up the only girl I knew I'd ever love. Five years later, I'm drumming in the hottest rock band in the country, but I live like a monk.

Fate hands me an opportunity to reconnect with my perfect girl, giving me one glorious night with Clio Barnes. Our chemistry is off the charts. Too bad fate plays by her own rules. When Clio hears my bandmate's idea of a joke, she believes I've used her, dissolved our love into a one-night stand, and she blows out of my life. When our tour ends, I'm determined to find her again, no matter how well she hides from me.

Clio

All my life, I've been invisible. For a brief moment five years ago, Jack Whitehorse saw me. And he made me feel like the center of his universe. But that was an illusion. Music was Jack's only love. A chance encounter after a Balefire concert allows us to reconnect, but once again, I'm playing second fiddle to his rock 'n' roll muse.

When the pregnancy test comes back positive, I decide to keep our baby secret. I can't force Jack to play for me—I wouldn't want to. Then he shows up unexpectedly one day, knocking on my door and demanding to be let in. He leaves me no choice but to tell him about the baby. Turns out, I wasn't the only one with a secret. But the one he's been keeping might end us for good.

For Bri Brasher Weigel
For all the laughs and your incredible support
You rock!

PROLOGUE

Five years ago
Jack

A S I STARED into the unblinking eyes of the shark, I couldn't escape the jaws of my own ambition. Harrison Barnes pushed the papers across the wide expanse of his mahogany desk. From the breast pocket inside his bespoke suit jacket, he produced a heavy gold-plated pen. Carefully, he placed it on top of the papers. I tried not to squirm in the deep leather chair as I stared at his fingers protectively—possessively—touching the cap end of that pen.

"Sign here."

The rain pounding silently against the insulated panes of the windows in Barnes's corner office froze into individual droplets. The pendulum directing the second hand of the antique wall clock stopped midmotion. One second before the eleventh hour. My breath hitched halfway into my lungs as my mind blurred into a vacuum of white space.

The pendulum finished its swing. Raindrops slid down the windowpane. The song "Nothing to Lose" played on a loop inside my head. I picked my hand up off my lap, reached across the desk, and grabbed that shiny pen. I pulled the cap off the tip and set it carefully aside. The page in front of me blurred for a second before righting itself as dark black ink flowed over the dotted line.

"And date it."

There was nothing ominous about scratching the numbers and slants, but something about seeing them beside my signature set off alarm bells in my head.

"And here."

Barnes slid another page across to me, and I repeated the ritual signing. At that moment, the jaws of the shark chomped down and bit me in two. "Of course, you read the fine print before you signed, correct?"

Fine print? What the hell? Trying to swallow my heart down my throat and back into my chest, I pulled the page closer and read.

"Are you kidding me? I can't talk to her in any form, anywhere? Not even to tell her about this?"

I didn't notice that I'd leaped at him across the expanse of his desk until I saw his hands braced against the edge of it, his body angled forward to meet mine, his eyes flashing a warning—or a challenge.

Yet his carefully modulated voice never changed inflection. "I believe that's how the contract reads. The one you just signed and dated."

I slammed my hand down on his expensive desk, the sound like a shot. "That's bullshit! You can't do this!"

"I can, son." His smile was feral. "Not only that, I did." He sat back and steepled his fingers over his chest. "Unless you'd rather not be the drummer in the hottest band to come out of Denver since Balefire. Unless you don't want to live your dream, take care of your family . . ."

Those alarm bells in my head crescendoed to give me a headache. "What's my family got to do with this?"

"As it turns out, your dad is in negotiations to be the subcontractor on the summer home I'm building on Mount Evans. Since this is a private rather than a government project, he can't claim his minority status to gain or maintain the contract. And I make final decisions on every aspect of the project . . ."

"You're saying if my dad is going to have work for the next year, if I'm going to have a shot at my dream, I don't talk to your daughter at all for the next two years." I deflated back into my chair, all the fight gone out of me at what Barnes could do to me and my family. At what my dreams cost me. "Why?"

"Because you're not the right man for her." He leaned forward, pinning me to my chair with his eyes. "And you never will be."

"You mean the man you want for her," I shot back through gritted teeth.

"It's the same thing."

When I'd walked into Harrison Barnes's office during my lunch break from classes, I thought I'd won the lottery. I was dating the perfect girl, and I was about to become the drummer for Rude Awakening and make some real money. When I graduated in a few weeks, I'd be on my way to giving her everything. When I walked back into my high school after my meeting, I couldn't even give Clio a smile when I saw her in the hall waiting for me.

"Jack, where have you been?"

I shook my head and kept walking.

"Jack? Are you in some kind of trouble?"

I nodded my head over my shoulder. Clio glanced behind me to see the goon in the three-piece suit Barnes sent to make sure I kept my word.

"Talk to me, Jack. Maybe I can help you."

"Can't." I swallowed against what had to come next. "We're done."

The hurt in her gorgeous gray eyes eviscerated me, and I had to get out of there. I sprinted down the hall in the direction of my history class as the tears in Clio's voice rang in my ears.

"Jack? Can we talk about this?" A sob stopped her voice. "Jack? What did I do?"

Dodging into a restroom outside my class, I barely made it to a stall before I heaved up my guts. A long time later when I finally had myself marginally together, I walked out to find Barnes's suit leaning against the wall, waiting for me. It was all I could do not to punch the look of elitist pity right off the guy's face. Instead, I went to class. I may have taken a step toward reaching my dream. I may have saved my family. But I sure as shit lost the only girl I knew I'd ever love.

CHAPTER ONE

Three Years Ago
Jack

DEZ GRABBED A handful of my leather jacket at the shoulder and tried to jerk me up from the nondescript chair I slumped down on in a generic room in a generic hotel in another generic town. We'd been on tour nonstop since I'd joined Rude Awakening at the end of my senior year in high school, and I needed a damn break. Mainly, I needed a break from the band. Not that our lead singer noticed—or cared.

"What the fuck, Whitehorse? We rocked the house tonight, and you're not joining the party. Again? What's up with you, man?"

"I don't feel like getting shitfaced tonight." I sighed. Truth was, drunk and stupid with the band wore on me. When I started playing with Rude Awakening, I partied because I thought I had to. After two years, I was over it.

"Yeah, like that's new," Dez complained, interrupting my thoughts. "There are some smokin' hot girls waiting down the hall in Ryan's room, and Blick scored some quality weed. You need to join us. Be a part of the band for once."

"Let it go, yeah? I left it all on the stage tonight, and I'm tired."

"You're twenty fuckin' years old. How the *fuck* can you be tired?"

I yanked away from his grip and stalked across the room, shoving my hands through my hair as I tried to control my temper. Ryan and Ross, the twins, and Blick, our manager, mostly left me alone, but Dez never gave up. "I said, let it go. I don't feel like partying. For the first time in a week I get to sleep in a real bed instead of a bunk on the bus, and I want to enjoy it for once."

"Fine, man. Have it your way. Jesus, when did you become such a fun-sucker?" he muttered as he headed for the door.

I flipped him the bird and headed into the bathroom to shower off the smoke and sweat of the concert. An actual shower instead of something out of a camper sounded almost as good as having a bed to myself. The bonus? Not dealing with the clank of bottles and the noxious stink of cigarettes and weed I usually put up with on the bus when I tried to sleep as we rolled down the road to the next gig.

'Course, Dez being Dez, I should have known he walked away too easy. I'd barely stepped under the spray and closed my eyes, letting the hot water ease my tense muscles when I felt cool air sliding over my body. Slitting open one eye, I was treated to the sight of a naked girl, all long golden hair and big tits. That's about all I could see of her through the steam.

Her breathy "Hey baby," seductive smile, and all that naked skin on offer should have turned me on in a heartbeat. I won't lie, my dick hardened up pretty fast. But a picture of intense gray eyes and a cascade of fire-red hair flashed across my brain, and another night of empty sex lost its appeal.

"Dez send you?"

"He said you were waiting for me. Looks like he was right."

She stepped closer and reached for me. I grabbed her hand before she could put it on the goods and held her away. "You probably shouldn't believe everything Dez says."

Reaching behind me, I turned off the spray, pushed the shower curtain aside, and stepped out. First, I handed her a towel, then I grabbed another and wrapped it around my waist. "Did you come from Ryan's room?"

"Yeah. He's really cute, but I wanted to be with you, Jack. You have so much power and energy onstage. I just know you're going to be something special in bed." Deliberately, she let the towel I handed her slip through her fingers.

"Here's the thing, darlin'. I don't want to be an asshole here, but I didn't ask for you, and I'm not sleeping with you."

"What do you mean? Am I not pretty enough for you?"

The pout on her face and the emotion in her voice alerted me to the inevitable waterworks. Back when I started with the band, tears would have made me give in, but after ten or twenty girls using that particular trick over the last two years, the ploy didn't work so much anymore. But she was a fan, and I had to think about social media and the band and all that happy shit. "You're gorgeous, a real hottie, but I'm beat. Tell me something. Did you even meet Ryan before Dez sent you to my room?"

"No, and I really wanted to meet him." The girl's lower lip covered her upper one as she pooched it out like a toddler on the edge of a tantrum. When she batted her eyes, I saw through the act.

The way she kind of lit up at Ryan's name gave me my out.

"Tell you what. Get dressed and I'll walk you back to Ryan's room. But I gotta tell you, Ross is the better lover of the two. I've heard that from every girl who's spent a night with him."

"Not you?" But she picked up the towel and started drying herself off.

"Oh, I'm awesome when I'm on my game. But I'm not on my game tonight, babe. Someone as pretty as you should be shown a super good time." I smiled at her as I let my eyes roam over her. Either I'm a much better actor than I thought or she was more drunk than she looked because she finished drying off and stepped back into her dress pretty fast. She wore only the tight red dress, a pair of damn sexy heels, and not a scrap of underwear. I had to hand it to her: the girl had come prepared for a good time.

After stepping back into my jeans, I pulled a clean T-shirt over my head and led Blondie by the hand back down to the party cranking in Ryan's room. We wove through the packed crowd until I found Ross with a beauty already seated on his lap.

"Ross this is—" I realized we hadn't made it to introductions before we'd seen each other naked, not that it mattered.

"Jade," the blonde supplied.

"Jade." Bending down, I whispered in his ear, "She has absolutely nothing on beneath that dress. Also, I might have mentioned how well you can satisfy a lady."

"You, Jack, are a gentleman and a scholar." Ross grinned. With renewed interest, he eyed Blondie down and up. "So, Jade, you like the show?"

"It was the best!" she gushed. "I don't know how you play all those notes so fast."

"I have talented hands. Why don't you sit down here and let me tell you about them?" He indicated his unoccupied knee, and the girl wasted no time perching there.

"Enjoy your evening, Ross," I said with a smirk.

"I'm sure I will, Jack. Don't bore yourself too much with *SportsCenter* or whatever it is you do by yourself."

I flipped him the finger, his laughter sounding in my ears as I walked over to the minibar. I grabbed a beer and made sure to catch Dez's eye as I tipped it back. A few minutes later, I slipped out through the crowd and wandered back to my room, locking the door with the deadbolt this time.

Tomorrow, we'd be back in Denver for a few days, right in time for Clio's high school graduation. And the end of my contract with Harrison Barnes. Dad had successfully bid on Barnes's luxury home construction, meaning he could put a little aside for my younger brother Cameron to go to college. So far, Barnes hadn't made good on his threat to blackball my dad's business, so I thought maybe I could take a chance. I hadn't talked to Clio in two long years, though I'd risked breaching my contract with her father whenever I Instagram stalked her via one of the guys' accounts. But I had to see her, or pictures of her at least, or I'd probably lose my damn mind.

In the two years since I walked away from her to follow my dream of drumming in a band, I worried she'd find someone else, someone in her social class who could set her up in the style she'd been raised in rather than someone who went to a private high school on scholarship. Maybe she'd hook up with someone who wouldn't take a chance on losing her to follow his dream. Of course, when I signed the contract with her father, I hadn't thought I'd have to give her up entirely. I thought I'd only be unable to date her physically for a while. We could still talk to each other at school and on the phone, text, communicate on social media. But Harrison Barnes wasn't a successful businessman because he skipped the fine print. Too bad I hadn't read it before I signed my ticket to stardom—and out of Clio's life completely.

From what I saw on her social media, it didn't look like she'd hooked up with anyone else during her last two years of high school. From the few posts she made, it seemed she only studied and worked on completing her required community service project for graduation. There were no new photos of her, though, and I wondered if she'd changed in the last two years. If anything, I bet she was even more beautiful than she was on our last date, her cheeks glowing, eyes shining, lips pink and swollen from my kisses. Thinking about her kisses left me hard, and for the thousandth time in the last two years, I wondered about my choices. Those kisses—tentative and soft one minute, demanding and hungry the next—turned me on more than any one-night stand I'd had since joining the band.

Before I met Clio my senior year, I thought music was the only girl I'd ever need. A life on the road, making music and scoring as much pussy as I wanted, the whole sex, drugs, and rock 'n' roll lifestyle, filled my dreams. Then one day she walked into my calculus class, this quiet sophomore with intense gray eyes, porcelain skin, and a gorgeous mane of auburn hair. The bonus was her scary-smart brain. It took me about a minute to figure out she was the whole package. Clio Barnes became my drug of choice, and I couldn't stay away from her.

For some reason, my interest in Clio surprised her, which made me want her even more. It took me a while to piece together that she was *that* Barnes, daughter of one of Denver's elite businessmen and heir to a multinational financial syndicate. Not that any of that mattered to me. Her beauty drew me in initially—I'm a guy after all—but her brains and goofy sense of humor kept me coming back for more. The way she kissed me, like she could never ever get enough? Yeah, that was a big draw. Whenever we were together, she made the rest of the world fade away.

This weekend, I was finally going to see her, talk to her, maybe explain some things, and I didn't have any room inside me to pretend interest in any other girl, even one as ready to give me sex as that groupie in my shower. Someone like Dez wouldn't understand my commitment to Clio, never in a million years.

♪

Thanks to the wild party the twins threw the night before, we rolled into Denver late the next morning. I didn't have time to stop at my parents' house before heading over to my old high school for the big event. When I arrived, I found the auditorium filled to capacity for Clio's graduation. Since I was late, I ended up standing against the back wall, but that was fine. I could still see the stage when the principal, some new guy since I graduated, introduced my baby as the valedictorian of her class.

When she stepped up to the podium, I lost my breath. All that beautiful hair I could remember tangling my hands in fell in soft curls and waves down her back. If anything, it looked like she'd let it grow even longer than when I'd seen her last. My hands itched to caress the porcelain skin of her cheeks, slide my fingers along the column of her neck. Even from a distance, her full pouty mouth begged me to kiss her for hours. Though her graduation robe hid her figure, she glided onto the stage with the grace of the dancer her mother always wanted her to be.

I don't remember much of what she said in her speech. She lost me in the husky timbre of her voice as she spoke clearly and confidently into the microphone. Another surprise. My sweet, quiet girl, the one who never wanted to draw attention to herself, didn't lack confidence. Apparently, she never saw the need to show off. Her father said something about breeding, how she would always stand out, attract lowlife guys like me because of her pedigree. Like she was some kind of showpony. Not even he understood how special she was. That much I figured out when he maneuvered me into giving her up.

I waited in the reception area right outside the auditorium, trying not to be rude to the few people who remembered me from high school or recognized me from Rude Awakening. When someone tried to engage me in conversation, I politely responded before discreetly moving away. It was a trick I'd had to learn dealing with groupies with cell phones who posted everything. I didn't want to be an asshole, but I had no intention of blowing my chance of seeing Clio, of talking to her.

I wasn't delusional. It had occurred to me on more than one occasion that she might not have any interest in talking to me. Scratch that. She'd probably blow me off after the way I disappeared from her life like I'd never known her. But that didn't mean I wouldn't seize the first opportunity I had to explain, to plead with her if necessary to listen to me, to give me another chance.

To trust me.

Unfortunately, Harrison Barnes spotted me before Clio looked my way. Abruptly, he hustled her out of the throng of people toward a door opposite where I stood waiting for her. It took me several minutes—and a couple of rude comments I wish I could have avoided—to force my way through the crowd to the door where I saw them leave. When I arrived there, I caught a glimpse of Clio's graduation robe as her parents all but pushed her into a waiting limousine. Before he joined his family, Harrison Barnes glanced back at the door. Seeing me standing there, he raised an eyebrow at me as if to say, *Did you honestly think I'd ever let you come back into my little girl's life?* Then he slid into the back of the car, the driver pulling away from the curb simultaneously with the finality of the slamming car door.

"Fuck!" I howled.

Sagging against the wall, I blew out a breath. As Harrison Barnes's long black limo rolled out of sight, I wondered if maybe he was right. Maybe I wasn't good enough for his beautiful girl.

CHAPTER TWO

Present Day
Clio

"SERIOUSLY, ANNABELLE, I don't think I want to start the semester hungover and missing class because of a concert," I said when the loudest and wildest of my sorority sisters made her offer of a free ticket to the Balefire concert in Denver.

"But Clio," she whined, "you love Balefire. I've seen your Spotify, and you have all their albums. At least one of their songs is on every playlist you listen to. Tell me again how you don't want to go to their concert with me." She batted her eyes and shot me her best grin.

"It's not that I don't want to go to their *concert*." I stretched out the last word. "I don't want to go on a Thursday night when I have a nine o'clock class Friday morning."

"It's the first week of classes. Honestly, Clio, how much are you going to miss?"

"Isn't there someone else in the house who wants to go?"

"Everyone wants to go, but I want to take you." She reached out and squeezed my hand. "Come on, Clio. The whole house knows you're the sole reason we've won the Panhellenic academic cup the last two years, but you're allowed some fun. That's what college is all about. Let your hair down for once and let's play." She turned her infectious grin up to full wattage.

Annabelle ricocheted around my small bedroom like an out-of-control ping-pong ball, mercifully only bouncing off my things rather than knocking my room into total chaos. I loved her. I truly did. But in small doses and with the buffer of several of our sorority sisters around us. She'd toned down about 150 percent since freshman year, but she still made the Energizer Bunny look anemic. The thought of spending an hour in a car with her plus the whole concert and the hour-long drive back from Denver exhausted me already, and I was still lounging comfortably on top of the plush duvet on my bed.

She picked up and put down my framed photo of Stacy and me when we pledged Chi Phi. Next, she ran her hand along the spines of the nursing books I'd shelved neatly at the back of my desk before she turned and picked up a sweater I'd tossed over a chair in the corner of the room. Holding it against her front, she checked herself out in the full-length mirror fastened to my closet door before she dropped the sweater on the floor.

"Clio." With her hands on her hips, she stared me down. "The concert is going to be epic, and no one else in the house is as big a fan of the band as you are. Which is why I *really* want you to go with me. Please?" She perched on the bed beside me and leaned over me, making the mattress bounce. "I'm driving and everything. Plus, my dad sprang for a hotel, so we can party and not worry about driving back until tomorrow afternoon." She ran her finger down my arm. Her tone wheedling, she said, "C'mon, Clio, you know you want to." She bounced once more on the edge of my bed and flopped herself down nearly on top of me.

A little part of me truly did want to go to the concert. A bigger part of me wanted to run to Wyoming and hide out like an outlaw in

South Pass or something until the band moved on to Seattle or Phoenix or LA or wherever they played their next show. What Annabelle didn't know—what none of my friends knew—was the boy who stole and stomped on my heart in high school had replaced Balefire's drummer when Dave Brubaker went into rehab two years ago. The thought of seeing Jack Whitehorse in the flesh, even from the safe distance of a packed concert venue, gave me an anxiety attack.

Still . . . I'd loved Balefire even before Jack abandoned his old band Rude Awakening to play with a group that had routinely filled stadiums for five years before he joined them. With the addition of his style of play, the band sounded even better, tighter, an opinion I shared with music critics all over rock radio and the internet. To see him again after nearly five years would be—what? A rush? A horror show? The biggest thrill ever?

Hearing that Jack had left Rude Awakening to join Balefire didn't surprise me. I knew all about how easily he could leave behind people he supposedly cared about. I'd been trying to forget him ever since he erased me from his life a couple of weeks after he took me to his senior prom. We'd dated exclusively for most of my sophomore year when one day he stopped calling, texting, talking to me. The next thing I knew, he'd unfriended me on social media and blocked my number on his phone. When I tried to talk to him in the math class we shared, he refused to even acknowledge me. I'd never felt so abandoned and humiliated in my life, and I couldn't figure out what I'd done to deserve it. Rather, I didn't want to believe Jack couldn't love me—that he saw me the same way everyone else did—quiet, unassuming, disappointing Clio Barnes. But the truth stared me in the face for the last two weeks of his senior year of high school and all the years since.

At the time, the news about him rocking an audition for Rude Awakening, an up-and-coming Denver rock band, blew through school, and it all clicked into place. He was moving on to much bigger things than a nerdy sophomore girlfriend. There would be all kinds of girls, most of them prettier and more experienced than I, groupies and minor celebrities and wild girls who wouldn't hesitate to give him anything he wanted. How could he pass that up to stay behind with someone he'd only dated for about a minute? Someone whose own parents considered her an afterthought?

It didn't matter that with his dark hair and sculpted body, incredible musical talent, and seemingly endless interest in me, he'd completely tilted my world on its axis. Apparently, I'd hidden my emotions exceptionally well. Or the chance at making his most precious dream come true took precedence. Either way, he hadn't thought twice about jettisoning me. A budding rock star didn't need the baggage of a girlfriend. Everyone knew that.

Still, erasing me from his life hurt even more than our breakup. If you could call it that. After all, I think people who break up with each other actually talk to each other or scream at each other or send a lame text to say it's over at least. Jack and I did none of those things. One day we were holding hands as we left math class, kissing each other outside the door to my science class before he sprinted to his band class because he couldn't stop kissing me to be on time. The next day, he made me invisible again. Exactly like I'd been before he discovered me. Exactly like I was at home.

If I went to the concert, the chances of being close enough for him to see me, let alone recognize me, were practically zero. The chance of talking to him even less than zero. Balefire would be playing at Red Rocks, which meant Annabelle and I would be so far back from the stage that all I'd probably see of Jack Whitehorse would be his drum kit and his flying sticks. So why shouldn't I go to the concert? What would it matter? I could see one of my all-time favorite bands and maybe erase my memories of Jack. Erase his kisses no other guy had been able to replicate no matter how many times I'd been kissed in the last five years. Maybe seeing him responding in his laidback, easygoing style to all the groupies vying for his attention would be the antidote to the love for him I hadn't been able to erase even after all this time.

What is it all the old people say about first love being the deepest, most intense? Yeah, that. Unfortunately, I could relate. No matter how many times I told myself I'd read too much into Jack's words when he told me how special I was or how unlike any other girl I was or how the best part of his day—even better than practicing his drums—was the time he spent with me, I'd remember the emotion in his eyes and still believe every word. Then I'd shake myself hard with the memories of a blocked phone number and the nasty comments of senior girls I passed in the halls at school when I wouldn't respond to the ugly rumors zipping across so many posts on Facebook.

I hated going to school after Jack dumped me.

"Hey, Clio. Where'd you go?" Annabelle asked, jerking me back to the present.

"Sorry. Trying to decide if missing classes tomorrow is worth it," I said, flinging my arm over my eyes with a melodramatic sigh. She couldn't read my mind, but I worried she could sense my heart racing at the thought of seeing Jack again after all this time.

"Oh, it's worth it, believe me."

Something knowing in her tone made me lift up on my elbows to stare closely at her, but in the next second, she pulled herself up to her knees and tossed her gorgeous mane of chestnut hair over her shoulder in one fluid movement.

"You know, Clio, with all your family's money, I don't understand why you still live here in the house," she said, glancing around my tiny third-floor room. "You could afford a sweet apartment off-campus, something cute down near Old Town."

"Yeah, but then I wouldn't have you and the other girls around for company, so what would be the point of being a member of Chi Phi?"

That was mostly true. What Annabelle and the others also never knew about me was that I paid for my education with a full-ride scholarship including any housing I wanted as long as it was university affiliated. My parents could afford to send me to Colorado State. Hell, my parents could afford to send me to Harvard, which was what they wanted. Harvard Business School, MBA, and a seat on the board of directors for Harrison's company. No thanks.

So, I'd disappointed them in the second biggest way possible— I'd taken the generous scholarship CSU offered and enrolled in the nursing program with a goal of becoming a nurse practitioner. A hands-on career helping others—that didn't include the word *doctor* in front of my name—would prove a colossal waste of my time and considerable brain, according to Harrison and Meredith.

Yeah, that considerable brain that should have been housed in a male body. I'd started life as a massive disappointment from the moment I took my first breath. Choosing nursing had been my rebellion against their elitist attitudes and a way to grab their attention, if only for a minute. Not that it lasted or even mattered in the end. Which was why my chosen profession mattered so much to me. I had to believe if my patients would *see* me, they'd appreciate me. My patients would matter to me—and I would matter to them.

In the sorority, I wasn't invisible, which was the main reason I loved living there. In the house, I mattered, if for no other reason than because I truly did carry the sorority's academics each semester. Taking honors classes covered that. Actually, attending my classes took care of that, I thought with an inward grin.

Yet . . . it had been almost five years since I'd seen Jack other than in concert videos on YouTube and Netflix. Yes, watching music videos of certain bands was a secret indulgence, videos that might or might not have been bookmarked on my computer. One of the perks of being an upperclassman in the sorority included a private room where I could crank up those videos and revel in the driving rhythms of Jack's drums without bothering a roommate or giving away my fantasies of a different ending—or no ending at all—to Jack's and my relationship.

Yet, maybe it was time to put away my rose-colored glasses and see my past for what it was—a painful lesson on the way to growing up. Facing one's demons described maturity, didn't it?

"What time is the concert?"

Annabelle's high-pitched squeal nearly split my eardrums in half as she pounced on me. "Clio! You're going with me! Yes! We're going to have so much fun," she shouted as she bounced off my bed. "Let's get ready together. I'll be right back with the outfits I'm thinking about, and we'll pick out something sexy for you too. I'll check with Stacy and see what she can loan you."

"Hey, are you implying I don't own anything sexy?" I said with a pout. I would have tried to sound hurt if I'd actually felt it.

"Does anyone ever try to raid your closet on the weekends?"

"No—"

"There's your answer. BRB!" Annabelle sang out as she dashed out of my room.

Sighing, I rolled over and buried my face in my pillow and seriously contemplated changing my mind. Before I could come up with an excuse, Annabelle reappeared in my room with an armload of clothes and my best friend Stacy Newhouse right behind her carrying more outfits. Turning my head to watch the procession crowding my space, I knew it was too late to back out.

"At least you have hot shoes, Clio. Whatever we pick out for you to wear, you'll have the right footwear," Stacy said as she dumped an armload of clothes on top of me.

"You're in on this plan too?" I asked.

"Annabelle said she wanted to take you to Balefire's concert. Knowing how much you love the band, I thought I'd help you get your groove on. Try this one." She handed me a sleeveless, black, sequined dress with fringe past the hem that pretended to hide that it barely covered my ass when I tried it on.

"Oooh, Clio, you look hot," Annabelle said as I tugged at the hem to avoid exposing my panties.

"That one shows off your coloring, but if you're going to tug at it all night, it's rather pointless." Stacy's grumpy voice left me trying to find a place for my hands anywhere but on the hem of her dress. She rolled her eyes and reached for another one. "Try this."

She handed me a lime-green dress with panels that crisscrossed my waist and fit me more like a swimsuit than a dress. Apparently when she'd dreamed up this one, the designer hadn't considered that the wearer might need to take a breath occasionally.

"I don't think I can go all night feeling like a sausage with legs. Especially not a lime-green sausage," I said as I sipped air. It took both of my friends to wrestle me out of that dress, leaving all three of us breathless.

Next came a black leather skirt and white bustier that I nixed without trying on even though both Stacy and Annabelle booed me. Stacy handed me a short periwinkle blue sheath dress with a lace overlay, cap sleeves, and a sweetheart neckline that hinted at my cleavage. It was classy and right at the edge of being too dressy for a concert. With my strappy silver stiletto sandals, the outfit bypassed sexy and ventured into mysteriously elegant. Annabelle stepped behind me and gathered my hair up into a messy bun, but left a few tendrils loose along the back of my neck. Even I had to admit the effect was pretty stunning.

"This is the one, Clio," Annabelle announced.

"You look so much better in that dress than I ever did. Consider it a gift," Stacy said with a smile.

"All right, Stace. You do Clio's makeup while I get dressed. The concert starts at seven, so we need to boogie out of here in the next half hour if we want to beat rush hour traffic and make it to the other side of Denver on time."

The two of them exchanged a look I couldn't follow before Stacy directed me to sit at my desk where the lighting was best. In all the clothes she carried, I hadn't noticed she'd also come prepared with her makeup bag. When it came to fixing her face, Stacy was the champ of all my sorority sisters. She turned my face in the light the way she wanted me, and I relaxed and let her work her magic. When I finally saw myself in the mirror ten minutes later, I couldn't believe the transformation. I looked like a kick-ass version of my real self.

A slow smile spread across my face. "Wow. I kind of look like me, but then again not. It's almost like I'm in disguise as my sexy alter ego."

"Yeah? Maybe you should spend the night *being* your sexy alter ego. Who knows what hot guy you might bring home?" Stacy winked at me in the mirror.

I stuck my tongue out at her. "Like that's gonna happen. I can already hear what Fern would have to say about me sneaking a guy into the house."

Our housemother, Fern, liked to play the part of sweet old lady with her soft-spoken Southern manners. But more than one of our sisters had found herself on the receiving end of a stern lecture whenever she tried to break a rule like sneak alcohol—or a man—into the house after hours or above the first floor. Having witnessed a couple of those lectures, I had no desire to experience one. Besides, I'd have to pick someone up and bring him all the way back to Fort Collins after the show. Not. Gonna. Happen.

The knowing look on Stacy's face said otherwise, and I huffed out a sigh.

"All I'm going to do is enjoy the concert. I've heard Balefire's pyrotechnics recreate the Fourth of July at every show." I laughed. "Like their music isn't enough. It's going to be fun—if I survive Annabelle's enthusiasm."

Stacy and I exchanged knowing grins.

At that moment, the woman in question bounded into the room, rocking a black leather-skirted dress. Though knee-length, the slit up the outside of her thigh showed off plenty of leg. A sheer black bodice pretended innocence with long sleeves and a Peter Pan collar buttoned up to her throat, but the black bandeau bra beneath it barely held in her girls. Somehow, she managed to look sexy rather than slutty even with her stacked-heel black leather ankle boots. It must have been the unstructured way she curled her hair and the light touch she'd taken with her makeup. At any rate, the girl looked stunning.

"You'd better pack an overnight bag quick, sister. We need to leave in ten minutes if we're going to move on the interstate at all," Annabelle said as she stepped in front of my mirror to check out her look.

I grabbed my duffel bag from the floor of my closet and stuffed in a pair of skinny jeans, a white tank top and a plain white button-up shirt, a pair of casual sandals, my toiletries bag, a pair of panties, and my makeup bag. "Quick enough for you?" I asked with a cocky grin.

"Don't forget your purse. Please tell me you have some condoms in it."

Shooting her a look, I said, "I won't need condoms, Annabelle."

"We're going to a concert for one of the biggest bands in the country. Literally thousands of cute guys will be there. Even you should be able to find one who meets your exacting standards." A smirk ruined her arch tone.

"Annabelle, make sure I have a key to our hotel room before you ditch me for a man, okay?" I sighed before turning to give Stacy a quick hug. "See you tomorrow, girlfriend."

"Tell me all about it," she said with a thumbs-up and a grin, but she was looking past me at Annabelle.

CHAPTER THREE

Clio

AS WE NEARED the city, Annabelle weaved her sweet blacked-out Mustang through the ever-intensifying traffic. Though I'd grown up in Denver, I never enjoyed driving there. Soon, three lanes became six, all of them filling up, the outside ones clogged and slow. The way the traffic moved, I wondered if we'd make it to the concert at all. Or maybe it was Annabelle's driving as she swerved back and forth between the lanes, revving up then slamming the brakes when her tailgating threatened her bumper. She drove like she did everything—with so much energy. After nearly sucking in all the air in the car, I yelled, "Look out!" as she cut off yet another driver, this time by inches.

Glancing over at me, she noticed my fists clenched in my lap. "You won't enjoy yourself at all if you don't relax. Check behind my seat. I might have brought along a little something to loosen you up."

"I don't need loosening. Maybe a distraction from your wild driving." I tried to soften my criticism with a smile, but she didn't buy it.

"There's nothing wrong with the way I drive. Traffic makes you tense. You started going quiet back at Loveland, and if you clench your hands any tighter in your lap, you might break bones." She bared her teeth. "Get over yourself and check out what I brought along for the ride."

Huffing out the rest of the air I was holding, I carefully unclenched my fists. The half-moons my nails left behind on my palms looked permanent. I twisted in my seat and reached behind hers to find a fifth of caramel vodka, one of my favorites.

"Did you include glasses with this deliciousness, or shall I risk us being pulled over by tipping up the bottle?"

"Solo cups are on the backseat, but you're going to have to pace yourself since you're getting a head start."

She looked away from the road and slid me a grin.

"You honestly don't think I'm sharing this with you while you're driving, do you?"

"Of course not," she huffed and returned her attention to the road. "Only enjoy enough to anticipate the show, but make sure I don't have to pour you into your seat when we reach Red Rocks."

I uncapped the bottle and poured a generous portion into a Solo cup, which I squeezed delicately between my knees as I recapped the bottle. Sipping my drink, I sat back in the silver-and-black leather bucket seat. The vodka went down sweet and smooth, warming my belly and relaxing my limbs in minutes. Soon, I joined Annabelle as she bopped along to the sounds of "Untraveled Road" by Thousand Foot Krutch cranking through her stereo and amping us up for the concert.

When we arrived at Red Rocks, Annabelle drove right up to the front. "What are you doing? This is the valet parking area for VIPs. We can't park here."

"Sure we can," she said with a grin. Reaching into her purse, she pulled out a VIP parking pass and placed it in the corner of her windshield.

Out of nowhere, a valet hustled up to the car and opened her door for her. She shot me a wicked smile before exiting her car and handing the valet her keys with a flourish. While I sat there gaping at my friend, I didn't notice someone had opened my door and patiently waited for me to exit the car. When I didn't respond at first, the valet discreetly cleared his throat, and I hurried out of the car, nearly bumping into him in the process.

Annabelle laughed at me. "Your dad is one of the richest, most influential men in Denver. Surely, you've experienced valet parking before."

"Of course I've experienced valet parking before, but never with one of my friends at a sold-out concert," I said as the first valet slid into the driver's seat and pulled away in Annabelle's Mustang.

"That's the first surprise. Come on, let's go in." Her grin hinted at all kinds of mischief as she linked her arm through mine and led me toward the front gates into Red Rocks Amphitheater.

At her words, something like dread—or maybe anticipation—coiled in my stomach. My heart rate ratcheted up, and a flush warmed my face. The pieces started falling into place. The weird looks I'd noticed Annabelle giving me, the secret smiles I caught Stacy and her exchanging, her insistence that I was the only girl in the house she wanted to take to the concert—she was up to something. But no one knew about my past. I was sure of it. No one knew how I'd dated Jack Whitehorse for one beautiful spring my sophomore year of high school. No one knew that as quickly and easily as he'd made me feel like his world revolved around me, he'd just as quickly and easily erased me from it. No one knew because I'd told no one at college about us.

Swallowing my dread, I concentrated on trying not to trip as Annabelle hustled me along.

When we reached the gates, she flashed another pass, and an usher directed us to a separate area marked *Band*. My heart tried to escape my chest while I thought longingly of that bottle of vodka on the back seat of Annabelle's Mustang. The way things were going, I should have finished at least half of it.

"Annabelle, how did you get your hands on backstage passes?" I asked as we followed the usher.

"Oh, I know someone on the crew," she replied airily. "I met him at a party freshman year. His older brother graduated from high school with Dakota and Blu and Tron, the three original members of the band. Didn't I tell you that before?" She batted her eyes innocently.

Huh.

"No, you didn't mention that. Do the other girls in the house know?"

"Maybe," she drawled.

The dread I experienced in front of the amphitheater ratcheted into heart-pounding fear. Or maybe excited anticipation. Thoughts of seeing Jack in person after five years made it hard to tell.

"Any special reason I have the honor of accompanying you backstage for this particular show?"

She glanced back at where I stopped, grabbed my hand, and tugged me along after her. "You mean other than your obsessive love for the band?"

"Yeah."

She hesitated for a fraction of a second before saying, "Nope. Like I said back at the house, I've seen your Spotify and your playlists on your phone, and Balefire is everywhere in your music choices. Out of everyone I know, you're the one who would appreciate this chance to meet the band the most."

Meet the band? I wanted to run full speed back to the parking lot and escape in Annabelle's fast car.

I wanted to do a happy dance at the chance to see the beautiful boy from my memories.

I kind of wanted to throw up.

I did none of those things as I let my friend's words roll through me.

Annabelle stopped in her tracks and stared me in the eyes. "You don't seem too happy about going backstage, Clio. What gives?"

"Nothing. This is a massive surprise. I guess I'm nervous about meeting the band." I shoved down my worry about seeing Jack again and shrugged. "Like you said, they're my all-time favorite. Maybe you could have given me a heads-up to prepare or something."

She laughed. "Are you kidding? Did you even look at yourself in the mirror before we left home?" She tugged me after her to where the usher had stopped to wait for us. "Girl, we are going to wow those boys so hard. They'll be begging us to attend their after-party."

"What are you talking about?"

"Their after-party. All bands have them after they play big shows, but Balefire's parties are legendary." Her excitement radiated off her like a light show. "As much as I want to see them in concert, I think I've been more excited for the after-party ever since Bailey scored me the tickets."

"Now I see where this is going. You're looking to hook up with one of the members of the band." A picture of a hot drummer with wide shoulders, thick black hair, and seafoam-green eyes flitted through my head, and I tried not to see him with his strong arms wrapped around Annabelle's gorgeous curves, currently on full display.

"Exactly. Why do you think I insisted you have condoms in your purse? Now stop stalling. We're watching the show from the front row, but there are other VIP pass holders too. I want to be front *and* center, so let's get going."

Annabelle grabbed my now clammy hand again and dragged me along behind her.

Backstage passes. Front row seats. Jack Whitehorse up close and personal after nearly five years. My heart raced like I tried to outrun the whole field of the Indy 500.

I was so not ready for this.

By the time we reached the front of the venue, my heart hammered so hard and fast I worried I'd embarrass myself and faint right there in the front row. Annabelle grinned at me and retrieved a flask from her purse. Another perk of backstage passes had been no security checks of our bags, which apparently, she knew.

Songs from Seether, one of my other favorite bands, pounded through the speakers, and lights flashed around the amphitheater, amping up the crowd and forcing Annabelle to lean in close to my ear. "I might have put one of these in your purse when you didn't notice. Check it out," she shouted before she uncapped her flask and took a pull.

My face must have revealed my surprise because she started laughing and nearly choked on her first drink. I flipped open the flap of my purse and reached inside it, discovering a pint-sized flask nestled in the bottom. I grinned at Annabelle, more in relief than anything else. At least I wouldn't have to face seeing Jack sober. The buzz from the vodka I'd drunk in the car had evaporated the minute she informed me we'd be meeting the band. No doubt that flask was my lifeline to sanity.

Not caring what I drank, I tipped my pint up for a big swallow. Happily, I discovered she'd filled it with more yummy vodka. Maybe if I drank the whole thing before the show started, I could survive seeing Jack again.

As I swallowed that first drink, it occurred to me he probably wouldn't see me at all from on top of his raised drum kit situated behind the rest of the band. Even if he did, he probably wouldn't recognize me after all this time. I'd changed some in the last five years. Moving out of Harrison and Meredith's house meant I could give up ballet and take up sports. After trying several, I discovered I could hold my own on a soccer field and joined the sorority's intramural team. The running involved in playing soccer coupled with the weight training I'd also taken up had changed my look from kind of skinny to toned and a bit curvy. I liked it. But Jack had shown interest in a dancer.

Shaking my head at my ridiculous thoughts, I took another long pull from my flask. Jack dumped a dancer, a nerd, a shy sophomore who was never in his league. That I'd done something stupid and fallen in love with him back then wouldn't have meant anything to him, I'm sure, even if I'd told him. Mercifully, I hadn't gone *that* far. Now I was a distant memory, if I rated that much. Who was I to think Jack Whitehorse would notice me in the mass of screaming fans let alone remember what I looked like way back when?

As I struggled with my thoughts, the amphitheater filled up behind us, the noise of the venue nearly deafening between the excited crowd laughing and shouting and the pounding rhythms blasting from the speakers at the sides of the stage. Energy pulsed in waves over the thousands of people thronging into the venue. Between my trepidation at seeing Jack again, the alcoholic buzz now blessedly coursing through my body, and the palpable energy generated by the people around me, my blood sizzled in my veins, and I worried I might self-combust.

The music suddenly stopped, the lights dropped, and the crowd held its breath for the opening riffs of the show. A flash of light, followed by the deep harsh punch of a drumstick on the surface of the tom-toms unleashed the collective breath of the crowd in one ear-popping roar. The concert had begun.

The show opened on Jack's ripping drum solo accompanied by cascading showers of multicolored fireworks and laser lights ricocheting across the stage, over the crowd, across the giant red rocks behind the stage, and up into the sky as Jack's massive drum kit rose from beneath the floor to tower over the stage. Like a master sorcerer, he struck each drumhead, cymbal, high hat, rim, tom-tom, and bass drum on exactly the right beat to command the emotions of the fans. No one in the amphitheater could resist responding to his masterful rhythms. The lights concentrated on the sorcerer, drawing every last vestige of the fans' attention to the man, the speed of whose drumsticks blurred the eyes and ears of everyone in the arena.

With the crowd's attention on Jack, the rest of the band appeared at the edge of the stage as if by magic. Adam Tron added his bass and Dakota Perri's monster guitar riffs joined Jack's drums before Blu Connolly's screaming vocals sent the crowd into a roaring frenzy.

Annabelle linked her arm through mine and squeezed. Based on the way her mouth formed, she was screaming, but I couldn't hear her over the rest of the crowd and the music. I smiled and squeezed her back before my eyes returned to the stage like magnets to true north. From where I stood, I could see between Dakota and Blu, a direct sight line to where Jack Whitehorse sat behind his massive drum set, the chrome scaffolding around it reflecting a rainbow of colors as the stage lights bounced off it.

From all the Balefire videos I'd watched, I knew Jack had let his hair grow from the short buzz cut he'd worn in high school to something shoulder length, so I was surprised to see he'd cut it. Now his hair lay right above the collar of his cutoff T-shirt. It looked to have been styled into soft messy waves before he started playing, his head moving in sync with the rhythms he created with his hands and feet. My fingers itched to slide through the warm silk of those waves, and I balled my hands into fists at my sides.

From video stalking him, I knew Jack now sported tattoos over his shoulder and down his right arm—something else that had changed about him since high school. Though his tight T-shirt hid part of that ink, all of it on his arm was on display, the tribal symbols and swirls sexy as hell. He closed his eyes, concentrating on the music, his sticks moving over the drumheads as though he and the drums were one entity. His playing mesmerized me as it always had. As desperately as I wanted to, I couldn't tear my eyes away from him, his biceps flexing, his broad sculpted chest visible above his drums, his whole body commanding the beat.

When the song ended, Dakota flipped guitar picks out at the roaring audience. Annabelle nearly ripped my arm off trying to disengage from me to snag one. I took the moment when she let go and Blu welcomed the crowd to Balefire's party to grab a quick swig from my flask. The vodka burned going down my throat, but

I welcomed the sting. It brought me back into the moment and stopped me from giving in to the lump that had formed in my throat the moment Jack touched his sticks to his skins.

A second later, my reprieve ended. Dakota struck a chord on his guitar, Jack answered with a flourish over his tom-toms, and exactly like back in high school, Jack's musicianship captured and held me. Without conscious thought, I moved and swayed to the rhythms he created, the percussions of his sticks on his skins reverberating through me. As the song played, I closed my eyes and became one with the rhythms of his drums. My body moved without my permission as waves of sound washed over and through me, and I became part of the rippling flood of music Jack and his band created.

The song ended with an explosion of fireworks and flashing lights of purple and chartreuse. I opened my eyes and, disoriented, staggered a little in the chaos of sound and light. Breathing heavily, I righted myself against Annabelle and looked up to discover Jack staring directly at me. At least I thought he stared at me. There were so many people around me I couldn't be sure he was even looking at me. Then he mouthed my name, and I dropped down hard onto the seat behind me.

When we arrived at the front row, I had a fleeting thought that the seats were superfluous. After I realized I now sat on one, I was grateful it spared me a more unfortunate drop directly to the floor. I closed my eyes, and for several long seconds, I concentrated on trying to breathe. At last I blinked my eyes open to see Jack standing up behind his drum kit. Blu, oblivious to the little drama playing out between Jack and me, blithely introduced the next song.

"Thank you, Red Rocks!" he shouted into his mic. "We're so fuckin' happy to be home tonight that we thought we'd debut a new song. You good with that?" he teased with a wicked grin, and all the girls in attendance nearly split the red rocks of the amphitheater with their screams. "Jack Whitehorse wrote this one. We hope you like it."

While Blu talked to the crowd, Jack never stopped staring at me. "You okay?" he mouthed.

I could barely manage a nod, but it seemed to satisfy him. After settling behind his drums again, he struck the opening riffs of the song. His timing was so impeccable he didn't miss a beat even when he clearly hadn't been ready to play on Blu's cue. His professionalism left me in awe, like him seeing and recognizing me hadn't been enough already. Leaving me behind five years ago had worked out well for Jack. He was born to be a professional musician. If I hadn't suspected as much when we were in high school, I had no doubt about it now.

The up-tempo song with Jack's driving drums and Dakota's scorching guitar licks dragged me up off the seat on which I'd landed so unceremoniously when Jack recognized me. Then Blu started singing the lyrics with Jack adding backing vocals.

Wait. I didn't know he sang too.

Then I listened to the words.

I've been too long without you, baby
Life's too short to live it apart.
Come back to me baby.
I know I fucked up, and I don't deserve it.
But I need your love,
I need your love tonight.
Come back to me baby.

Jack's voice sounded a plea when he echoed Blu on "Come back to me baby," and he stared at me throughout the song. It felt as though he sang to me only, but if that were the case, the words made no sense. I never left him. He walked away from me. He erased *me* from *his* life. I opened my flask and downed the rest of the vodka in it, wishing Annabelle had had the foresight to slip two flasks into my purse.

When the song ended, the woman standing on the side of me opposite Annabelle stepped in front of me, and I let her. She made a scene of slipping her hands up her shirt and divesting herself of her lacy red bra. Directing her little show at Dakota, she bounced up and down swinging her bra around above her head and screaming his name until at last, he acknowledged her. When he did, she flung her underwear at him, a bra strap miraculously catching on the pegs of his guitar. He laughed delightedly and flipped a guitar pick at her. For all of the next song, he played with her bra dangling from his axe.

The crowd roared its approval of both the woman's and Dakota's antics, which only encouraged copycats. Soon, bras and panties of all styles, colors, and sizes carpeted the stage in front of the band and a fair amount of the floor along the front row. A couple of pieces of lingerie landed on and near me, so I obligingly tossed them up to join the rest onstage. Somewhere, I heard Balefire encouraged the tossing of lingerie, and apparently, Annabelle knew that as well as she reached into her purse, pulled out a black lace thong, and shot it directly at Dakota's microphone, landing it perfectly and earning her a naughty grin from the man.

Catching her attention, I raised an eyebrow in question, but she only shrugged and gazed back at Dakota. She obviously had plans for the after-party. And for some reason, her attention to Dakota and not to Jack made me happy.

All the underwear mayhem distracted me from Jack for the space of a song. Then the girl who started it all moved back to her spot beside me, and I found myself riveted by his unwavering stare while Blu transitioned the band and the crowd to the next tune. Mercifully, the song involved complicated syncopated rhythms requiring Jack's full concentration. He focused on his drums, releasing me from his eyes, and I looked around for somewhere to hide. Though the crowd seethed and screamed around me, the very VIPness of the front row left me vulnerable, exposed to his inscrutable intensity.

Bumping into Annabelle to snag her attention, I leaned close to her ear and shouted, "Got any more vodka? I'm out."

With a grin, she handed me her flask. I didn't think I could drink enough vodka to overcome the emotions surging inside me. But it was worth a shot anyway. I downed most of what Annabelle had left in her flask, which surprisingly, was quite a bit, and hoped it would dull my heart enough to finish the concert.

Somewhere in my silly schoolgirl brain, I discovered that if I closed my eyes, I could lose myself in the music and not in Jack Whitehorse. Even if keeping my eyes closed made me look ridiculous, it didn't matter as long as I didn't have to see him. The maneuver allowed me the fiction of listening to a live concert on my Spotify rather than face the reality of standing a mere thirty feet or so from the one man who had ever mattered to me.

After a little while, all the vodka I'd drunk started to do its job, and I discovered I could remain upright while still keeping my eyes closed by moving with the crowd swaying around me. In what seemed like a few minutes after I'd made my discoveries, the band finished its set. I glanced up as Jack came out from behind his drums to join the others at the front of the stage for a final bow. When he stood up straight again, he looked right at me and smiled like I was the only person in the entire amphitheater.

I had no idea what to do with that.

Chapter Four

Clio

THAT WAS EPIC! I've never seen such an incredible show in my life!" Annabelle gushed as we made our way toward the VIP corridor.

"Balefire is amazing in concert," I agreed, the buzz from the vodka and music simultaneously mellowing me, leaving me euphoric. Which made no sense at all considering the emotional turmoil roiling through me for most of the show.

When we reached the corridor, an usher met us and led us toward the backstage area, and my euphoria evaporated in a nano-second. No-no-no. I was so not ready for this.

"They hold the after-party at the venue?" I couldn't help the way my voice squeaked on the question.

"No, silly. The party is at the Marriott downtown, where the band is staying tonight. We're riding to that party in a Town Car." Annabelle danced a little happy dance and grinned.

"But what about your Mustang? You're not leaving it here, are you?"

What I lacked the courage to ask was, were we riding with the band? I figured the after-party would be a rather raucous and wild event, giving me an opportunity to hide from Jack and watch him surreptitiously. Recognizing me during the show didn't mean he wanted his old history showing up at his party. It occurred to me that other people from our high school were likely to be in attendance, and wasn't that going to be awkward? Riding in a Town Car with him and the other members of Balefire? I hadn't drunk nearly enough vodka for that.

"A valet is driving it over to the hotel for me. Now stop worrying and stalling. Let's get the party started!" She grabbed my hand and pulled me along with her behind the usher. "I don't get you, Clio. You seemed to be having a great time at the concert. Now the real fun begins, and you're holding back. Why are you acting so weird?"

"I'm nervous, I guess. You love the spotlight, but I'm everyone's sidekick. It's why we're such good friends." I nudged her playfully, trying to distract her.

"Tonight, sister, I have a feeling you're going to be a whole lot more than anyone's sidekick."

"Annabelle, what aren't you telling me?"

She didn't have the chance to answer as we exited the corridor into a room where several other people excitedly waited for Town Cars too. I relaxed a fraction. We wouldn't be riding to the party with the band after all. I had more time to compose myself or drink more. The second idea seemed the best until I admitted to myself that so far, I wasn't smashed. After all the vodka I'd drunk already, it's a wonder I was coherent.

On some magical cue, the large group moved as one to an exit where a parade of limousines lined up to take us into the city and the party. Annabelle tugged me toward one of the front cars where we joined two couples and two chattering girls.

"Check it out, man. There's a fully stocked minibar in this ride. Who wants a drink?" one of the guys asked as he grabbed and uncapped a beer.

Several people talked at once, and the guy, I later learned his name was Joey, started handing out beers like he was hosting the party.

After everyone had a libation and made introductions all around, one of the chatty girls, I think she introduced herself as Hayley, said, "Oh God, did you see the way Dakota smiled when my bra landed on his guitar?" As she spoke, I realized she was the girl who saved me from Jack's mesmerizing gaze during the show.

"That red lacy bra was yours?" asked a guy who introduced himself as Sean or Shane or something.

"Of course you noticed that," his girlfriend snarled before she elbowed him in the side, crossed her arms over her chest, and turned away to pout.

The others in the car laughed while Hayley's friend addressed Annabelle. "Didn't you toss a black thong at Dakota?"

"Yeah. Judging from the hot look he shot me, he liked it too," she said with a self-satisfied grin.

"Looks like you have some competition tonight, Hayley," her friend said in a tone so catty I couldn't understand how they were friends. She leaned back against the plush cushion of the leather seats and eyed me next. "Which band member do you have your eye on, Red?"

When I didn't immediately respond, Annabelle spoke for me. "Clio only has eyes for Jack Whitehorse."

Gasping at her words, I sat forward and turned my head to look back at her. "What are you talking about?" I squeaked. "I haven't said a word about him." I caught myself and sat back, crossing my arms over my chest. "And unlike the rest of you, I wasn't throwing my underwear onstage."

"You didn't have to say a word. The way you were staring at him said it all." Annabelle smirked.

Pushing deeper into the pillowy softness of the plush upholstered seat, I attempted to hide inside my bottle of beer. Still, I endured the scrutiny of the other people in the car.

"That boy can hammer a set of drums, that's for sure," said Sean or Shane. I might have kissed him in gratitude had I been sure his girlfriend wouldn't throw a punch.

"Yeah, I was afraid when Dave Brubaker left the band that Balefire would stop playing. Instead, they go out and find Jack Whitehorse and play even better," said the Joey guy.

"Jack's definitely hot," Hayley added. "I didn't realize that until he joined the others at the edge of the stage after the encore. All those yummy muscles and tats." She ran her tongue over her lips, and I worked not to fist my hands.

"Well, if your plans with Dakota don't work out, you can always make a run at Jack," the catty girl said, giving me a what-are-you-going-to-do-about-that? look.

I abandoned the conversation to stare out the window at the passing lights along the city streets. The Town Cars traveled at speed, indicating we had an escort or were taking an alternate route to skirt the post-concert traffic. At the rate we were traveling, we'd arrive at the hotel in a few minutes, and I broke out in a sweat. After all this time apart with no communication between us, what would I even say to him if I saw him up close and personal?

The cars pulled up one after the next under the hotel canopy and the passengers began exiting. Being seated next to the door, I had no choice but to leave the car first to let the others out of it though I wished I could jump back in and take a ride to wherever. Somewhere I wouldn't have to face my past. Somewhere I wouldn't have to discover why Jack had not only dumped me, but also thoroughly erased me from his life.

As if she read my thoughts, Annabelle linked her arm through mine and walked us through the front doors and into the opulent lobby of the hotel. For a moment, I considered sinking into the depths of the cushions of one of the inviting brown leather couches. Or disappearing behind a giant potted palm. Before I could act on a plan, security guards met us and escorted us to the elevators. More than anything, I wanted to take a minute and sit on one of the love seats or deep round chairs artfully placed in tête-à-tête arrangements throughout the lobby, catch my breath, hyperventilate in private maybe. Instead, the rest of the VIPs herded me with them onto an elevator that jetted us to a playroom on the penthouse floor.

As we exited the elevator, the deafening excitement of the others increased by twenty decibels—enough to hear it over the music pulsing from behind a set of double doors. When two security guards opened the doors to let us in, the sound waves of the room nearly flattened me. I staggered back into the arms of a guy from our Town Car, Joey I think. He laughed and righted me before pushing me through the doors ahead of him.

"Clio, isn't this awesome?" Annabelle shouted over the sounds of the party.

I managed a lame smile and nodded.

She squeezed my hand and spoke directly in my ear. "I'm on a mission. You going to be okay?"

Again I nodded, and with a grin, she disappeared into the throng, in search of Dakota Perri no doubt, leaving me standing alone on the edge of the crowd. Feeling anything but okay, I slipped back along a wall and stood still for several minutes, attempting to adjust to the people and the noise. To my delight and, weirdly, my disappointment, the room was packed with revelers. I could hide so easily in this crush, but I might not have a chance to talk to—or even to see Jack amid all these people.

Then again, if groupies surrounded him—or worse, if he'd already hooked up with someone—I didn't think I wanted to see that.

A waiter shouldering a tray of drinks passed near me. Automatically, I reached for one, more to have something to do with my hands than to have something to drink. My vodka buzz had largely worn off, and I'd given up on alcohol doing the job of dulling my senses—or my memories. Looking into Jack's eyes as he played the show brought back so much I thought I'd repressed in fuzzy images

and nebulous dreams. When he mouthed my name at the beginning of the concert, I could hear his voice as it had sounded long ago whispering my name against the shell of my ear before he trailed soft kisses along my jaw on his way to my mouth. I could feel his lips moving on mine, firm and demanding, his kisses drugging me with a desire I couldn't understand at the time and hadn't experienced with anyone else since.

Annabelle's earlier insistence about having condoms in my purse meant she assumed carrying them was routine for me, that I actually needed them. Truth was, the only person I'd ever been interested in sharing my body with had erased me from his life as soon as he had the chance to pursue his one real dream. Of course, if I actually ran into him, talking's all that would happen. Annabelle's optimism could be ridiculous sometimes. I wouldn't need condoms.

Back when we were together, I should have seen the end coming. After all, he talked all the time about how he wanted to join a rock band and make the big time. As talented as he was back then, I had no doubt he'd realize his dream. It should have come as no surprise then, to a girl who'd grown up invisible to those who mattered most to her, that she'd be easy for him to erase in favor of following that dream.

Though I'd dated pretty regularly since high school, I hadn't become involved enough with anyone to want to have sex with him. One look from Jack Whitehorse, my name mouthed over the top of his massive drum set, and I wondered if Annabelle had any spare condoms in her purse.

I gave myself a stern mental shake and downed half the flute of champagne I'd snagged from the waiter. Was I seriously contemplating having sex with Jack Whitehorse after not seeing or speaking to him in five long years? After he walked away from me without a backward glance, without a thanks-that-was-fun-but-I'm-moving-on? *Get a grip, Clio. The man is exposed to all kinds of women on a nightly basis, all of whom are more interesting—and far more experienced than you. Chill, enjoy the party, and forget about Jack Whitehorse.*

After my severe private pep talk, I decided to wander around the party, see if I couldn't find Annabelle and at least enjoy her little show as she tried to entice Dakota Perri into her panties. If she got anywhere near the man, I had no doubt she'd win her prize. However, he had a reputation for being a man whore, and she might have to wait her turn or share him. Even as wild as I knew Annabelle to be, I didn't think either scenario would suit her. At any rate, it would certainly be fun watching.

As I navigated my way around the clusters of people seated at tables at the edges of the party, I noticed several professional sports players from Denver-area teams. Since Harrison regularly sought out those guys as clients, I had a working knowledge of the men who played for the Nuggets basketball team, the Broncos football team, the Avalanche hockey team, and the Rapids soccer team. I nodded at a couple of basketball players I'd met at one of Harrison's functions last summer as I walked past their table, but I wasn't comfortable enough to stop to chat.

Nearby, a buffet table nearly groaned aloud with all the food piled on top of it. The sight of acres of an eclectic array of snacks and appetizers rumbled my stomach, and I remembered I hadn't eaten since lunch, which was almost a day ago. Shrimp cocktail, oysters on the half shell, fancy stuffed jalapeno canapés, fruit platters, vegetable platters, hot wings, onion rings, and trays of mini sliders were only the beginning of what was on offer. Trailing my eyes down the table, I noticed a pair of chefs carving slices off of some sort of stuffed meat roll and a party-sized prime rib.

It occurred to me as I checked out the food that maybe I should eat something to soak up the alcohol in my system. As I joined the others lined up along the buffet, I noticed a gorgeous buff guy about my age, with intense dark eyes and tawny skin wearing a cutoff Balefire T-shirt and a beanie staring at me from across the table.

"Hey, aren't you Annabelle Stewart's friend?" he asked.

"Yes," I replied hesitantly. "Do I know you?"

"I'm Bailey Saunders."

"Hey Bailey." I smiled. "Thanks for the VIP tickets to the concert and everything." I nodded around at the party in full swing. "Annabelle said you were the one who gave them to us."

"You're welcome. A friend of mine made it easy for me to do him a favor with those tickets." He glanced behind me. "So, where is Annabelle? She made it to the party, didn't she?"

By this point in our conversation, we'd reached the chef station, so we had to pause our convo to make our requests. Bailey opted for a little of each. I only wanted the prime rib. With the chef station situated at the end of the buffet, Bailey motioned me to follow him to a pedestal table where we could set down our plates and drinks though we'd be enjoying our meal standing up.

"What happened to Annabelle?"

Something accusatory in his tone told me he and Annabelle hadn't been on the same page when he'd given her those tickets. As bad as I felt for him, my loyalty lay with my friend.

"She's here somewhere. Somehow, I lost her in this crowd. Imagine that," I replied with a playful grin as I waved my fork at the crush around us. "You're a roadie with the band? How is it you're at this party? Do you tear down tomorrow?" I asked, deliberately changing the subject.

"Actually, I'm the head road engineer for all of Balefire's live shows."

"I'm sorry. I guess I misunderstood what Annabelle told me."

His broad smile told me he took no offense at the way I'd inadvertently demoted him. "The road crew takes turns attending the after-parties. Tonight, most of the team will be here since we aren't going back out on the road until the day after tomorrow." He tipped up his bottle and swallowed some beer. "We'll wait till morning to load the gear. Our next show's in Phoenix on Monday."

"It's cool you get to attend the parties. Are they always like this?"

"You mean this big?" Bailey asked, looking around the room for a minute.

"And the catering with the chefs and all the waitstaff and the drinks . . ." I trailed off as I caught his grin.

"Nah, this one's special since we're home. The guys have tons of friends and family here, so they're celebrating extra."

"That's cool. I guess I didn't think about that."

Bailey didn't mean to stick a knife in me with that remark, but I felt a stabbing pain in my chest all the same. I gave my total concentration to my food, which had been going down easily before but now stuck in my throat. Oblivious to my distress, he said, "Balefire's based here in Denver, but being a big fan of theirs, I bet you already knew that."

I nodded as I downed the last of my drink and pushed my plate away, my previous hunger replaced by a churning in my stomach that echoed my churning emotions. Like I needed the reminder of Jack's geographical proximity to me all this time. The emotional distance between us was planetary, which rendered our physical proximity meaningless. Still, he was somewhere in this room, and to my horror, I very much wanted to see him. Somehow, I thought, if I could see him up close and personal, I could loosen the hold he'd had on me since my sophomore year of high school.

"Hey, hey, hey. We can't have that," Bailey chided me.

Startled at what my face must have revealed, I tried to smile away his assumptions. "Oh, I—"

"You're out of champagne. That will never do."

He signaled a passing waiter and grabbed two fresh flutes of champagne from his tray, setting both in front of me. "This is a Balefire party, Clio. You can never be out of a drink." He winked at me before he finished the last of the food on his plate.

"You gonna finish that?" With his fork, he indicated an oyster and a couple of shrimp I'd left behind.

"Help yourself."

He didn't even bother to transfer the food to his own plate, instead eating directly off mine. I imagined the crew shared a lot of things, so helping himself to my leftovers would be completely natural for him, even if I found it a little strange.

"You have any idea where in this crowd I might find Annabelle?"

I shrugged. "You're the after-party expert here, not me. I have yet to make a full circuit of the room." I tipped back some champagne, more to divert an uncomfortable conversation than because I wanted more to drink.

A local band started warming up on a dais opposite the doors into the room, and I leaned across the table so he could hear me over the additional noise. "If there's a band playing, chances are pretty good Annabelle will be dancing. You might start there," I said. "Thanks for sharing dinner with me, Bailey. It was nice to meet you. And thanks again for the tickets to the concert."

"My pleasure. Nice to meet you too Clio. Maybe I'll see you around later."

"Sure," I said and downed one glass of champagne before grabbing the other and wandering off toward the sounds of the band. Maybe I could lose myself and my memories on the dance floor—or find myself staring up into a pair of seafoam-green eyes that had haunted me for five long years.

CHAPTER FIVE

Jack

CLIO STOOD TO the side of the dance floor, sipping a flute of champagne and looking so stunning she nearly broke my heart—again.

I wanted to study her, take all of her in for a few minutes before I broke the spell and actually talked to her. What do you say to the only person who ever really mattered after you dumped her with no explanation whatsoever? After the way she dropped on her ass when I caught her attention at the concert, I had to wonder how she was going to react to talking to me.

Then again, maybe she went down because of the booze she'd been drinking. I barely took my eyes off her from the moment I spotted her in the front row at the show, so I saw how she finished her flask then finished off her friend's. Now she had a half-full glass of champagne in her hand, and I couldn't tell if she was swaying to the music or trying to remain upright.

Jesus, tipsy or not, her beauty stunned me. That dress she had on wore me out. All that delicate lace hinted at her pretty curves and showed off her legs, which her sexy sandals emphasized. I couldn't guess the length of her hair since she was wearing it up, but I was glad she apparently hadn't cut it. The style exposed the neck I'd loved touching and kissing, making her shiver and snuggle closer to me for more. As the memories washed over me, I smiled before I heard Dakota talking from somewhere behind me.

"Oh, yeah, I'd like to tap that," he said, and I wondered which girl would be the starter for his evening. Then he boiled my blood. "That redhead in the blue lace dress is one seriously sexy woman."

"I think she's spoken for, dude. You're going to have to look somewhere else," Tron said as he materialized next to me.

"Just 'cause there's a goalie doesn't mean you can't score," Dakota said with a laugh.

I flexed my fists as I considered clocking him when Tron put a restraining hand on my arm. Clenching my jaw, I didn't turn my head to look at him, but I uncoiled slightly. Of the three other guys in the band, I was closest to Tron. He was steady and levelheaded, and he didn't mind at all that I didn't drink much and never spent private time with the army of groupies who followed Balefire like it was their job.

"She belongs to the monk, Dakota. That's one goalie you don't want to mess with."

"The monk has a girl? How did I not know this?" Dakota turned a wide-eyed stare on me.

"With any luck, I'll have *that* girl, so back off," I growled.

"You haven't made a move yet? That makes her fair game." Dakota took a step in Clio's direction.

"I invited her to this party, so no, she's not fair game. If you don't want me to mess up your pretty face, back the fuck off," I gritted out, staring him down.

Dakota raised his hands in surrender. "Whoa, man. No need to get your shorts in a knot over a woman. The room is full of 'em." His eyes wandered the room and all the ladies on offer. "Why, there's another sweet little number walking over to talk to Red. The brunette off-limits too?"

"Knock yourself out. I'll even introduce you," I said. Maybe with the buffer of other people, I could survive this initial reconnection with Clio.

Then again, maybe it was a much bigger deal to me than it would be to her. For all I knew, Harrison Barnes had fed her a truckload of shit about me, and now she couldn't give a flying fuck if I talked to her or not.

"You've been stirred up about seeing her again since you found her friend and set up this opportunity, dude. Probably better do something about it now that you have the chance," Tron said quietly into my ear.

I nodded and turned to Dakota. "Let's go talk to some nice girls for a change."

"Seriously? What fun will that be?"

The stricken look on Dakota's face cracked me up, and I felt lighter than I had all night. "God, you're such a fuck boy. If Clio's friend is too nice for you, I'm sure you can find the girl who belongs with the red bra you kept from the show."

"You saw that, did you?" A grin broke over his face.

"Bet her phone number is written in great big digits over the inside of the cups."

"Nah, they're all lace."

I raised a brow and waited for the punch line.

"It's written along the straps. Since all the VIPs in the front row got invited to this little soiree of ours, I know she's here somewhere. But first, the angel in the naughty black leather dress."

I burst out laughing at the melodramatic villain way he rubbed his hands together, and we were all right again.

Glancing back to where Clio and her friend stood, I sucked in a breath, squared my shoulders, and willed my feet to move. Walking beside me, Tron snorted out a laugh. "Jesus, dude, she's a beautiful woman, not a firing squad. Relax already."

Inclining my head in Tron's direction, I didn't have to look at his face to see his smirk. With Dakota and Tron dogging me, I couldn't falter, couldn't slow down. I was within two steps of her before Annabelle noticed us, her face lighting up with a hundred-watt smile. Judging from the rigid way she held herself, Clio had noticed me sooner and chosen not to let on. Funny how after so many years apart, I could still read her.

"Oh my God, Clio! It's the whole band," Annabelle squealed.

At long last, Clio turned her head to acknowledge me. The pain in her eyes arrowed directly into my solar plexus.

"Hello, Clio," I choked out, my voice harsh to my ears.

"Hello, Jack." Like a balm, her soft voice washed over me.

"You *do* know her. I thought you were fuckin' with us, man," Dakota said. "Dakota Perri. Very"—he dragged the word out—"pleased to meet you. Quite honestly, we thought the monk here didn't know any girls, let alone two such fine women as yourselves."

The way Dakota stared at Clio's breasts had me balling my fists again, something Tron must have noticed too.

"Adam Tron, but I go by Tron. I don't think I caught your names," he said as he extended his hand across to Annabelle, cutting off Dakota's view of Clio.

"Annabelle Stewart, and this is Clio Barnes." Annabelle shook Tron's hand. "But you knew that already," she said, addressing me and turning to Clio. "You've been holding out on me, sister. You never let on for one second that you actually *knew* Jack Whitehorse."

"We went to the same high school," Clio said, noncommittally. "Nice to meet you Tron, Dakota."

She shook their hands, and Dakota jerked my chain again by holding Clio's hand too long. About the time I thought I might have to damage his million-dollar fingers, he let go and reached for Annabelle. "Since these two are old friends, maybe you and I should wander off and let them catch up. Annabelle, tell me about your very fine self," he said as he wrapped an arm around her waist and led her away from the group.

Annabelle turned her head to wink at Clio, and I noticed she slipped an arm around Dakota as they walked away. When I returned my attention to Clio, she studiously avoided looking at me, instead directing her eyes to the people on the dance floor.

Tron interrupted the awkward silence left in Dakota and Annabelle's wake. "Hope you enjoy the party Clio. See you around." Then he disappeared too, leaving Clio and me alone surrounded by strangers.

"So—"

"Look, Jack. When Annabelle invited me to your concert, she left out the part about backstage passes to your after-party. She, of course, had a mission, one I think she's currently accomplishing. I wouldn't have come along if I'd known there was a chance of finding myself here."

My heart might have dropped to my knees. Clio hated me.

"Please don't let me cramp your style. I'm only here as Annabelle's wingwoman, and I'm used to entertaining myself at parties." She tossed off the last of her champagne before she set her empty glass on a passing waiter's tray and grabbed a fresh drink.

She gave me no choice but to go all in. "I asked Annabelle to bring you."

"*What?*" she sputtered. "She acted like she didn't know you and had no idea you and I knew each other."

I blew out a breath, then laid out all my cards. "Actually, I did just meet her. Our head road engineer, Bailey Saunders, went to a party once and met Annabelle. You were there too." Clio shot me a look. "I saw you in the background of one of Bailey's photos on his phone when he was telling me about a hot girl he met. So, I looked up your friend, saw you in lots of pictures on her Instagram page, and realized you hadn't moved far away to go to college like

I always thought you would." I blew out a breath. "Anyway, I gave Bailey the tickets for Annabelle with the requirement that she bring you with her."

"Why do you want to see me now?" She fisted her hand on her hip. "It's been five years, Jack."

I could tell she was trying to be tough, but I could also hear the hurt in her voice. It killed me. And it gave me hope. "Listen, can we go somewhere quiet—and private—to talk about this?"

"You engineered this whole evening to talk to me? You couldn't, oh, I don't know, pick up a phone, give me a call even once in all this time? Like when you were tired of me in high school and walked away?" She downed half the flute of champagne in her hand. "Jesus, Jack, I don't know what I'm doing standing here still talking to you."

She was about to take another drink of her champagne, but I needed her sober, so I snagged the glass out of her hand and set it on a table. Before she could finish spitting her indignation, I grabbed her hand and started walking toward the side doors where I knew I could sneak us out. No doubt, it was a caveman move, my grip on Clio's hand giving her no choice but to follow me. But I needed to talk to her, explain myself. Beg for a second chance.

When we reached the hallway, she half-heartedly tried to pull away, but I didn't let go.

"Jack, you can't force me to come with you. I'm not some groupie who can't wait to share your bed."

"Who said anything about sharing a bed? I need to talk to you, and I don't want to do it in front of an audience." The idea of sharing a bed had definitely entered my head regularly over the past five years and probably ten or a hundred more times since I first set eyes on her at the concert tonight. But we needed to talk first.

I pulled her along with me to the bank of elevators and punched in the number for the band's reserved floor.

"You still haven't answered my question, Jack. Why now?"

With the subdued ding of a bell, the elevator arrived, and I tugged Clio into it with me, crowding her toward the back of the car so she wouldn't try to slip back out of it. That's when I finally started talking. "I tried to see you three years ago at your high school graduation, but you left right after you gave your speech. I tried to call you, but your number didn't work. I looked your number up online, but you're not listed anywhere, and I think the last time you updated your Instagram page was in high school."

Though we were alone in the elevator, I didn't let go of her hand. As I talked, I gave her fingers a squeeze, trying to communicate physically what my words weren't doing so well for me, judging from the skeptical look on her face. "I've been touring nearly nonstop since I graduated, so it's been hard to reconnect with you, but I have tried."

The elevator stopped on my floor, and mercifully, Clio exited the car with me without a fight, so I could stop feeling like a caveman dragging her behind me.

"Which must be obvious since you're here right now," I said, finishing my explanation.

She said nothing as we walked to my door. I fished the key card from my pocket and let us into my suite, flipping on the lights as she walked ahead of me into the outer room.

Clio stood in the middle of the suite looking like an angel even with her arms protectively covering her chest. "It seems you hit the jackpot, accomplished your dreams. Drumming in a big-time band, partying with all kinds of people, staying in fancy hotel rooms like this."

I watched her as she took in the high-end reproductions of fine art on the walls, the plush white couches, the minimalist black-and-chrome tables scattered conveniently around the room. When I caught her sneaking a glance at the partially opened door to the bedroom, I had to suppress a smile. Yeah, maybe I wasn't the only one who'd thought about us together in bed.

"Did you enjoy the show?"

"At the risk of overinflating your ego, the show was fantastic."

A ghost of a smile crossed her face. "I've been a fan of Balefire since I first heard them my senior year of high school. The original band with Dave Brubaker behind the drums rocked, but when you joined them, you elevated their sound."

"Thank you."

She refused to raise her eyes above my chest as she gracefully seated herself on the edge of one of the couches.

I stepped over to the minibar to pour us each a glass of ice water, handing her one as I sat beside her.

"What happened, Jack? What did I do to make you walk away without a backward glance? Erase me from your life the way you did?"

I caught the hitch in her voice even though she tried to cover it by taking a sip of her water.

So, she didn't know. Without risking my dad's business, I wasn't in a position to tell her. *Fuck.*

"I was under contract. Part of the terms included walking away from my old life."

"Just like that?" The snap of her fingers rang in my ears.

Beneath the anger, she sounded so forlorn, she cracked my heart wide open.

"I didn't have a choice." I begged her with my eyes to hear the truth in my words. "After I won the audition with Rude Awakening, I headed out on tour almost immediately. I'd had my high school experience. I wanted to let you have yours. I couldn't expect you to wait around for me when there'd be times when even I didn't know where I'd be going next or for how long."

"Don't you think that should have been my decision?"

Oh, yeah, most definitely. Too bad your father didn't agree.

"I was trying to do the right thing, Clio." My hand had a mind of its own, and it slid over the back of the couch. "You were talking Ivy League schools and medicine. I didn't want to hold you back."

She white-knuckled both hands around her water hard enough

to worry me. "Sounds more like the other way around, Jack. Sounds more like I was going to hold you back from your sex-drugs-and-rock-n-roll dream."

"You know what the guys in the band call me?"

She shook her head.

"They call me the monk. Wanna know why?"

She shrugged, but the look she slid me told me she only pretended indifference.

"They call me the monk because I don't drink much, I don't do drugs, and I haven't been with a groupie even once since I joined them." I set my water on the table in front of us. "One day after I'd been touring with them for a few months, I overheard Blu and Dakota talking, wondering whether I preferred guys. I burst out laughing, and that was the end of that conversation."

"Why don't you do those things?"

Leaning back into the cushions, I gazed up at the ceiling. "Rude Awakening was all about the party. The whole lifestyle came before the music, which is why they'll always be a warm-up band and never the main attraction." I glanced over my shoulder at her. She needed my eyes when I told her the truth. "They expected me to party with them, and being young and desperate to play, I participated."

Pain flashed across her face before she hid it behind a sip of water.

I pretended not to notice and continued. "It wasn't as much fun as advertised. In fact, my eventual lack of enthusiasm for the party grated on my mates in Rude Awakening." Sitting forward, I sipped some water then set my glass back on the table in front of us. "The guys in Balefire may party hard, but Blu, Dakota, and Tron are dedicated to the music. Balefire replaced Dave Brubaker because he couldn't separate the party from real life. Even though they nick-named me the monk, the guys like that I put the music first."

She whispered, "I wasn't as important as the music." Her pretty mouth turned down in sorrow. "You could have told me that. It would have hurt, but not any more than your silence. Ironic. You dumped me for your music and left me without a sound."

"Clio, baby. It wasn't like that." When I reached for her, she flinched, and I dropped my hand to my knee.

"Yeah, Jack, it was. I was there, remember?" She closed in on herself. "And don't call me baby."

I smiled. Harrison Barnes may have stolen almost five years from us, but Clio still had some fight in her. Good. "You used to like it when I called you baby," I said, coaxing her with a grin.

"I used to like a lot of things." She took another sip of water before carefully setting the glass on the coffee table in front of us.

I couldn't take my eyes off her. She'd changed from the pretty girl who rocked my world into a beautiful woman whose gorgeous curves made my hands itch to touch her. I wanted to shove my fingers into her hair, mess up her careful styling, and let all that auburn fire lick and flow over my hands. I wanted to trail kisses along the long smooth column of her throat, listen to her moan at my touch, feel her pulse race beneath my lips, taste the sweetness of her skin with my tongue.

"Stop looking at me like that."

"How am I looking at you, Clio?"

"Like I'm the center of your universe." She wrapped her arms around herself. "You used to be good at making me feel like I was. Now I know better."

"What do you mean?"

She laughed, but there was only pain there. "One day you were looking at me like you are now. The next day you weren't looking at me at all."

She stood and wandered over to the floor-to-ceiling windows, turning her back to me as she gazed out at the lights of the city below. I'd schemed too much for this chance to reconnect to let her walk away from me now. In two strides, I stood behind her, close enough to touch.

CHAPTER SIX

Clio

WHAT WAS IT about Jack Whitehorse that made me lose every last vestige of reason and common sense? Why did I let him drag me up to his hotel room? Oh, yeah, because masochist that I am, I couldn't walk away from a few minutes alone with him. What did I expect him to say? I fell in love with him for precisely who he was. A smile tugged at my lips as I remembered playing the part of groupie when I stood at the front of the crowd while his high school band played for school dances. After five years, not much had changed.

As I stared out at miles of twinkling lights, I didn't hear Jack as he padded across the sumptuous white carpet to stand close behind me. Instead, I felt his heat radiating over me, goose-bumping my skin. I shivered and rubbed my hands up and down my arms. When he skimmed his hands along my arms, internally, I rejoiced that I already held myself, or I might have flown apart into a million pieces.

"I've never stopped looking at you Clio. You're the most beautiful girl I've ever known," he whispered.

"Right," I said, dragging the word out. "'Cause you haven't

met any supermodels or actresses or pro athletes since you became a famous rock star." I snorted.

"Doesn't matter who they are or who they know or what they do," he said quietly. "For me, no other woman has ever come close to you. Seeing you again after all this time is a dream come true." Gently, he pulled me back into his chest and wrapped his arms over mine. "You're shivering. Are you cold?"

"N-no."

"Ah."

I don't know what he thought, but it didn't matter when his lips butterflied the skin where my neck and shoulder met. I tightened my arms over my chest and tried to quell the sensations his touch demanded from me. Had always demanded from me. When he flicked his tongue out and tasted me, I couldn't hold back the tiny moan that escaped my lips. It was as though time and life and experience hadn't happened at all. Being held in Jack Whitehorse's arms was so natural, so right. Experiencing his kisses was like coming home, or what I imagined coming home would be like.

Without my permission, my body responded to his touch, melting back into him, my head dropping to one side to give him easier access to my neck. He took advantage, trailing soft kisses along my pulse to the sensitive spot behind my ear where he licked and sucked my skin. When he did that, my knees gave way, but he held me so close I didn't fall.

Carefully, he turned me and wrapped his arms around me. "I dream about you all the time, Clio. And when I dream about you, I dream about this."

Lowering his head, he set his lips on mine, sipping me, tasting me, enticing me to join him. He'd disappeared from my life for five long years, only to reappear in it like a summer storm. God, I wanted to resist him so damn much, pretend he didn't matter, pretend I hadn't thought about him every single day since he walked out of my life.

But I wasn't that strong.

Leaning into him, I kissed him back. My response did something to him, and he groaned deep in his throat before he opened his mouth and slid his tongue over the seam of my lips. Accepting his request, I opened my mouth and met his tongue, firing the soft kiss into an inferno that burned away all the years since the last time he'd kissed me.

No one could kiss me like Jack. No one but Jack Whitehorse could turn me into a hot mess merely by touching his tongue to mine. His hands roamed my back, from my shoulders to my waist, holding me, urging me closer to his hard body. He slid his hands over my ass, kneading me and pulling me against the erection pushing hard between us. I moaned into his mouth and tightened my arms around his neck, desperately trying to meld myself into him.

Then he pulled out all the stops, sliding his hands up my waist, skimming the curves of my breasts on his way to my neck. He cupped his big palms on the sides of my neck, his fingertips meeting at my nape while he skimmed his calloused thumbs along my jaw. All the while, he deepened the kiss, undoing me with his touch. I never could resist that one move, and he knew it.

Keeping his hands on my neck, he started walking me backward, stealing kisses between checking his navigation over my shoulder.

"What, where are we—?"

Jack preempted my questions with more kisses.

Something solid gave way at my back. We'd pushed through the door, left the sitting room, and entered the bedroom. Still, he kept walking me backward until the backs of my thighs bumped the soft edge of the bed. At last, he dropped his hands from my neck to grasp my hips, silently urging me back, and I fell slowly onto the mattress with him coming down on top of me.

"Jack."

His mouth returned to mine, making me forget what I'd wanted to say.

Somehow, he worked the zipper on the back of my dress free before he slid off me and sat up on his knees. Desire darkened his eyes as he reached for the neck of my dress. "May I?"

I answered the question with a single nod, and slowly, he tugged my dress down. The callouses on his palms played over my skin as he skimmed his hands across my collarbone, over my shoulders, and down my arms behind the lace of my dress, his touch driving me as wild as his kisses. Writhing beneath his hands, I helped him divest me of the pretty periwinkle confection, which he tossed over a nearby chair.

For a few seconds, he stared at me lying in the middle of his bed in nothing but my plain white bra and bikini panties and silver sandals. Being so exposed should have made me self-conscious, but I was with Jack, and the hungry look on his face emboldened me. I trailed my hand along the top of his thigh, enjoying the power of muscles I could feel beneath the fabric of his jeans.

He sucked in a breath before reaching behind his head and grabbing the collar of his T-shirt in the way guys do, pulling it over his head and off his body to drop on the floor beside the bed. His broad sculpted shoulders and deep chest hinted at the kind of shape he was in. In the dim light glowing from the sitting room beyond the bedroom door, I could see the outlines of a tattoo over his shoulder. As I reached up to trace it, Jack bent down to kiss me again, stretching out beside me as he took his time with my mouth.

He nibbled at the side of my lips, working his way slowly across my mouth while his calloused hand toured my body. Starting with the bare skin of my waist, he explored my torso from the edge of my panties to the underwires of my bra before dropping lower again to the top of my thigh. Involuntarily, I shifted under his touch, pulling my knee up and opening my center to him.

He smiled against my mouth and moved his hand around to my back. When he plunged his tongue inside my lips, I met him with the desperation of wanting him for five long years. With my hands buried in his silky dark hair, I held his mouth to mine as we kissed each other crazy. Cool air flowed over my nipples, alerting me Jack had unhooked my bra. He lifted away from me enough to strip me of that scrap of fabric and bent his head to one tight nipple. I arched off the bed at the touch of his lips tugging me into his mouth, sucking me and ripping a scream from me.

Deep in his throat, he chuckled at my response before he transferred his attention to my other nipple. My belly tightened and hummed, and I thought I might come from his attentions to my breasts alone. He mesmerized me with his talented mouth and left me begging when he pulled away to stand beside the bed.

"Where are you going?" I whimpered.

"Nowhere, Clio. I'm staying right here."

He toed off his Converse and unzipped the fly of his jeans. Hooking his fingers in the waistbands of both his jeans and his boxers, he slid the whole works over his lean hips and down his long legs before straightening up and stepping out of them. The evidence of his response to me stood proudly erect at the apex of his thighs, and my eyes nearly popped out of my head at the size of him. He picked up his jeans, retrieved his wallet, and pulled a condom from it, setting it on the nightstand beside the bed. Instead of rejoining me like I thought he would, he walked around to the foot of the bed and raked my body with his eyes from my face to my feet.

"I think I want you to leave these on," Jack said with a grin as he palmed my sandals.

The way he smoothed his hands along the outsides of my legs had me digging my heels into the mattress to lift my hips in anticipation of his destination. Smiling at my eagerness, he slipped his fingers inside the waistband of my panties and smoothed them down my legs.

"Jesus, Clio. You're even more beautiful than I dreamed, and that's saying something. I've got to taste you."

It took me several seconds to process what he meant, time he spent slipping his hands beneath my knees to raise them off the bed, widening my thighs enough for his broad shoulders to fit between them. When I figured out what he meant to do, I tried to push my thighs together, but his dark laugh met my surprise. He held my legs apart with his shoulders as he lowered his head to my center. Having never experienced a man's mouth so intimately before, and considering it was Jack's mouth, maybe I should have been at least a little prepared for what he would do to me. But I wasn't. What his kisses did to me when he trailed them along my neck, on my breasts, on my mouth were pink sensations compared to the deep dark vermillion thrill of his mouth on my pussy.

I cried out and arched into him, dragging a moan from him as he tightened his grip on my thighs and continued to lick and kiss my sex. When he turned his full attention to my clit, tonguing and nipping, sucking and kissing me, I lost my mind. As if from some great distance, I heard myself whimpering his name, heard his dark laugh rumbling in his throat. "That's it, Clio. Come all over my face."

At little time later when my heart slowed from warp speed to a race, he let me go, only to crawl up the bed beside me to grab the condom off the nightstand. Lying on his back, he tore open the packet and smoothed the condom over his cock before he rolled over on top of me again. After nudging my thighs apart with his knee, he settled himself between them, the head of his cock twitching against my clit.

He pushed up on his elbows and smiled down at me. "You tasted even sweeter than I imagined. Want me to show you?"

I couldn't understand what he meant until he leaned down and kissed me, and I tasted myself on his lips, smelled my arousal on his face. Somehow whenever I'd imagined a man doing to me what Jack had just done, I'd thought it might be vaguely disgusting to taste myself, smell myself, but on Jack, those smells and that taste only intensified the tightening low in my belly, the anticipation of what would happen next.

Shifting my thighs farther apart, I gave him better access to my pussy. I wanted him so much, even though I didn't understand what that truly meant. A hollowness, a deep longing drew my body to his, and I instinctively lifted my hips to encourage him to fill me. Clinically, I knew we'd fit together, but nothing could prepare me for the sting as he stretched me and popped my cherry with the first thrust of his impressive cock.

Closing my eyes tight, I hissed in air through gritted teeth and tried not to cry out.

After seating himself deep inside me, Jack stopped moving. "Clio? What is it? Am I hurting you?" The concern in his voice forced my eyes open, and he saw the truth there.

His Adam's apple bobbed as he swallowed hard. "This is your first time, isn't it?" he asked, his voice raspy.

I nodded.

He closed his eyes, sucked in a breath, and dropped his forehead to mine. After a minute, he lifted his head and gazed into my eyes. "Do you want to stop, baby? Because if that's what you want, that's what we'll do."

So of course, I fell in love with him all over again. "No. Give me a second to adjust to you." I pulled in a breath, held it, and let it go. "You're kinda big, you know, even if I was experienced."

He grinned at my compliment before he leaned down and took my nipple in his mouth, laving and sucking and arrowing pleasure straight to my core. Involuntarily, I tightened my pussy around him. Jack groaned into my skin and pulled most of the way out of me before he plunged back in. This time his thrust stretched me, but without the sting. There was so much of him, but I discovered that when I tightened my inner muscles around him, hot, dark, incredible sensations shot through me.

"Oh fuck, Clio. You catch on quick. And it's been so long for me. If you don't cool it, I'm going to have no choice but to finish before you do." Jack panted. He stopped moving and held himself rigid above me, the cords in his neck standing out in relief as he fought for control.

"It feels good to you too when I do this?" I clamped myself around him again, and he moaned.

"Jesus, you have no idea how good, baby."

I smiled and ran my hands up over his sculpted chest and broad shoulders to his neck, which I held the same way I liked him to hold me. "Come here. I need a kiss."

Jack bent down and gave me what I wanted, his kiss lighting me up as always, and I arched into him. Of their own volition, my legs wrapped around him, and he started pumping into me. The first sting of his body entering mine became a distant memory as the pressure built deep in my belly. Soon, I was lost as wave and after wave of pleasure washed over me, and I cried his name over and over like a song.

"Clio!" Jack shouted as he joined me, our bodies fused into one being of completeness.

When at last my body stopped pulsing and the green lights no longer flashed behind my eyelids and I could breathe somewhat normally again, I relaxed my arms from their tight hold around his shoulders to smooth my hands up and down the warm, resilient skin and muscles of his broad back. Sighing in contentment, I brushed a kiss where his shoulder met his neck and smiled into his skin.

"Are you alive?" I asked, a smile in my voice.

"Barely." His reply was muffled by his face-plant in the pillow beneath my head.

"That was amazing, Jack. I never understood what the big deal was before. Now I think I do."

He lifted his head to stare into my eyes. "Clio." He stopped and dropped his head back onto the pillow beside mine. "You have no idea how big a deal you are," he mumbled.

At least that's what I thought he said. I couldn't be completely sure with his face buried in the pillow. Finally, he rolled off me, the loss of his heat leaving a trail of goose bumps over my skin. He slid off the bed and ambled into the bathroom to dispose of the condom.

Somehow, we'd wrestled the sheets and blankets down on the bed, and I slipped off my sandals before pulling up the covers and burrowing beneath them. As I lay there replaying what had happened between us, the mattress sagged as Jack returned to bed. He gathered me to him, spooning himself behind me, his arm protectively wrapped around my middle. "Sleep a little, babe," he whispered into my neck.

I settled back into him and drifted into a doze. The next thing I knew, Jack's hand was between my legs, his clever fingers gliding over my wet center. When I wiggled against him, I could feel his hard arousal snugged tightly in the cleft of my ass. "About time you woke up, Clio." The smile in his voice as he spoke into my neck warned me we weren't done.

He pulled away from me enough so he could roll me onto my back. With a grin, he climbed on top of me and kissed me crazy. In the space of a breath, I went from sound asleep to wildly needing to touch him everywhere. I couldn't keep my hands still, and he laughed into my mouth. "I like the way you wake up, babe."

Reaching across the bed to the nightstand, he retrieved another condom from a box in the drawer there, and a troubling thought flitted through my mind as I watched him tear open the packet and roll it over his erection. Another smile into my eyes chased all thought from my head. Parting my legs, he pushed into me slowly, testing my readiness for him, my level of comfort. When I lifted my hips, silently inviting him all the way in, I didn't have to ask twice.

Though I braced myself for a repeat of the sting, it didn't come. Instead, I sensed a perfect fullness through my entire body as I pulsed around Jack's thick length. Knowing where we were headed this time, I participated with my whole self, touching him everywhere I could reach, kissing his mouth, his neck, his shoulders, his chest. I dragged my nails up and down his broad back as he increased his rhythm in response to my touch. When we came together the second time, I shattered into a million tiny stars and fell asleep with Jack still inside me.

♪

Daylight streaming into the room and the sound of Jack's voice singing something I couldn't quite distinguish over the spray of the shower pulled me gently from sleep. When I snuggled back down into the covers to remain for a few more minutes in my semiconscious cocoon, the jarring clamor of a phone catapulted me into full wakefulness.

I bolted out of bed, dragging the sheet with me and wrapping it around me as I raced out to the sitting area to find the ringing phone. Finally locating it on top of the minibar, I answered it without even thinking. I listened to the person on the other end of the call leaving a message, one I heard quite distinctly—and pain lanced through me like a blade.

"Jack baby. I missed you last night. I'll be waiting for you at breakfast. Don't be late," a sexy female voice said. Before I could say anything, she clicked off.

For several long seconds after the woman ended the call, I stood rooted to the floor while random conversations from the previous night flashed through my head. "I haven't been with anyone since I joined the band over two years ago." "Clio, I've missed you so much." "Clio, I've been trying to catch up with you." And a *box* of condoms waiting in the nightstand drawer.

"I am so dumb. So amazingly stupid," I whispered to the empty room.

On autopilot, I started moving, dropping the sheet on my way back to the bedroom. It took me a few minutes to locate my panties and bra. Ruthlessly, I dragged them on before I grabbed my dress from the chair where it had landed the night before and tugged it over my head. I grabbed my sandals from the foot of the bed and hurried out to the sitting room in search of my purse, tugging up the zipper on my dress as I scrambled to leave Jack's suite.

I could hear him still singing softly in the shower, so I looked around for a notepad, and finding one on a side table, I dashed off a note:

> *It seems you forgot about your breakfast*
> *date. Good luck on tour. —Clio*

I left the note by his phone and let myself out of the room. When I was safely inside the elevator—mercifully alone—I slipped on my sandals and tried to smooth down my wild tangle of hair. Anything to distract myself from the emotions roiling through me. How, how, how could I have been so stupid? To give myself to a rock star, to a man who'd walked away from me before without a backward glance? Without an explanation? Why did I think I could trust anything he said? What had I been thinking?

Oh, yeah, I hadn't been thinking. From the minute Jack White-horse wrapped me in his arms and put his mouth on my neck, all my coherent brain functions had taken a minibreak while my body took over running the show. For a few minutes last night, I even thought I still loved him.

Watching the numbers of the floors count down, I stifled a sob. Who was I kidding? I'd never stopped loving him. That's why it had been so easy to give in to him, so easy to let him off the hook without a real explanation for why he walked away from me when we were in high school. So easy to be yet another one-night stand in his rock 'n' roll dream.

As I exited the elevator into the lobby of the hotel, I fished my phone from my purse and discovered several texts from Annabelle. Her name above the texts was all I could read as I lost my focus in the tears swimming in my eyes. It took me a minute to catch on that several people waiting for or exiting the elevators had stopped to stare at me. I dashed the heels of my hands across my face, squared my shoulders, and brazened out my walk of shame through the front doors of the hotel. Hailing a taxi, I gave the driver the address of the hotel Annabelle had booked us into for the night before and willed myself to hold it together until I reached the safety of my friend.

CHAPTER SEVEN

Clio

"LOOK WHAT THE cat dragged in," Annabelle said as she let me into the room I should have shared with her after the concert. "I take it you had an interesting night. I hope you used a condom." She smirked.

"I don't want to talk about it, Annabelle. What I want is a shower and a ride back to Fort Collins."

Something in my tone—or maybe the puffiness of my eyes—stopped her short, and her playful tone jumped into the backseat. "Hey. What happened?" She stuck her face right into mine, demanding my attention. "He didn't force himself on you or something?" The ferociousness of her concern made me feel better. Though she went through life like a tornado, her friends could count on her to stop and fight for them when they needed her. Right now, I needed her to take me home.

"Jack would never do that to me." *He'd never have to take what I so willingly would give.*

"Then why do you look like death warmed over?"

"That bad, huh? I've never done the walk of shame before,

Annabelle. Cut me some slack. Did you bring my little duffel bag in by chance?" I asked, changing the subject as I headed to the bathroom.

"It's on the other side of the *un-slept-in* bed. Checkout's in an hour."

"I'll be ready in fifteen minutes."

♪

It was closer to forty-five minutes when I finally declared myself ready to leave. I stood in the shower and let the silent tears fall for twenty minutes before I could gather myself enough to shower off my night with Jack Whitehorse.

When he dumped me back when we were actually dating, I thought I'd never find all the pieces of my shattered heart. But somehow over the years, I found them and glued them back together enough to be a functional human being, even finding a few other guys interesting enough to date along the way. One night with him ripped all that hard work to shreds. My only consolation was that no one but Annabelle knew, and I wasn't sharing anything with her about what had happened after Jack dragged me away from the party. The less I thought about how easily he'd played me, the better off I'd be.

"Did he at least give you breakfast?" she asked as we loaded our bags into the trunk of her Mustang.

The mention of breakfast brought back the memory of the message I listened to on Jack's phone, and I stumbled a step on my way around the back of her car. "I wasn't hungry. Still don't feel much like eating, but I could go for a venti Starbucks."

She laughed as she revved the engine of her Mustang and drove us out onto the road. "You were hitting the vodka rather hard last night," she said with a grin before she sobered. "Are you sure that's all it is? You're not acting like yourself, Clio."

"All right, since I can tell you're not going to let this go, here it is." I stared straight ahead at the passing traffic. "Jack Whitehorse and I dated for like five minutes when he was a senior in high school. We broke up right before he graduated, and last night was the first time we'd seen each other since then. And we spent the night rediscovering why we broke up."

"Whoa! You used to date Jack Whitehorse?" Annabelle's eyes saucered.

"Eyes on the road please. I'd like to make it home in one piece."

Ignoring my sarcasm, she said, "Holy shit, Clio. That's some secret you've been keeping. Why didn't you tell anyone after he joined Balefire?" Her brow creased. "I thought we were sisters. You don't hold out on something that big with your sisters."

"Since I had no way to prove it, it didn't seem like I should bring it up." I shrugged. "Besides, it wasn't that big of a deal," I said, almost choking on the lie. Jack Whitehorse would always be a big deal. I could see that even more clearly now than I could back when he was the center of my universe. When I thought I was the center of his.

"So how did your night go?" I asked, deflecting the conversation away from Jack and me. "Did you accomplish your goal of scoring with Dakota Perri?"

"What do you think?" She slid me a sly grin.

"Way to go, girlfriend," I said with a slow clap. "I suppose you have photographic proof?"

"Of course."

"And your heart's not broken?"

"Like Dakota, I was only in it for the sex. Which was spectacular. He thought so too and even walked me out to my car in the wee hours so I didn't have to do the walk of shame." We high-fived across the console between us.

"Do me a favor. If anyone in the band asks for my number, don't give it to them."

"You mean Jack didn't ask for it?" Any other time, the indignation in her tone would have comforted me. Right now, my own stupidity took precedence.

"Like I said, we rediscovered why we broke up. Then his girl-friend called and reminded him about their date for breakfast, and I excused myself to keep things from becoming more awkward." I stared at the buildings passing outside the Mustang's blacked-out windows. "I doubt Jack wants my number, but if he changes his mind, I'm not interested in giving it to him." I turned in my seat to face her. "You'll honor that, right?"

She frowned at me before returning her attention to the road. "Yeah, I'll honor that Clio. But judging from the way you looked when you arrived at our hotel, I'm not sure that's what you really want."

"Don't tell me what I want," I snapped and regretted my tone immediately.

We lapsed into a tense silence that she finally broke by turning up the stereo. Of course, the latest Balefire song blasted through the speakers, the one Blu Connolly said Jack had written. I stared blindly at the city passing by and tried not to listen. When we returned to campus, I disappeared into my room and spent a couple of hours deleting every Balefire song and video I'd ever bought from all my devices.

♪

Two months later

After we returned to school, Annabelle proved herself a loyal friend when she said nothing about me spending the night with Jack White-horse. In fact, she spun a story of nonsense about Joey and Shane—it turned out that was the guy's name—and everyone believed her.

The beginning of a new semester with new classes distracted me from thinking about my night with Jack—for part of each day anyway. But even the brutal workload in organic chemistry couldn't steal all thoughts of him from my mind. About a month after the concert, though, he grabbed top billing in my head.

At first, I thought I had the flu. But after a week of nonstop vomiting immediately after I woke up each morning, I had to consider another possibility. A trip to the student health center confirmed my suspicions. I believed the box of condoms in Jack's nightstand at the hotel were probably new. But the one in his wallet? The things have expiration dates for a reason.

I gathered my closest friends in my tiny third-floor room to share my news. And to sound them out on what they thought I should do. I was two months pregnant.

"Are you sure, Clio?" Stacy asked, the concern in her voice mirrored on Annabelle's face.

"Positive. Just like the little plus sign on the four sticks I brought home from the pharmacy and the one the nurse showed me at the student health center."

"Wow. I thought you said you used a condom," Annabelle said.

My shoulders sagged. "We did. But I guess I should have been prepared with some backup."

Though I tried to act matter-of-fact, the truth was, my *condition* scared the hell out of me. I had a little more than a year and a half left to finish my first degree. I'd need grad school to reach my goal of becoming a nurse practitioner. A baby definitely complicated that plan. Then a picture of the tiny life growing inside me flashed through my mind. I'd created a little person with Jack Whitehorse, and my fears for the future faded slightly. Jack's baby. Our baby. It felt simultaneously unreal and right.

Ever the practical one, Stacy asked, "Have you told your parents?"

"Not yet. Honestly, having the baby terrifies me less than telling Harrison and Meredith I'm pregnant. They're already disappointed in my life choices so far." I flopped back on my bed and stared at the ceiling.

"Do you plan to have it?" Annabelle asked.

"Yes."

"Are you keeping it?"

"Yes."

"Have you told the baby's father? If you're keeping it, he's going to have a right and a responsibility to know," Stacy said in a determined tone that had me sitting up again.

"I haven't told him, and as far as I'm concerned, he doesn't have a right to know if I'm not going to hit him up for child support. Which I'm not," I added emphatically. I couldn't imagine that Jack would welcome the complication of a baby in his life. Even more than having a girlfriend, being a father would seriously damage his rock 'n' roll hottie reputation.

"Well, then. You'd better tell your parents. After all, you're going to need their help." Annabelle picked up one of my nursing books from my desk chair, flipped through a few pages, set it on the floor, and sat down. "When are you due?"

"May, right after finals." I laughed hollowly. "At least the baby's timing is good."

"You know you're going to have to move out of the house," she said, her tone sad.

Swinging my legs over the side of the bed, I faced her. "Oh. Oh, wow. You're right. I hadn't thought about that."

"Seems you haven't thought about a lot of things. Are you sure having this baby is the right thing to do?" Annabelle asked.

A gentle calm stole over me as I contemplated her question. "Yes. I've never taken a big risk before, but of all the times to try one, this one seems totally right."

"If that's how you feel, we'll support you all the way," Stacy said as she leaned across my bed where we sat together and hugged me. Annabelle joined us on the bed for a group hug, and I found myself tearing up at the unconditional support of my friends.

♪

"You're *what?*" Meredith shouted at me the following Tuesday when I told my parents my news over dinner.

"I'm pregnant."

Harrison picked up the embroidered cloth napkin from his lap and delicately wiped his mouth before asking, "How far along are you?"

"About two months."

"Then you can easily get rid of it," Meredith sneered before she reached for her goblet of wine and downed half of it in one long swallow.

For a woman who prided herself on her manners and composure, gulping her wine was quite unladylike. Her response to my news should have given me my first clue about where our conversation would end up. Of course, I'd always underestimated my parents' self-centeredness.

Straightening my spine, I said, "I'm having this baby."

"Talk to her, Harrison. Make her understand how she cannot go through with this asinine idea of becoming a single mother."

"If she aborts it, there will be a scandal, darling," Harrison said, his tone insufferably reasonable. "If she gives it up for adoption, there will be a scandal. If she keeps it, of course there will be a scandal. These things have a way of not staying quiet."

"I'm right here," I huffed. "Stop talking about me as though I'm invisible."

"But if she has it and keeps it, we'll become pariahs among all our friends. You are in delicate negotiations with that conservative church organization. Our family cannot become involved in scandal, especially one so immoral. You must do something about this, Harrison." Meredith smashed her napkin down on the exquisite Belgian lace tablecloth and tried to dig her perfect manicure into the cherrywood tabletop. With a huff, she finished her glass of wine and held it out for our butler to refill for her.

"I'm not sure what that can be, darling. Unfortunately, I don't have access to a time machine so we can send Clio back to where she can unmake her egregious mistake."

That unwaveringly logical tone of his grated on my every last nerve. He always tried to sound so rational. He made me want to smash something. *Egregious* mistake? Seriously?

"Who is the father of this baby?" Meredith demanded.

"None of your business."

Somewhere deep in my subconscious I knew I only exacerbated my own problems. Of course, I expected they'd be disappointed in me, but I never expected such an all-out attack. Something inside me rose up in defense of the tiny life growing innocently inside my womb—and in defense of the man who put it there, a man who had taken precautions to avoid this exact event.

Meredith came to a decision, one she imparted to Harrison with a look. Standing from the table, she repaired to the sitting room next door to the dining room. I knew I was in real trouble then.

Harrison and I followed Meredith and found her seated on the edge of the love seat she preferred whenever she wanted to scold me like I was still a six-year-old. She intended for me to feel small, which she accomplished with too much ease. Harrison took the wingback chair immediately to her right and indicated I was to remain standing. Twenty-one years old, and they planned to dress me down like they had when I was eight and had the audacity to tell my favorite nanny Maria that I loved her. The dread I felt at the moment mirrored that long-ago time, memories of Maria's tearful departure that very afternoon flashing into my head.

"Since you can't unmake your mistake, and you can't ameliorate it in any way that doesn't bring scandal down on this family, you must leave this house and never return," Meredith said. The coldness in her voice did more to ice the blood in my veins than her words, which took a few more seconds to register. "Hutchins will oversee your packing, which you will commence as soon as we're finished here. You may take only those things which are personal to you, nothing that rightfully belongs in this house."

"Additionally," Harrison said, "you will no longer have access to any of our money, be that bank accounts, trusts, credit cards, or insurance we have set up for you. You are on your own."

I stared stupidly at them. I'd made one big mistake in my life, and they were disowning me? No, they were erasing me as though I'd never been a part of their lives, as though I didn't share their DNA. There they sat in all their monied splendor dismissing me, their own daughter—their only child—as though I'd been nothing more than a maid—or my nanny.

Not trusting myself to speak, I nodded and stiffly walked out of the room. If nothing else, I still had my dignity, and I refused to fall apart—or worse—beg them to treat me as though they'd ever actually loved me.

Hutchins, my parents' butler since before my birth, awaited me in my bedroom. Tears I refused to shed blurred my vision as I grabbed a suitcase from the top shelf of my walk-in closet and began filling it with random clothes, framed photos, a stuffed rabbit Maria had given me one Christmas that I'd steadfastly refused to give up. An empty box sat on my bed, appearing as though by magic, and I filled it with my high school yearbooks and favorite childhood storybooks. Most everything I truly valued I'd already taken to college—my journals, my music, my favorite pillow.

Without a backward glance, I followed Hutchins as he carried my heavy suitcase down the stairs to the front foyer. I half expected Harrison and Meredith to be standing at the front door witnessing my usual obedience or miraculously changing their minds. However, we walked through a deserted foyer before Hutchins opened the door for me to precede him out of the house.

For reasons I could never understand, my parents had always been cold people. Cold to each other. Cold to me. The only warmth, the only affection I could ever remember came from the servants. Even in this moment of my greatest distress, Hutchins didn't let me down.

Carefully, he loaded my few possessions into the back of my

car. As he did so, he spoke to me in a low tone. "Your mother is already three glasses of wine into the evening," he said as he opened the back hatch to my SUV. "I suggest you go online and raid your savings tonight. Open a new account and transfer your funds." He slid my suitcase into the back and took the box from my hands. "I believe this car is in your name. Don't let them try to convince you otherwise." He stowed the box beside my suitcase and walked me around to the driver's door. "Check with your university about your other needs—housing, insurance. Someone there can help you." He held the door for me to climb into my car.

"Why are you telling me these things?"

"Because I've watched you grow into a fine young woman in spite of the fact your parents treated you like furniture. They dumped their disappointments in themselves on you. You never deserved that, and you certainly don't deserve what they're doing to you now. If you need assistance, let me know. I'll do what I can."

"I won't jeopardize your position. I remember exactly what Harrison and Meredith do to employees they believe have betrayed them. Thank you for everything."

More than anything, I wanted to give Hutchins a hug, but fearing one or both of my parents watching from behind a curtained window, I held back. One person losing a position because of me had been enough.

Instead, I closed my car door, pulled around the circular drive in front of the Barnes mansion, and drove down the block, where I pulled over, parked, and gave in to the sobs I'd held in since I'd severely disappointed my parents for the third time in my life.

CHAPTER EIGHT

Jack

SOMEONE POUNDED HARD enough on the door to my hotel suite that it rattled on its hinges. I could guess who.

"Open up, Jack."

"Fuck you."

"It's Tron. Let me in, dude."

Sighing, I dragged myself off the couch where I'd flopped down a few minutes before and wandered over to the door. Without acknowledging him, I let him in and lay back down on the couch.

"We need to talk."

I jacked a brow. "Is this one of those relationship interventions or some shit?"

"Seriously, dude. You're driving the whole band fucking crazy. Ever since Red Rocks, you've been in a bad mood. You gonna tell me what happened?" he asked as he seated himself comfortably in a chair like he might be moving in with me.

We were in Dallas or Houston or Austin. It didn't matter. The towns and days and shows had become one big blur. The only thing I could focus on was that note Clio left the morning after the most glorious night of my life. She'd given me her virginity, for fuck's sake. That had to mean something.

Or not.

She heard that message on my phone and walked out without a backward glance. She decided I'd used her and offered me no chance to defend myself, explain to her Dakota's idea of a joke. That he woke me up every morning with whatever message she heard or something else like it. The band called me the monk for a reason. There were no women in my life.

I'd been waiting for her.

"You want to know what's been bugging me?" I sat up and stared him down. "It's fuckin' Dakota and his stupid idea of a fuckin' joke. He keeps stealing my phone and programming a wake-up call into it. Or having his most recent conquest call to wake me in the morning. After Red Rocks, I asked him not to leave the breakfast message on my phone anymore, but he won't let up. In fact, it's only gotten more explicit after each show." I tugged at my hair in frustration. "I'm sick of it, all right? He needs to let it go."

"Can I hear it?"

"I delete it every damn time. But you know what? When he sends it again tomorrow morning, I'll forward it to you for your listening pleasure."

"It's not the message, is it man?"

Something about Tron's steadiness, his straight man to Blu's lead singer preening and Dakota's over-the-top clowning drew me to him, made me trust him. He'd been asking about my state of mind for the past two months. Carrying around my hurt and confusion at the way things didn't work out with Clio after all my careful planning had worn me down. Truth was, I needed someone to talk to.

"Look, if I tell you something, can you keep it to yourself?"

"Sure man. You can trust me."

"Those other two clowns don't take anything seriously. I don't want this getting back to them, and the three of you go way back. I don't need their grief, Tron," I said, glaring at him.

"If it helps you deal with the bug up your ass, I'll take an oath on my very fine bass-playing fingers to keep my mouth shut. Now tell me what the fuck's going on with you."

I took a deep breath and plunged in. "Remember that girl I introduced you to after Red Rocks?"

"The hot redhead in the blue lace dress? Hard to forget that one."

"Yeah, keep it in your pants. She's spoken for."

"The monk ain't so celibate after all, huh?" Tron asked with a smirk.

I backhanded his thigh. "Stop being crude. We're talking about someone special here, not some random hookup."

He put up his hands. "Sorry."

"Clio and I go back to high school. We were really into each other back then, and even though we were so young, I was pretty damn sure she was the one, you know?" I flopped back against the couch cushions. "Anyway, her dad's a rich bastard, and her mom's a high-society bitch."

"No stereotype there at all." He grinned, and I half-heartedly flipped him the bird.

"Clio's parents are the poster children for rich stereotypes. Only they took it a step farther. Her parents were older when they had her, and I guess they couldn't have any other kids. She was born a girl when her parents wanted a boy, so she spent her life growing up invisible in her own home. Punished for being the wrong gender." Flexing my fists, I indulged in a nanosecond fantasy of planting them in Harrison Barnes's smug face. "Her parents trotted her out to show her off whenever she aced some academic test or danced a perfect ballet—then they put her away again." I blew out a breath. "On our first date, I think she said maybe five words."

Tron rested his elbows on his thighs and cocked his head. "You *are* talking about that gorgeous girl you introduced me to at the after-party, right?"

"Yeah."

He blew out a breath. "Jesus. How could they miss that?"

I shared a look with him. "I know, right? Anyway, her parents must have decided she liked me a little too much, and maybe the feelings were mutual, and they were in a position to do something about it."

Tron quirked a brow but remained silent.

"They had plans for her to attend Harvard Business School, come home, and join the board of directors for her father's company. And probably marry some rich bastard handpicked by dear old dad. Which meant, she had no business having an interest in a *musician*."

"You say that like it's a dirty word."

"Harrison Barnes's inflection, not mine," I growled. Memories washed over me. "One day a couple of weeks before my graduation, Barnes called me downtown to his office. Told me all about how he'd heard me play, knew talent when he saw it, and would I be interested in an opportunity to join a real band?" I couldn't help the mirthless laugh that came with the thought of the "real band" he'd meant.

"Of course, I said yes, and he offered me a contract with Rude Awakening. It came with strings attached, as I knew it would." Running my hands through my hair, I sighed. "I didn't read the fine print. When I signed the contract he'd drawn up, I realized I'd traded Clio for the opportunity to chase my dreams and a chance for my dad to maintain his business."

"Damn, that's harsh, Jack."

"Man, was I pissed. But it was my signature on the dotted line, so there was nothing I could do about it."

Tron stood and walked over to the minibar. He grabbed a couple of waters and wandered back over to his chair, handing me one as he sat.

"What did your dad's business have to do with it?"

"Dad's proud of his Native American heritage." I uncapped my water, slugged back half of it, and wiped my mouth with the back of my hand.

Tron slanted me a look. "As he should be." As the other member of the band with brown skin, he understood exactly what I meant.

"I know you know. But you also know how hard it can be sometimes to get work. The playing field isn't always even."

He nodded and tipped back his water, taking a long pull.

"Barnes had a big project, and my dad bid on it as a subcontractor. Barnes threatened to drop my dad's bid—and worse, blackball him for shading his bids—if I tried to go back on my word."

He choked, almost spitting out the drink he'd taken. "Jesus. That's fuckin' crazy. You were what, eighteen?"

"Yeah. And I had nothing, no experience, no leverage. Anyway, according to the terms of the contract, I had to wait until Clio graduated high school before I could even look her up on Instagram." Unable to sit still anymore, I stood and paced the room. "I went to her high school graduation, heard her give a kick-ass valedictorian speech, and watched her parents jerk her right out of the graduation party the minute her dad laid eyes on me there."

"Does she know any of this?"

"I never had the chance to tell her. Barnes can't do anything to me anymore, but he's still threatening my dad. With a kid in college and three more boys at home, my dad can't afford to lose work." With an eye roll, I preempted what I knew my friend would say. "Dad's too proud to take any help from me."

Tron clasped his hands between his legs and stared out the window.

"Judging from some things she said in Denver, I don't think Clio has a clue what her dad has done—or is perfectly willing to do—to control her life."

He glanced up at me. "That's the problem?"

"The problem is she heard Dakota's breakfast message, decided

I'd played her, and walked out before I could tell her anything, get her number, or even find out where exactly she's going to college."

Tron grinned. "I take it the two of you didn't talk much that night."

"Oh, we talked." The laugh that escaped me held no humor. "But like a dumbass, I thought I had more time with her. Since the band had a day off following Red Rocks, I had plans to spend it with her. Talk some things out. I was in the shower when Dakota sent his wake-up call, and when I got out, Clio was gone. I tried to contact her, but she blocked me in every media I tried."

"That explains things."

I nodded.

He tossed his empty water bottle at the trash can near the door, missed, and walked over to pick it up. "How did you arrange for her to be at the party?"

"One day, Bailey Saunders showed me some photos on his phone of a hot girl he met at some party in Denver. Clio was in the photos too. I casually asked him about the girl—you met her. Annabelle? I think she ended up spending the night with Dakota."

Tron nodded as he gave his water bottle another toss at the trash. "The one in the tight leather dress who was with your girl."

"That's the one. Anyway, I talked Bailey into hooking Annabelle up with tickets to the show and backstage passes to the party on the condition she bring Clio. Only neither girl could know it was my idea."

"Nothing could possibly go wrong with that." His voice dripped sarcasm.

I crossed my arms over my chest. "Bailey was all over it 'cause he thought he'd score with Annabelle. He had her number and arranged the tickets for her, and that's how I finally reconnected with Clio."

"You've still got it bad for her."

I blew out a breath. "Yeah."

He zeroed in on the obvious question. "Why haven't you gotten Annabelle's number from Bailey?"

"I did, and I called her, but she won't give me Clio's number."

"Why not?" One dark eyebrow rose. "She pissed about how her night with Dakota ended and taking it out on you?"

"That wouldn't be a surprise." I huffed out a mirthless laugh. "But no. Turns out Clio told her not to give it out, and Annabelle's being all loyal or some shit."

"Listen, buddy, we'll figure out some way for you to contact your girl." Tron hauled himself up out of his chair and grinned at me. "In the meantime, could you at least try to act like a human being sometimes? I mean, after everything you've told me, I get your bad mood and all. But this music gig is supposed to be fun."

He clapped a hand on my shoulder. "We have a night off. Let's go grab dinner and some beers and see what else this town has to offer."

I shot him a look.

He held up his hands. "Not girls. Maybe we can catch a pro game or something. It's Sunday. We'll have Garrett make some calls, see who's playing, score us some tickets."

I couldn't decide if Tron's good nature or the talking had lightened my mood, but for the first time since I'd walked out of the bathroom into an empty hotel suite in Denver, I felt better.

I grinned back at him. "What the fuck. Besides, Garrett needs to earn that manager's salary we pay him. Let's see if there's a football game in town tonight."

CHAPTER NINE

Clio

I PLOPPED DOWN ON a chair in the common room of the sorority. "Well, that's the first thing I can cross off my list," I said to Stacy.

"What did you do today? Find an apartment?"

"Almost as good. I found a job. I start the weekend after Thanksgiving actually, which is pretty decent considering I have no employment history." Privately, I wondered about anyone hiring me with my complete lack of understanding about what it meant to work. Of course, in short order, I was going to find out exactly what it was to have a schedule and hope for extra hours like several of my friends seemed to do.

"Rich girls aren't supposed to work. Didn't you learn anything in finishing school?" she sassed with an impish grin at me over the top of her sociology book.

Melodramatically, I threw my arm across my forehead. "I flunked finishing school. Another reason Meredith despaired of me." I sighed.

Though it was easy to make fun, the truth was my only real skills outside of studying were the kinds of things Meredith and her country club ladies cared about—knowing where the dessert spoon went, which fork to use for which course, how to say hello to the queen. None of which would keep me fed, clothed, and housed now that the Barneses withheld their money.

Mentioning my egg donor's name left a dull ache in my chest. Which was a ginormous improvement over the stabbing pain piercing my heart when I told my friends almost two months ago that Harrison and Meredith had disowned me. I think it was a full month after that terrible night before my heart climbed out of my stomach where it landed when they kicked me out of their lives. After another month of twenty-four-hour anxiety, I'd finally started working on what I needed to learn and do to survive on my own. Lucky for me, I had my sorority sisters who rallied around me and went to work to help me figure out what I had to do for myself and my baby after the Barneses jettisoned me from their lives.

Stacy let her book thunk to the table. "So, where are you working?"

Puffing out my chest, I pointed to myself and said, "You're looking at the new night desk clerk at the freshman dorm." Before she could open her mouth, I preempted her next question. "Yes, I told my supervisor I was pregnant when I interviewed, and he hired me anyway."

A genuine smile lit up my friend's face. "That's great, Clio. Congratulations."

"The best part is after I have it, I can bring the baby with me to work. Since I'll be giving birth between spring and summer semesters, I'll even have a little time off without having to inconvenience anyone with trading shifts or anything. It's pretty sweet."

Though I was nearly four months along, I had yet to show. All those hours at the barre when I was growing up followed by three years of workouts in the weight room had kept my abs tight in spite of my growing baby. Last week was the first time I'd had to pop the top button of my jeans. Weekend and overnight desk clerking meant it was unlikely anyone would notice my pregnancy even after my belly gave the appearance that I'd swallowed a basketball.

"Will you make enough to cover your expenses?"

Since Harrison and Meredith had cut me loose, my practical friends who hadn't grown up in a mansion with servants and access to a platinum credit card in their name had been teaching me how to budget and live within a limited income. So far, I'd been a quick study, walking to places I'd normally drive and skipping morning lattes. Though I hated to admit it, those changes made me feel physically better, ameliorating some of my morning sickness. Without access to a credit card, it went without saying that my shoe-shopping binges were over.

Thanks to Hutchins's advice, I'd rescued my savings account, though it wouldn't be enough by itself to see me through nearly two years of school—even with my scholarships.

"It pays minimum wage and is only twenty hours a week, which is about as much as I can handle and still keep my grades up, I think." Honestly, having never had a job before, I didn't have a clue if I could handle it. But I also didn't have a choice. The Barneses saw to that when they disowned me.

"Face it, Clio. You're going to have to join the rest of us poor saps and take out a loan. You can come with me to the financial aid office tomorrow since I need to meet with my advisor there anyway."

"I didn't know you had a loan, Stacy."

Having had access to Harrison Barnes's money all my life had evidently made me a snob who didn't notice other people's money issues. My heart slammed into my ribs. How would I ever repay a loan on minimum wage?

"It's actually not something one advertises, especially when one lives in a sorority, Clio." She quirked a brow. "Let's keep it that way."

A flush heated my neck and cheeks.

Mercifully, Stacy changed the subject. "About Thanksgiving. You're still planning to come home with me, aren't you?"

"You sure it's all right with your parents? I won't be in the way or anything?"

"You won't be in the way." Her sigh sounded a touch exasperated. "My mother will smother you. My little brother will fall madly in love with you. My dad will only pay attention to you if you make the mistake of walking in front of the television, impeding his view of the Lions-Packers game."

"Thanks," I said laughing. "Your family sounds wonderful."

Her wistful smile tore at my insides. "They truly are. It's going to be so much fun sharing them with you."

I made an excuse about studying so I could exit the room before she caught me tearing up. Though I blamed pregnancy hormones, I knew her generosity lay at the heart of my emotions. That and the fear about money issues swirling through my head.

For the first time since I discovered my pregnancy, I wondered how I was truly going to do it all—work, go to school, be a mom. I didn't have the first clue. As I raced up the stairs to my room, I willed my thoughts to slow down. Sagging against my closed door, I struggled to hold back the tears demanding to fall.

One thing at a time. I had a job. I still had a roof over my head. I had somewhere to go for the holidays. It was going to be all right. It had to be.

From the moment I'd joined the sorority, I'd kept myself a little apart from the other girls in the house. Making friends had always been a struggle for me. Growing up with people as monied and cold as Harrison and Meredith Barnes had taught me not to trust in relationships. It seemed whenever I formed one with a maid or more importantly, a nanny, that person would disappear from my life. The only constants I had were Hutchins, our butler, and Baxter, our chef, both of whom were masterfully circumspect about doling out their affection for me.

Thinking about Baxter brought to mind his secret recipe for sugar cookies, and I determined I'd make a batch to take to Stacy's for Thanksgiving. As thank-you gifts went, it wouldn't be much. However, I was learning that money was expensive but maybe not nearly as valuable as the things it couldn't buy. Like friendship and love and character. Besides, outside of pouring a bowl of cereal or shaking salad from a bag, Baxter's cookies were the only food item I knew how to make.

Pushing away from the door, I took two steps across my room, dropped down on my bed, and thought about the last time I baked cookies. For Jack. For Valentine's Day. A lifetime ago. Before Red Rocks, I'd convinced myself Jack had some character. His popularity in high school stemmed not only from his incredible musical skills but also from the way he treated people. He genuinely seemed to like them as he went out of his way to laugh and joke with everyone. It's how he'd convinced me to go out with him the first time. Now I wondered if I projected good qualities onto him because he was so gorgeous and talented and paid so much attention to me. Maybe he really was like so many of the others, pretending an interest in me that only went as far as Harrison Barnes's bank accounts.

A derisive laugh snorted out of me to echo in the silence of my room. Obviously, he didn't need Harrison's money now—how ironic Jack and I had switched places. Now he had all the wealth while I had to be ever so careful with every dime. Considering my finances caused me to wonder whether I might have to improvise Baxter's cookies if his secret ingredients exceeded my budget.

Even visions of sugar cookies couldn't stop intrusive thoughts about the night of the concert when I'd given Jack everything—my friendship, my love, my body. Maybe the draw for him had only been to put another notch on his headboard. He'd finally managed to bed his old high school sweetheart, the rich man's daughter—notch—now he could move on. Too bad I couldn't move on too. My inability to leave the past behind didn't have as much to do with the little life growing inside me as with the memories of the night Jack and I had spent together.

His strong, muscular body moving over mine, initiating me so blissfully into the mystery of sex. His possessive expression when he realized what he'd done. His musky male smell that invaded my senses. The way he brought my skin to life when he skimmed his calloused hands over me. What had happened between us was so much more for me than experiencing sex for the first time. What we did could only be described as making love. At least for me.

He said the guys in the band called him the monk because he didn't bang groupies, but the evidence in his room suggested otherwise. The readily available condom in his wallet and the drawer full of them in the nightstand beside the bed should have alerted me that I was just another willing body for him. Never mind that phone call.

Jack had tripped me up in high school, and I'd never fully regained my footing. The night of the concert proved that. One look at him, and I couldn't breathe. One touch, and I only pretended not to follow him. One kiss, and I willingly gave him everything he wanted. What troubled me most about it all was I feared if he walked through my door today, I'd repeat all my mistakes, give him everything all over again.

Jesus, what was wrong with me?

When it came to Jack Whitehorse, my lack of self-control proved I'd done the right thing by blocking him from my life. Clearly, I couldn't trust him—and I couldn't trust me either.

♪

We arrived at the Newhouse family's home late in the afternoon the day before Thanksgiving. Stacy had grown up in a small town in northern Wyoming, so we skipped our morning classes to make the drive. Even though I grew up in Denver and went to college an hour from the Colorado-Wyoming border, I'd never been to Wyoming. Though Stacy took it for granted, the trip was one big adventure for me.

After bucking hurricane-force headwinds from Cheyenne to

Casper, I understood why Stacy drove a gas-guzzling, three-quarter-ton, four-wheel-drive pickup truck. The fact she looked totally badass behind the wheel of such a behemoth, all five feet two of her, was a bonus. At Casper, we veered off the freeway to drive through miles of endless sagebrush over a flat, barren landscape. Having made the drive dozens of times, she hardly noticed the view, but the stark beauty of so much open space stole my breath.

Our arrival at her family's ranch at dusk caused a stir among the horde of dogs in residence, and she squealed in delight as she exited the truck to their barking cacophony. Not having grown up with pets, I was a bit more reticent about leaving the safe confines of the cab.

"Don't worry. None of them bite. They might try to lick you to death, though," she said, laughing as they wriggled and jumped around her.

Stacy's parents were no less affectionate than her pets when she walked into her house.

"Oh, baby, you're finally home!" Mrs. Newhouse gushed as she enveloped Stacy in a hug that brought tears to my eyes. What must it be like to be loved so hard, I wondered.

Mr. Newhouse wrapped his arms around both of his girls and said, "'Bout time. Good to have you home, Stace."

"Hello, Tardface," a lanky teenage boy said from his place at the table. "She's here. Can we eat now, Mom?"

"You're a senior in high school and still calling me junior high names," Stacy said with a scowl. "Nice to see you too, Chase." She mussed her brother's hair and jumped away with a grin when he slapped at her.

My heart squeezed in my chest at the family scene in front of me. Even her brother's affected nonchalance radiated the love this family harbored for each other. Sure, I'd visited other friends' homes, met their families, understood the icebox that passed for the Barnes residence wasn't normal. But somehow, the love so evident in Stacy's home smacked me right in the solar plexus.

As I watched the Newhouses with each other, I determined I'd create something similar in my own family. Only when I saw Stacy giving me a pointed look did I notice I'd covered my belly with my hand. Stepping forward, I extended my hand toward Mrs. Newhouse.

"Hello. I'm Clio, the stray Stacy dragged home for Thanksgiving. Thank you for having me."

"Clio! Stacy's told us so much about you. We're so happy you could join us," Mrs. Newhouse gushed as she took my outstretched hand to tug me into her embrace.

"Nice to meet you, Clio," Mr. Newhouse added from behind his wife.

Chase hastily stood up from his place at the table and flashed an accusing stare at his sister. "Geez, Stace. You didn't say anything about how hot your friend was, or I might have showered right after practice. 'Scuse me."

He hustled out of the kitchen to a bathroom I supposed while the rest of his family burst into gales of laughter.

"Told you, Clio. Chase is already in love with you," Stacy said.

♪

Thanksgiving Day began so well. My morning sickness had passed, and like I'd read in my nursing books, I entered my second trimester with a million watts of energy. Translation: Mrs. Newhouse didn't have nearly enough for me to do. First, I helped her and Stacy with dinner preparations. After they showed me how, I peeled sweet potatoes and chopped vegetables for turkey dressing. Next, I set the table with stoneware featuring a hunting motif. Mrs. Newhouse told me her husband had given the set to her as a joke one Christmas, and in retaliation, she'd used it every Thanksgiving since.

Afterward, Stacy and I joined Chase outside for a rousing snowball fight. I'd witnessed Stacy's pitching talent during Panhellenic intramural softball tournaments the last two spring semesters.

Watching her winging snowballs at her little brother, I discovered how my friend must have honed her talent. At well over six feet, Chase wasn't all that little. However, since he played basketball, his sport didn't prepare him well for hurling snowballs. Plus, we outnumbered him two to one. When we finally trouped back into the house for dinner, Chase looked more like a yeti than Stacy's younger brother.

Following dinner, we all took up space on the two couches and the two recliners filling the living room to watch football. Since no one in my family had anything to do with sports other than my father investing pro players' money, the game baffled me. The Newhouses, even Stacy, loved it though, cheering and groaning in turns for reasons I absolutely couldn't follow.

Replete from the delicious meal, sleepy from all the predinner exercise, and a tiny bit bored watching the game, I drifted into a doze. The intermittent shouting and moaning of the football fans in the room prevented me from dropping off into a full-fledged nap though, so I came wide awake when Chase shouted, "Sweet! Balefire's the headliner of the halftime show." He turned up the volume on the television as the first chords of Dakota's guitar introduced the new Balefire song currently tearing up the charts.

"Clio had a backstage pass to their show at Red Rocks last summer," Stacy informed her brother with a teasing grin. Apparently, he was a big fan of the band.

He looked at me with even more interest than he had when I first met him. "Lucky! I bet that was epic!"

"Yeah. They were pretty great," I said, trying to sound enthusiastic.

The TV cameras panned over the entire band before zooming in on Jack as he performed a short drum solo in the middle of the song. I tried to look away from the screen, but his rhythms, the wild intensity of his music, ensnared me as always. Why did he have to be so beautiful? That thick dark hair shifting over his head as he moved with the beat, the Celtic tribal tattoo seeming to writhe up and down his arm as he raised and lowered it to strike his drums, his whole body involved in driving the band's sound made him irresistible.

More than anything, I wished I could resist him, but it seemed Jack Whitehorse had, without even caring, made a home for himself in my heart. Watching him and his band tear it up on national television ached my heart. It took a long pull from my mug of apple cider to tamp down the lump in my throat. The scene before me drove home the truth—there was no room in Jack's dreams for a bookish girl from the suburbs.

The after-party for a national TV appearance would be phenomenal. No doubt, the number of celebrities in attendance would probably keep the band busy through the weekend. Thinking about Jack and some actress made my stomach hurt. Still, I couldn't wrest my eyes away from the show.

Afterward, I caught Stacy looking at me funny, and I worried I'd given myself away. I smiled my most winning smile at her and said, "Wow! That was excellent. They were that good at Red Rocks too, for sure."

"You had backstage passes? Did you meet the band?" Chase's eagerness to know my experience rescued me—at least for the moment—from his sister's scrutiny.

"Yeah, I met them. Well, all but Blu. But I met the others. Dakota is kind of a wild man."

"Considering how he shreds the lead guitar, that makes sense," Chase said.

Mrs. Newhouse saved me from having to discuss Balefire any further when she announced dessert. Never in my life could I remember wanting a slice of pumpkin pie more than I did in that moment.

The rest of our minibreak passed quickly. Stacy's pack of dogs and I made friends as I helped her walk them in the mornings. Chase declared I was the coolest of the friends Stacy had brought home so far since I made kick-ass sugar cookies and had met most of the members of Balefire. Mr. and Mrs. Newhouse invited me back for another visit. When Stacy turned her big truck south for our return to Colorado, I wished more than anything that I'd grown up in a middle-class family in a small town in Wyoming instead of alone in a cold mansion in Denver.

CHAPTER TEN

Jack

"SERIOUSLY, GARRETT? YOU booked us over Christmas? Again? I haven't had Christmas with my family since I joined the band," I said when our manager announced our current tour extension through the holidays and well into the New Year.

"What can I say? You guys are the hottest show playing right now. I wouldn't be doing my job as your manager if I didn't help you take advantage of that." Garrett grinned. "Besides, playing New York City over the holidays is fucking huge. Those dates will launch your Asian tour like a rocket."

"New York at Christmas?" Dakota asked as he sprawled across a leather recliner in Garrett's suite at our Chicago hotel. "Cool. I've always wanted to see New York at Christmas. See if all that 'Yes, Virginia, there is a Santa Claus' bullshit might actually be real." He smirked at me and tipped back the beer he'd cracked open when Garrett called us together for a meeting in his suite.

"By the time I see my family again, my youngest brother is going to have white Santa hair and a beard to match. Jay's fifteen, by the way," I grumbled as I flopped down beside Blu on a nearby couch.

"Not spending Christmas with your family the last two years didn't seem to bother you much. Can't help wondering what's changed. Couldn't have something to do with a certain hot red-head you reluctantly introduced me to after we played that concert at Red Rocks, could it?" Dakota prodded.

"Fuck you, Dakota. And leave Clio out of it."

"Clio, that's the one." He nodded. "Blu said he saw you dragging her out of the party like you couldn't wait to get into her panties. Then no one saw either of you for the rest of the night. Since that night, you haven't been any fun at all." He took a swig of his beer. "She blue-ball you or something?"

My hands tightened into fists, and I was halfway off the couch when Blu grabbed me and pulled me back down. He shook his head at me and kept a restraining hand on my arm.

"Leave it alone, Dakota. It would fuck up our tour if one of you two broke a hand on the other one," Tron warned from where he leaned against the minibar. Though his stance said casual, his tone brooked no argument. At least not from a sane individual. The jury remained out on Dakota's state of mind.

"I'm only sayin' Jackie-boy didn't have attitude before we played Denver, and he's had nothin' but attitude since."

"That wouldn't have anything to do with your wake-up calls, even after he's asked you for months to lay off, would it?" Again, a sane man might have paid attention to Blu's sarcasm.

Not Dakota. "Aw, come on guys. I'm just having a little fun with him. Being the youngest and newest one of us, Jack needs some hazing, yeah?" Dakota whined.

"He's been part of the band for almost three years," Tron reminded him. "Look, we all know how tight you and Dave were, but Dave walked away. None of us asked him to leave. He needed to sober up, and this life wouldn't let him do that. You have to stop taking it out on Jack."

Seeming to ignore Tron, Dakota said, "It'd help if you weren't such a monk. Jesus, women throw themselves at you, and you play 'em like dodge ball."

"I don't know why that bugs you so much, Dakota. It just leaves more pussy for you," I said.

"Whatever." He snorted and finished off his beer.

Tron handed me a beer. "His rhythms make you sound damn good, Dakota. Stop bein' such a dick and let him up."

Garrett clapped his hands together and said, "Now that we've finished the catfight portion of this meeting, maybe we can talk logistics and plan for the New York dates. Did I mention I've booked you guys on both Fallon and Colbert while we're in the city?"

Following Garrett's understated announcement, the four of us started talking at once.

"No shit!"

"Are you fuckin' kidding me?"

"No fuckin' way!"

"Man, I love Fallon. You're a fuckin' genius, Garrett," Dakota said with a huge grin while Blu and I high-fived each other on the couch. Tron cracked open a beer and toasted Garrett with it.

Garrett's announcement shifted the whole mood of the meeting.

"Maybe you can work on the new song Jack wrote. That one has potential. You might even debut it on one of those shows," Garrett said.

Though we'd decided to spend a rare day off during the tour by taking in the sights, Garrett's announcement sent us into a studio to rehearse. The howling winds Lake Michigan sent to attack Chicago might have contributed to our change of plans too. Mostly, we were all excited about the opportunity to meet some popular late-night talk show hosts and score more television time. Playing in front of a national audience on Thanksgiving had been a rush for us, letting the world know we'd arrived. The whole band was eager for more of that.

As we left the hotel, I wondered for the hundredth time if Clio had seen the show on Thanksgiving. I'd finally convinced Annabelle to give me Clio's number right before we played that pro football game halftime show, so I'd called her to ask if she'd tune in to watch. But Annabelle must have been messing with me because the number she gave me was no longer in service. Maybe Clio would catch one of the talk shows. Maybe she'd try to get in touch with me. Maybe my dreams were too big.

♪

"We rock Australia and go home," Blu said as he flopped down beside me on one of the plush leather couches on the jet.

"You say that like it's a bad thing," I replied, laughing.

"Even in your monkish state with women, you gotta admit, Jack, this tour has been one helluva party."

I nodded. "It has been at that, Blu. It has been at that."

He cracked open the beer he'd grabbed from the always-stocked bar on the private jet Balefire owned and finished half of it in one swig.

I stared out the window at the expanse of azure sky above and midnight blue water below as we flew over the South Pacific en route to Sydney from Hong Kong. *Who would have thought all those years ago when Mom and Dad gave me that beginner drum set for Christmas that I'd end up here?*

Quick on the heels of that thought came another, one that showed up in some form several times a day. *What is Clio doing right now? Does she ever think about that night? About me? What can I ever do to get her to trust me again? Why couldn't she give me a chance?*

I remembered every detail from that night. How I should have done what I'd set out to do—explain why I walked away from her in high school. Tell her about her dad's part in my decision. Trust that she wouldn't reject me for him and all his money and influence.

She'd looked so beautiful standing there in the window with the glow of the city lights haloing her, and she'd felt so right in my arms. Her skin was like satin, her taste strawberry sweet. Her pretty ass, which spooned perfectly against my groin in the middle of the night, tempted me to wake her up so I could have her pulsing wildly around me again. The sounds she made as I moved inside her made my temperature rise. The most intense memory that never left me alone was the way her gray eyes darkened into a storm of desire when she gazed into mine while I was balls deep inside her. She made me feel like Superman. I ran my hand down my face. Jesus, how I wanted her back in my life.

I shifted in my seat to keep my body from revealing where my thoughts inevitably took me. The guys called me the monk because they thought I had some kind of iron will or something wrong with me. I kept pretending the former when in fact loving Clio from a distance for such a long time had definitely fucked me up. Especially the part where I hadn't even talked to her in nine long months. Damn Dakota and his stupid morning wake-up calls. Damn Annabelle and that disconnected number and being literally half a world away from Clio.

Hell, it was all my fault. If only I could figure out how she'd react to finding out what her father did. Would she choose me over him? Back then? Now? Would she ever believe I didn't want to leave her? As usual, the questions with no answers played on a loop in my head.

"Hey buddy, where'd you go?" Blu asked from his seat beside me.

"Huh?" I blinked myself back into the present. "Sorry. You were sayin' somethin'?"

"Yeah, I was wondering if an Aussie accent might loosen you up enough to show some pretty sheila a good time while we're there. You can't go on an international tour and not partake in some exotic pussy at least once."

I started to laugh when Dakota butted in.

"Awww, leave the monk alone. He's savin' himself for some

redhead back in Denver. She must be a spectacular piece of ass for Jackie-boy to pass up all the gorgeous opportunities who've thrown themselves at him from Thailand to Japan and back again the past six months."

My fist would have connected with Dakota's smirk if I wasn't seated at such an awkward angle from him. Which gave Blu a chance to intercept me and save Dakota's looks.

"Stop baiting him, Dakota."

From somewhere in the cabin behind us, Tron spoke up. "One of these times, you're going to push him when neither of us is around to stop him from pounding your pretty face into a pulp. For the thousandth time, let up on Jack about that girl."

"You know, Dakota," Blu said conversationally from beside me where he still had a hold of my arm, "the way you keep bothering Jack about his love life makes me wonder if you have a thing for him. Is that it? You harboring a secret crush on our drummer?"

"Fuck you, Blu. You're not funny."

"No, he kinda is," Tron said. "Dakota has a boner for Jack."

I cracked up. "Maybe I need to create a breakfast message to leave on your phone, Dakota. See what the girls you bed think about something like, 'Morning, Dakota. Wanna come over to my room and beat my drum?'"

Turning the tables on him had the desired effect on my temper, and I relaxed enough that Blu let go of my arm.

"You're an asshole. You're all assholes," Dakota pouted as he walked to the back of the cabin and threw himself into a recliner.

"And you're a diva," Tron said, grinning at Blu and me. "Guess that's why you play lead and struggle so much with rhythm."

Dakota flipped him the bird before pushing back his recliner, closing his eyes, and pretending to ignore the rest of us.

Tron, Blu, and I burst out laughing. Dakota rewarded us by flipping us two birds. Though he didn't open his eyes, his lips twitched as he tried to suppress a grin. Tron handed me a beer, and the little squall brewing inside the cabin of our jet blew over. By the time we landed in Australia, we were all pleasantly buzzed and looking forward to the start of the last leg of our tour.

CHAPTER ELEVEN

Clio

I LAUGHED AS STACY and Annabelle helped me unload the last of my few belongings into my new apartment. "When I dreamed of moving into my own place one day, married student housing on campus wasn't in the picture."

After doing a little research, Stacy had discovered that single parents could apply to live in married student housing. Before the end of fall semester, I applied and received my acceptance letter right before I went home with Stacy to spend Christmas break with her and her family. By Christmas, I'd thickened through the middle, and Stacy's mom figured out my situation pretty fast.

"I had these packed away after I bought some new things. I planned to donate them to Goodwill, but it seems you can put them to use too," she'd said as she loaded a box of dishes and another of pots and pans into the back of Stacy's truck before we headed back to campus. Even though I had no cooking skills whatsoever, I teared up at Mrs. Newhouse's generosity.

When we returned to campus the weekend before spring semester began, Stacy took me on a tour of secondhand stores where I found a decent double bed, a dresser, a couch, and a coffee table. The efficiency kitchen in my apartment included an island, and the couple who'd moved out had left behind their barstools, which meant I didn't need a dining table and chairs. It wouldn't be much, but thanks to Stacy, I was able to wade through the murk of student financial aid, and my furniture purchases didn't dent the loan I'd secured much.

The way my friends rallied around me constricted my throat whenever I stopped to think about it. Though I had no idea how I'd made such great friends, I had no doubt about how lucky I was to have these women in my life. To say they saved me was a massive understatement. As lifelines went, my girlfriends were steel cables.

As we sprawled on the floor and couch in my new place, Annabelle announced, "This is a monumentous occasion. We need to celebrate."

"Monumentous, Annabelle?" Stacy laughed.

"Absolutely. Clio is the first of us to have her own place. Carve it into Mount Rushmore," she said with a slashing gesture and an Annabelle-sized grin.

She called in an order with a local pizza delivery shop we all kept on speed dial before she walked out the door without a word. Stacy and I stared at each other in bewilderment before we burst out laughing. Whatever Annabelle was up to wouldn't surprise us. We'd learned a long time ago not to try to predict what she'd do next.

A short while later, she showed up simultaneously with the pizza delivery guy.

"What did you order?" I asked as I grabbed the boxes of pizza and tipped the driver.

"Something for everyone," she said. "Of course, you'll have to be the designated mom tonight—as usual these days—so here's your ginger ale."

She handed me a two-liter bottle and a bag of plastic cups.

"The rest of us will enjoy a classic Italian dinner including wine."

From the carrier bag in her hand, she produced three bottles of red, and I groaned in frustration. "Someone needs to rethink the whole staying sober part of being pregnant. I didn't discover how much fun drinking wine with the girls was until I met you ladies. Now I only get to watch. It's so unfair," I said with a pout.

"After you have the baby, you're going to have to switch over to drinking beer," Annabelle said as she uncorked the first bottle by carefully punching the cork down into the bottle with the stiletto heel of her boot. She accomplished the maneuver so effortlessly that I think she may have invented the sorority corkscrew. Yes, the girl had helped me carry heavy boxes while wearing stilettos. Annabelle truly was a wonder.

Stacy wrinkled her nose. "Why will she have to drink beer?" she asked as she opened a box of pizza. "Oh, yum! You ordered taco pizza. But does that go with wine?"

"All pizza goes with wine," Annabelle pronounced with an eye roll. "Clio will have to drink beer to make thick milk for the baby. Bet that's even in one of your nursing textbooks, huh?"

"That's an old wives' tale, Annababy," I said with a grin. "Besides, I was kidding. Now that I have someone else to worry about besides myself, I'll have to party vicariously through you."

I reached for the unopened box of pizza and found to my delight that my friend had ordered Hawaiian, my favorite. Ginger ale didn't complement it like a nice red, but my happiness in sharing the moment with my two favorite people gave the simple meal the flavor of a gourmet feast.

The way Annabelle improvised a corkscrew demanded the two of them finish each bottle of wine they opened, which meant they finished all three and were in no shape to drive back across campus to the sorority house. The couch I'd bought unfolded into a bed, so they shared it while I retired to my double bed that took up most of my bedroom. We'd had to unpack several boxes before we found the one with the thousand-thread-count sheets and cashmere blankets

I managed to have with me already when Harrison and Meredith kicked me out. The linens made our small beds cozy at least.

By the time the girls left me the following day, we'd unpacked and put away my clothes, books, the dishes Stacy's mom had given me, and the box of baby things I'd started collecting. Before they went back to the sorority house, I hugged my friends tightly and fought the tears threatening to give away how much I was going to miss seeing them every day. Living in the sorority for two and a half years had been a highlight of my life. The noise of the constant coming and going of a houseful of women, the shared laughter and commiseration, jostling for time in the bathroom, the comfortable knowledge of someone always being around made me feel safe, like I belonged. For once, I'd felt visible.

Now I was truly on my own. Loneliness gathered around me like a black cloak, and I wondered what I'd do with myself. I knew I could always visit the sorority, and I would. I also knew Stacy and Annabelle would never desert me. But nothing would ever be the same as it had been before I reconnected with Jack Whitehorse for one unforgettable night.

Nothing. Would. Ever. Be. The. Same.

Nothing.

As though I'd lost control of my will, I found myself in front of my computer pulling up Balefire's official website. Reduced to cyberstalking, I checked out the band's current tour and discovered that over the holidays, when I'd been too busy to watch television, Balefire had guested on late-night TV. A link on their website took me to the recordings of their performances, and I couldn't help myself. I had to watch.

There they were, all four of them seated on Jimmy Fallon's studio couch, chatting about their upcoming tour through Asia. Dakota and Blu did most of the talking, so the cameras focused on them. When Jack came on screen, I paused the recording and stared at him. He looked so at ease, so beautiful. As I catalogued his features, my mind drifted to our baby, and I wondered if he or she would look more like Jack or like me. His sculpted cheekbones and square jaw would be striking on a boy or a girl. His light brown skin combined with my auburn hair and gray eyes would be gorgeous. His long-sleeved T-shirt stretched over defined muscles, and I hoped our baby would inherit his strength.

I placed my hand on my belly and felt a tiny fluttering. "Oh, Jack," I whispered, "our baby's moving. It feels incredible. Like butterfly wings." I closed my eyes and let myself daydream that if Jack were with me now, he'd be thrilled to feel the baby moving inside me for the first time. Our baby. I knew better, of course. But for a little moment, I indulged in my new favorite fantasy.

As usual, my emotions threatened to overcome me, so I hit play again on the computer, and the recording skipped to the band on stage debuting their newest single. Blu had made a big deal about how Jack had written the tune, so I cranked up the sound on my computer.

The song opened with a blistering guitar solo. Even though I'd only talked to Dakota for a couple of minutes once, I knew from following the band what a showman and attention hog he was. Jack opening his song with Dakota's guitar showed how tight he was with the band. After a few bars, Dakota turned it down enough for Blu to sing the lyrics. Jack supplied the harmonies, a fact that still stymied me. We'd dated for months, and he'd played his rhythms every time we were together, either on an actual drum set or on the steering wheel and dash of his truck or on a desktop with or without drumsticks. He'd even work out rhythms with his hands and fingers on my back as he held me, and sometimes when he was being especially playful, on my ass. I smiled at the memories.

However, in all those times, I'd never once heard him sing. Now, as I listened to his song, I lost myself in the beauty of his tenor voice softly backing Blu's melancholy baritone. The music itself mesmerized me so much at first that I didn't pay attention to the words until I heard, "Our love lost in opportunities." That line hauled me up short.

I scrolled the recording back to the beginning of the song and listened intently to the words.

You were everything I ever wanted.
You were everything I ever needed.
But I let my dreams get in the way.

You were everything I ever wanted.
You were everything I ever needed.
Such a damn high price to pay.

And now I'm missing you every day.

Life on the road is long.
I'm so far from my home.
I can't return in my memories.

Havin' you by my side,
You don't know how hard I tried.
Our love lost in opportunities.

You were everything I ever wanted.
You were everything I ever needed.
But I let my dreams get in the way.

You were everything I ever wanted.
You were everything I ever needed.
Such a damn high price to pay.

And now I'm missing you every day.

Jack dropped the hammer on the tom-toms on the "havin' you by my side" lyric, a rhythm I knew and understood. The tom-toms had always drawn me to him when he played back in high school, and I couldn't help but respond to their sound and key on the lyrics accompanying them.

I repeated the song, this time catching Jimmy Fallon's introduction. "We're so excited that Balefire's debuting their new song with us tonight. Give it up for 'Missing You.'" I focused my ear on the lyrics rather than on the rhythms of Jack's drums, and something inside me broke. When the song ended, I dashed the heel of my hand at the tears silently flowing down my face. Jack's song, so sorrowful, so powerful, Blu's voice, so melancholy, tore at me. Someone had come along after me and broken Jack's heart. Boy, did I know how that felt.

Somehow knowing I needed comfort, my little one fluttered inside me again, and I sniffed back my tears. Jack Whitehorse had broken my heart—twice—but he left me something special to remember him by. As much as my baby had already disrupted my life, and as much as I could imagine she or he would continue to disrupt it, the little person growing inside me made me truly happy. My baby's response to my distress over Balefire's new song proved to me the two of us were already a team. Life might have taken a hard ninety, but maybe this new direction was where I was meant to go.

♪

My due date loomed on this day of lasts—last day of regular classes and the last day of my childbirth classes. After finishing both, Stacy and I sat in the coffee shop of the student union. I dropped my head to the table and sighed.

"Thanks again for agreeing to be my birth coach and attending the extra classes with me." Glancing up, I said, "I gotta tell you though, between school and work and this acrobat inside me, I'm exhausted."

"You know, Clio, you're so petite, you look like you swallowed a basketball," Stacy said with a laugh.

Dropping my head again, I didn't even try to suppress the annoyance I knew masked my face.

"Your baby has nowhere to go but out. From the back, you don't even look pregnant, and you're due any minute," she said in a tone meant to mollify me.

I sat up quick. "Don't say that! My water might break right here, right now, and how embarrassing would that be?"

She laughed again. Glad someone was enjoying herself at the moment. "At least you'd have an interesting story to tell your kid's friends one day."

"I think I'll let my kid do all of her own embarrassing things and record them on my phone to show all her friends."

"You've decided you're having a girl?"

"That's the special for today. We'll see how much the little beggar thinks it needs to move tomorrow."

"What do you mean?"

"When the baby's being especially acrobatic, I decide I'm having a very busy boy. When the baby's being calm, I decide I'm having a demure little girl. Today is a demure day."

"You could have solved the mystery with one easy procedure, you know." Since I'd asked her to be my birth coach, Stacy had made it her personal mission to learn all things pregnancy related and share them with me. Like I wasn't a nursing major or anything.

Early in my pregnancy, I'd had the standard ultrasound to make sure the baby was fine, but it had been too early to determine the gender. Having another ultrasound solely for the purpose of discovering the baby's sex was an unnecessary expense, which Stacy should have been proud of me for avoiding. Besides, unlike my biological donors, I didn't give a care which sex I gave birth to as long as my baby was healthy. Obviously, I knew—and understood—very little about boys, but I figured if I had a boy, he'd teach me all about them. If I had a girl, I'd raise her to be strong and happy in herself. Either way, in a short time I would have a person in my life who would welcome all the love I had in my heart to give. Such a novel circumstance was one I couldn't wait to experience.

"It doesn't matter, Stace. I'm not giving him or her back," I said with a grin.

She smiled back at me then sobered. "You know, Clio, I don't think it's good for you to be alone in your apartment this close to your due date. I was thinking I could sleep on your couch during finals."

"Oh, Stace." I reached across the table and squeezed her hand. "You're the world's best friend, but I couldn't ask you to give up your comfy bed during finals week when you need to sleep. I'm going to feel terrible enough as it is if the baby decides to come a week early and disrupts your exams."

"I've already cleared it with my professors, so stop worrying about it. But I'm going to sleep better knowing I'm right there with you if you go into labor in the middle of the night."

Out of all my friends, she'd proven the steadiest. However, since we started taking the birthing classes, she'd become more neurotic than the most nervous father on the planet. Luckily for both of us, my pregnancy had been pretty easy. For Stacy's sake, I hoped the baby's birth would be textbook perfect too, or she might not want to become a mom someday.

In the course of her research, Stacy hadn't only read up on pregnancy tests and procedures, but also on birth horror stories. Because learning about pregnancy and childbirth was part of my nursing program, I'd read those same types of stories from a clinical view. Which made them far less and far more terrifying. I finally had to insist she not read any more of them when she started trying to attach herself to my side.

I did have to admit, though, it had become increasingly difficult to be alone. More and more often, I found myself longing for Jack and wishing I could share this experience with him. Not that I thought for a second that he'd welcome it if he knew. Still, I loved him. I'd loved him since I was sixteen years old, and sharing my pregnancy and the birth of our baby with him would have been such a rush if he'd felt the same way about me. Which he clearly did not.

On that morose thought, my resolve not to be a burden to my friends weakened. "Okay, you can sleep on my couch. But you can't cook any of your deep-fried favorites at my place. That oily smell gags me." I rubbed my round belly. "I don't think the baby likes anything fried."

A wicked smile flashed over her features. "For that, I'm ordering a triple-shot espresso and savoring all of it in front of you."

"That's downright mean, and you know it."

"I also know how much you love your coffee and how much your baby hates it," she added with an evil grin.

"I won't be pregnant forever, even though it feels that way right now." I slouched back in my chair and sighed.

"Hey, it's only coffee. At least I didn't drag you out to a bar so you could watch me enjoy a giant goblet of wine."

"Ugh!" I threw my hands up. "Why are we friends again?"

"Because we had the good sense to choose each other as room-mates the first semester after we pledged Chi Phi." She pushed out her chair and stood. "Now be a good girl and sit with me while I enjoy my coffee."

While Stacy ordered her triple espresso, Baby Barnes decided to stretch to her full length inside me. When Stacy returned to our table, she took one look at me and said, "You're not going to let me finish this, are you?"

"You have it all wrong." I panted. "I'm perfectly fine with you finishing your latte, but I don't think I'm in charge anymore." With a groan, I pushed out my chair and leaned heavily on the table to stand. "As we discussed earlier, my baby isn't a big fan of coffee."

The first contraction rolled through me, and I gasped in a breath. A couple seated beside each other at the next table glanced up from their phones. The one guy dropped his phone in his lap, while the blood drained from his boyfriend's face. I might have laughed at their expressions if my teeth weren't ground together to keep from screaming.

"Oh, crap! You're having the baby now," my friend announced loudly enough to stop all conversation around us in the busy union.

My snarky retort died on my lips as another wave of pain rippled over my belly. All morning, I'd experienced a dull ache low in my abdomen. The speed of my contractions at the moment told me I should have paid more attention to that ache. I panted a couple of breaths and nodded at Stacy.

By then, the two guys from the next table were standing beside Stacy and asking what they could do to help. Between the three of them, they hustled me out of the coffee shop and across the street to the lot where I'd parked my car. Stacy steadied her nerves with one hand on the wheel and the other wrapped around her espresso, which she only gave up when the attending obstetrics nurse pried it from her grip as we entered the maternity ward in the hospital.

CHAPTER TWELVE

Clio

ANGEL CLAIRE BARNES decided to make her debut the weekend before finals. Fortunately for me, my professors allowed me extensions for completing my exams. Stacy wanted to stay with me and help with the baby after we came home from the hospital, but I insisted she sleep in her own bed at the sorority. Angel and I needed to establish a routine. It took us the better part of a month for her to arrange her days and nights in a way that made sleep possible for me, let alone for my friend. Stacy's professors didn't see any reason why she needed extensions for her exams since I'd given birth early on a Saturday morning.

Even with the initial sleep deprivation, I couldn't believe what a rush it was to be a mom. I spent hours sitting on the couch in my tiny apartment, Angel in my arms, the two of us staring into each other's eyes, connecting. Though obviously I did all the talking, I knew she absorbed every word. Whenever one of my friends came to visit and insisted on holding her, she looked around for me, and I knew that for one person in the world, I mattered more than anything else. For the first time in my life, I came first in the life of someone I loved. And I loved Angel desperately, fiercely, with an all-consuming devotion I didn't understand—or question.

Though my life became exponentially more complicated once I was responsible for the well-being of someone so precious to me, I still found myself at odd times—and every single night before I fell asleep—thinking about Jack Whitehorse. I wondered if his dreams were everything he'd hoped they'd be. Occasionally, I looked the band up online. Fine. I followed them on Instagram, so I knew they were on hiatus for a while after returning from their Asian tour. As I spent yet another afternoon staring at Jack's handsome half-Native American features, I wondered what he'd do if he ever found out about Angel.

The thought terrified me, and I did my best to put it out of my mind whenever it intruded there. I couldn't imagine any scenario where Jack welcomed the news that he had a daughter with my hair and heart-shaped face and his beautiful brown skin and seafoam-green eyes. At only a month old, Angel possessed striking looks. More than once, total strangers had stopped me in the grocery store, on campus, and on the street to stare at my daughter and comment on her beauty. As beautiful as Angel was, she'd only be in the way of Jack's rock 'n' roll lifestyle—that much I knew as sure as I knew I'd been nothing more to him than another groupie.

Though other people agreed with my biased view of my daughter's looks, my sole interest lay in her happiness. More than anything, I wanted Angel to grow up strong and confident, knowing that no matter what, her mom would be right there supporting her. Giving birth to Angel and spending that first month with her made me wonder for the millionth time how Meredith could give birth to me and be so indifferent and sometimes downright hostile toward me. What had been so wrong with me that the people who looked so happy in the photos I'd seen of a pregnant Meredith had never shown me affection and apparently equated love with material things? Becoming a mom myself made me question Harrison and Meredith's self-centered detachment from me even more.

It made me wonder again how Jack would react to seeing his baby. From the band's Instagram page, I knew they'd be heading home any day now after their tour through Asia. I wondered if Jack would be back in Denver. The thought of him being so close terrified me with how much I wanted to see him, even if it was only a glimpse. Sometimes, I truly worried about where my thoughts wandered.

I'd just finished nursing Angel and put her down for her afternoon nap when Annabelle texted me. As I read her text, my heart lodged in my throat while my mind froze.

I didn't give out your phone number, but Jack Whitehorse dropped by the house looking for you. He's on his way to your place now.

Jack was in town? Jack was coming here? To my apartment? Now?

So I'd been right about the band heading home after their tour. But why would Jack seek me out? After the way our one night together ended, what could he possibly want with me? *How will he respond when he finds out about Angel?*

More than anything, I wanted to run away, but Angel slept contentedly in her little bassinet in my bedroom, and I wouldn't disrupt her schedule to run from Jack. Besides, doing so would only put off the inevitable. But oh God, what was I going to say to him?

I didn't have a chance to think about it before the doorbell echoed through my apartment, and I jumped and covered my scream with my hand. After a quick scan for any telltale signs a baby lived here, I grabbed a baby blanket from the back of the couch and a stuffed kitten off the floor. I raced to my room to check on Angel to make sure the loud chiming hadn't awakened her, dropped her baby things on my bed, gulped a breath, and hotfooted it to the door before Jack could ring the bell again.

"Jack! What are you doing here?"

"Must be a big place you've got that you're out of breath answering the door," he said laughing. "May I come in?"

Having no real choice, I opened the door wider and stood aside as he strode past me. While he took up all the space in my tiny apartment, I stood at my open door, staring at him. Though his tall, broad-shouldered body seemed to fill up my living area, I struggled to process that he stood in the middle of it.

"Did I catch you working out or something?"

"Um, no. I don't get many visitors, so the sound of my doorbell in the middle of the afternoon startled me." With a swallow, I tried to compose myself as I closed the door. "What are you doing here? Aren't you supposed to be on tour or something?"

"Just got back from six months in Asia. Before that, we toured for four months here at home. Before that, we were in Europe for a couple months."

As I watched him glance around my home, I wondered what was going through his mind. Was he cataloging my used furniture, the lack of art on the walls, the dollhouse size of it?

"Wow. Sounds exciting. Everything you ever wanted." I stuffed my hands in the front pockets of my shorts. "What are you doing in Fort Collins?"

"Finding you."

The deep timbre of his voice rippled through me on those two words, and I nearly reached out to him. But I caught myself, remembering the breathy voice of woman on his phone, and I walked around my island instead. "You want something to drink? I'm afraid I don't have anything stronger than soda or iced tea."

"I want to talk to you, Clio."

I faced him with the safety of the island between us. "About what?" Panic made my heart race. Had he found out about Angel somehow?

"About that night after our concert at Red Rocks."

Putting on a brave face, I said, "Listen, Jack, I get it. You were playing a huge show for the home crowd. Everyone was there, and you forgot you had someone else lined up when you ran into me."

I waved a hand in front of my face and finished with a lie. "Don't worry about it."

His gorgeous eyes blazed green fire. "Did you forget the whole part where I engineered your presence at that party? I explained to you then what I did to get you there."

Suddenly, my bar didn't feel like a barrier at all.

"I'm sure your friend Annabelle told you. You were the only woman I had 'lined up,'" he said, air-quoting the words. "That message you heard on my phone the next morning was Dakota's idea of a joke. The fact that I don't sleep with all the groupies who throw themselves at us on tour grates on his nerves." He pulled his trucker hat off his head, ran his hand over his thick, dark hair, and replaced his hat. "He thinks it's funny to have whatever woman he spends the night with record a message, which he forwards to me as a wake-up call."

Crossing my arms over my chest, I stared at him for a beat. "Sure. That absolutely explains the box of condoms in the drawer in the nightstand too, Jack. Come on. Give me a little credit. I'm not completely naïve."

He leaned on the counter, his square jaw jutting out as he said through clenched teeth, "What about the part where I set up the evening with you did you miss, Clio? I had plans for us for that night, plans that included being responsible."

"Why, Jack? Why did you have plans for us that night after you didn't even think about me for nearly five years?" I tried to keep the piercing hurt that I'd buried for so long out of my voice, but the words stuck in my throat all the same.

He sat heavily on a barstool. "Believe me, Clio. I've thought about you constantly for all that time. There were"—he hesitated—"things that got in the way of us. But those things aren't there anymore, and I want to reconnect. That's what I was trying to do after the show at Red Rocks." His eyes pleaded with me. "The timing when we were in the middle of the US tour wasn't great, but I was so close to you, I had to give it a shot. Now I'm off the road for at least a month, and I want to spend time with you."

I tightened my arms around myself. "Just like that, huh? You walk through my door like you own the place and announce that you want us to 'reconnect,'" I air-quoted him. "It's not that easy Jack. What if I have someone else in my life now?"

He stood up again. "He'll have to prove he's the better man, that he wants you more, that he cares about you more than I do. Frankly, Clio, I doubt that's possible for anyone else to do."

Jack took one step, two steps, toward me as he spoke until he'd rounded the island and backed me up against the counter between the sink and the fridge. Still, I kept my arms protectively crossed over my chest and stared up at him defiantly. No matter how much I wanted to believe him, not only did I have my heart to shield, but also my little girl innocently sleeping in the next room.

Slowly, Jack reached for me, like someone trying to coax a wounded bird into his hand. He ran one gentle finger over my cheek and tucked a stray strand of hair that had escaped my ponytail behind my ear. I sucked in air at his touch but otherwise pretended his nearness didn't affect me. He must have sensed the lie as his nostrils flared, and he dropped his beautiful long-fingered hand to his side.

"The thing is, Clio, there isn't anyone else. Not for me. Not for you. That much was obvious when you let me be your first lover." He stared at my mouth for a beat. "I suspect I've been your only lover."

I clamped my lips shut at his not-so-subtle comment.

"What I don't understand is why you're living here, in married student housing, rather than in your sorority house. When I asked your friend Annabelle, she was about as helpful with that information as she was with giving me your number. Which, by the way, I'd like you to give me now."

He pulled his phone from his pocket and started typing into it. When I didn't talk right away, he stopped and raised an expectant eyebrow at me. "Your number?"

Sighing, I rattled off the numbers even though a little voice in the back of my head kept reminding me he'd probably delete me the minute he found out about our baby.

"Now, where is your phone?"

I pulled my phone from the back pocket of my jean shorts. "Here."

He snatched it from my hand and programmed his number into it.

Handing my phone back to me, he said, "There. Now we can communicate like normal people since you apparently do nothing on social media."

"Some of us are more private than others," I responded to his veiled question.

Jack let that go as he took two long-legged strides to the couch, sitting in the middle of it and giving me room to breathe for the first time since I'd received Annabelle's text.

"What kind of pop do you have?" he asked casually as he made himself at home by taking up most of my couch with his tattooed arm draped across the back of it and one knee drawn up on the cushion.

"Diet Coke, root beer, a cream soda Stacy must have left here when she stayed with—" I stopped myself before I blurted Angel's name. Stacy had watched her when I took my last final last week.

Oblivious to my blunder, Jack said, "I love root beer. Do you have ice?"

I pulled a glass from the cupboard by the fridge, filled it with ice from a tray in the freezer, and poured his root beer over it. Then I poured myself a glass of iced tea and joined him on the couch, sitting in the far corner opposite him, my knee drawn up protectively between us.

His demeanor made it clear he intended to stay for a while, which meant the chances of Angel making her presence known increased by the second. Somehow, I needed to tell him about the third person currently in my apartment. Jack gave me my opening.

"Tell me again why you're living here?"

Carefully, I placed my drink on the coffee table in front of me, took a deep breath, and said, "I don't live here by myself, and the dorms and the sorority don't allow children to live in them."

Now it was Jack's turn to sit forward and put his drink on the coffee table.

"Children? What are you talking about, Clio?"

On cue, a noise erupted from the peanut gallery, and Angel took care of introducing herself.

"Just one. Child that is. Excuse me."

I stood and walked into my bedroom to check on Angel, who must have heard our voices and awakened early from her nap. She looked up at me from her bassinet and smiled. She'd started doing that recently, smiling, and my heart melted every time. "Hello, beautiful girl. Did you wake up early? Come here. There's someone I need to introduce you to."

Jack's eyes rounded to saucers, and he came to his feet in a rush when I reentered the living room with Angel cradled in my arms.

"This is my daughter, Angel Claire. She's the reason I live in married student housing."

Jack blinked, his mouth agape. After several long seconds, he finally choked out, "Your daughter?"

I could tell from his expression he couldn't wrap his head around what he could see right in front of him.

"My daughter."

He ran his hand down his face. "How can you have a baby, Clio?"

His voice cracked on the question, and my biggest fears formed a lump in my throat, one I had to swallow over a couple of times before I could push out words to answer him. "The usual way. I spent a night with a man, and nine months later, I gave birth to Angel."

"When?" He swallowed and tried again. "When did you have her?" he croaked out.

I noticed he kept balling his hands into fists at his sides, then opening and flexing them like he wanted to hit something. But I held my ground.

"Angel's a month old." I waited for the fireworks.

Fascinatedly, I watched as Jack did the math.

"But you were a virgin." He blew out a breath. "And we used condoms."

"Virginity can't prevent pregnancy, and condoms aren't one hundred percent pregnancy protection."

"So, she's mine."

I nodded.

Then he shocked me. "May I hold her?"

He extended his hands to me, and I walked over to him. Gently, he took Angel from my arms and stared down into the seafoam green of his own eyes. Instead of running away screaming like I worried he would, Jack sat carefully on the couch and laid Angel in his lap. He counted her fingers and gently ran his index finger across the ends of her feet covered in her footy pajamas, counting her toes. While cupping her head in his big hands, he cradled her body between his forearms resting on his lap. As I watched Jack fall in love with our daughter, I fell more deeply in love with him.

Without looking away from Angel, he whispered, "Were you going to tell me?"

"Yes."

He quirked a dubious brow at me as I sat near him on the edge of the couch.

"I just hadn't figured out how. Until a few minutes ago, I didn't have your number."

Like he couldn't help himself, he returned to staring at our baby. "You could have called my parents," he said softly. "They would have given it to you." He didn't take his eyes off Angel, who studied him with the same intensity.

"Are you sure about that?" I didn't bother to keep the sarcasm out of my tone. "How many women call your parents every week claiming to know you? Claiming to have children you've fathered?"

He glanced up at that. "Good point." Clearing his throat, he said, "Annabelle had my number."

"She did?" I tried to cover my squeak with a shrug. "Besides, telling you over the phone when you were on tour didn't sound like a great idea."

"Who else knows about us? About our baby?"

"Annabelle. My friend Stacy from the sorority. They suspect you're her father, but they don't know for sure because I haven't told anyone who Angel's father is."

The abject expression on his face tore at me. "Sounds like you maybe weren't going to tell me about my daughter. Are you ashamed I'm Angel's father?"

Hurt? Anger? I thought I heard both in his voice.

"Of course not."

"Then why keep it a secret?"

Tipping a look at the ceiling, I gathered my thoughts. With Jack holding Angel like she meant everything to him, I knew I only had one chance to say everything right. "For starters, my friends would believe me, but no one else I know would. Then there's the press. Someone would see an opportunity to make money, and the next thing you know, it's all over Twitter, *TMZ*, *Entertainment Tonight*." I leaned forward, willing him to understand where I was coming from, that I was trying to do everything right. "Some reporter is shoving a microphone in your face and asking all sorts of intrusive questions you don't have a clue how to answer. How would you have felt if that was the way you found out?"

"I—"

"If the existence of my baby were splashed across the pages of the local news, which it would be considering who you are and who Harrison Barnes is, then Harrison and Meredith would know all about her too, and I don't want them anywhere near Angel," I finished in a rush.

He jerked his head like I'd slapped him. "Your parents know nothing about her? How can that be?"

Closing my eyes, I sucked a long breath in through my nose and let it out slowly. Opening my eyes again, I gave him a level stare. "They disowned me the day I told them I was pregnant."

"They did *what?*"

Angel startled at Jack's outburst, and he gave his attention to soothing her for a minute before returning his eyes to me.

"Beyond knowing about my pregnancy, they know nothing about me, about you, about Angel. They cut me off with nothing but my car, which it turns out they'd foolishly put in my name when they gave it to me for high school graduation. Otherwise, they cut off everything. Especially contact with them." I wrapped my arms around myself. "It's as though I never existed. If they knew you were Angel's father, it might even be worse than no contact."

"What do you mean by that?" Jack's tone was low—and dangerous.

I sucked in a breath and spilled the ugly truth. "When I told Harrison and Meredith you were taking me to prom sophomore year, Meredith's exact words were: 'You're going to prom with a boy named Whitehorse? Really? Is he—an Indian?' She made it sound like your race was a social disease."

Jack flexed his hands into fists and growled, "I suppose she wanted you to go with someone named Carlyle?"

Angel let out a squawk, reminding Jack she still lay in his lap, and I watched him slowly relax for her.

"If I hadn't done something so socially unacceptable as to become pregnant outside of marriage, she'd probably still like me to be dating someone named Carlyle." I let out a snort. "In fact, before they erased me from their lives, they invited Michael Carlyle to every social event for which I needed an escort. No subtlety whatsoever." I rolled my eyes. "Which made it awkward for everyone when I ignored him for the entirety of those events."

"At least you have good taste," Jack said. We shared a feral grin.

"Actually, when Meredith saw you in your tux when you picked me up for prom, she commented on how incredibly handsome you were. 'Too bad he has the last name Whitehorse and no money,' she said."

"After nearly three years with Balefire, I can probably buy and sell your parents." His tone switched from partly sunny to deadly frigid in a heartbeat.

Mine matched his. "Stop calling them my parents. Parents care about their kids. Parents take care of their kids when their kids need them. Parents don't raise their kids to be invisible except when the parents need to show them off at social functions. Parents don't disown their kids when their kids disappoint them." Angel startled at my raised voice, and I worked to lower it a couple of octaves. "Harrison and Meredith Barnes are my biological donors. They are *not* my parents."

I'd ranted myself into a state and needed to take a couple of laps around my apartment to calm down. Angel continued to fuss, and Jack automatically put her on his shoulder and patted her gently, soothing her.

"Jesus, Clio."

We stared at each other in awkward silence before he finally broke it. "Well, that explains your apartment."

I looked around at my sparsely furnished place and realized how it must look to someone who'd spent the better part of the last three years living in hotel suites with bathrooms as big as my living room and kitchen combo. Embarrassed heat suffused my face, and I dug my nails into my palms.

"I'm on scholarship, so school is paid for. I took out a loan for living expenses since my part-time job only pays minimum wage. This place is clean, and Angel has everything she needs," I said, daring him.

A pained look crossed his face. "You could have asked me, Clio.

I would have taken care of you," he said quietly. "I'll start now, if you'll let me."

It was the way he said it that defeated me. Plus the fact that he looked so handsome, so perfect sitting there holding Angel effortlessly, like handling a tiny baby was just another part of his day.

"Why, Jack? Why did you walk away from me without a backward glance?" I hated how small my voice sounded, but after all this time, the hurt had never left me.

An answering pain flashed in his gorgeous eyes. "Part of my plan that night at Red Rocks included an explanation. But one thing led to another—" He shrugged. "The truth is, I never wanted to walk away from you."

"Then why did you?"

Before he could answer, Angel stiffened her teeny body and tore off an earsplitting scream. He flinched and held her closer to his shoulder as she followed her scream with a pitiful wail.

I came around the coffee table and reached for my daughter. Reluctantly, Jack handed her to me. "I didn't hurt her, I swear."

"No, you didn't," I agreed. "Someone has gas. It's a little intestinal trouble she's had since birth. The doctor said she'll outgrow it in the next month or so. In the meanwhile, she needs a little massage, don't you, baby girl?"

I sat back down on the couch in the opposite corner from him and laid Angel across my lap to massage her sides the way the pediatric nurse showed me. After a couple of minutes, her cries subsided into hiccups and then into cooing sounds that told me the pain had passed.

"Does she scream like that in the middle of the night?"

I laughed. "Not often. When she does, she certainly grabs your attention," I said, smiling down at my daughter. "Fortunately, I finished my last makeup final last week, so I only have to worry about being awake for work." Because I loved touching her, I continued to rub her sides. The baby noises she made told me she enjoyed the extra massage too. "Since I work mostly evenings and nights, her occasional evening attacks shouldn't be a problem either. Unless I'm in the middle of someone else's meltdown. Then things could become dicey."

"You work nights?" Jack growled. "Where?"

Ignoring his tone, I said, "I'm a night desk clerk at the freshman dorm. It's an easy gig, and I can have Angel with me, which is great. I'll only have to leave her in daycare while I'm in classes this year."

His thunderous expression leveled me.

"Don't even start, Jack. You just walked back into my life, and you know nothing about what I've had to learn in the last year. I might have been a spoiled rich girl before, but I don't have that luxury anymore." He opened his mouth, but I plowed on. "And you know what? I'm glad. I'm proud of myself for finding a job and my own place and being able to stay in school while taking care of my daughter. You have no right to judge me."

"Whoa, Clio." He gestured at me to hold it down. "I wasn't judging you. I think we have some things to work out is all."

We? We have some things to work out? What the hell?

CHAPTER THIRTEEN

Jack

HOLY SHIT. I was a father. My girl had given birth to an Angel. And I was her dad. The whole situation probably should have terrified me. Truthfully, it did a little. But this was Clio, the only woman I'd ever loved. And this was Angel—my beautiful daughter with my eyes and her mom's face. We had so much shit to work out, but one thing was sure—our baby meant we were always going to be in each other's lives.

Angel was my daughter. I had a daughter, a precious little girl to love and take care of. The idea of Clio leaving my daughter in a daycare didn't sit well. Not even a little bit. Even if she could ignore it, I couldn't ignore who her parents were, who I was now. Being related to well-known people, celebrities, would make Angel an enticing target for some enterprising lowlife when Clio had to leave her in the care of others. The idea drove me crazy already, and I'd only known about her for a minute.

"Talk to me about this daycare."

"It's on campus. It's a drop-in service for nontraditional students. Early childhood development majors run it. It serves as a kind of field station for experiments in early childhood education," she said like it was no big deal.

"Sorry I can't share your enthusiasm for other people experimenting on my kid."

Clio slanted me a look. "It's a great facility with a top-notch reputation. The work they do there is cutting-edge. People outside the university are on a waiting list to put their kids in the center whenever there's an opening," she said, her tone defensive. "I toured it as part of my nursing program before I became pregnant, and the place impressed the hell out of me."

I put up my hands to slow her roll. "I wasn't criticizing your judgment. I only want Angel to be safe."

Those clear gray eyes stared at me for a long time before she said softly, "Me too."

"She better? May I hold her again?"

She handed our baby back to me. Our baby. Wow. As I stared into the mirror of my eyes, I couldn't believe it. Yet it felt exactly right. Angel was so tiny, but I could feel strength in her. She also liked my voice. I could tell by the way she tracked me when I spoke. I stroked the pad of my finger over her features. Like her mom, she had the softest skin. Like her mom, she also smelled so damn good. In another life, like yesterday, sitting on the couch in Clio's shoebox of an apartment and holding a baby would have sounded about as appealing as watching grass grow. Normally, I needed to keep moving, maintain a rhythm.

Today, holding my daughter, I discovered I wanted to do nothing more than to live in the stillness. Sit quietly and look at her. She was the most incredible person on the planet, and I'd helped to make her. I found myself checking out of the conversation because I was too busy staring at Angel. Then I'd look up and catch Clio smiling at me, and I thought maybe we had a chance.

After what seemed only a few minutes but had actually been an hour, Angel decided she wanted to eat. When she started making noise, Clio took her from me and disappeared into her bedroom to change Angel's diaper. Without invitation, I followed, curious about my daughter—and her mother.

Clio placed Angel on a pad on top of her double bed. As I stared at the bed, I wondered how the two of us were going to sleep in it together. *Slow down, Cowboy. She's not there yet. Besides, for what you have in mind, a single bed would get the job done.*

She looked up, caught me grinning, and shot me a perplexed look. When she returned her attention to grabbing a diaper from the box beside a bassinet, I reached down discreetly to adjust myself. Thoughts of what the two of us could get up to in that bed wouldn't leave me alone, though.

"I'm not sure what I have in the fridge that you'd like. At home, we had a chef. At the sorority, we had a chef. Cooking is a new experience for me, and I'm not very good at it yet. But if you see something you think you'd like, I can try to make it after I feed Angel."

"Or I can go out and grab us something. How 'bout that?"

"That sounds great, actually."

The way Clio said that had me looking more carefully at her. Her being my girl and me being a guy, the size of her breasts had drawn most of my attention. Now that I looked at her closely as she bent over Angel on the bed, I noticed she seemed thinner than when I'd seen her, held her last summer.

"All right. I'll go pick up some grub and be back in a few minutes. Any preferences?"

"Nothing spicy. Angel doesn't like it."

What?

"Um, I didn't think she ate anything but mama's milk."

"Exactly. Whatever I eat, she eats, and she doesn't like spicy," Clio said with a grin.

"Got it. My girls don't do spicy. See you in a few."

Out of curiosity, I took a little tour of Clio's fridge before I headed out the door. From what I could see, she was living on fruit, vegetables, milk, and eggs. There wasn't any meat in sight, though there was a bowl of something that looked vaguely like pasta, but the lumps could have been potatoes or dumplings or congealed soup. In any case, it didn't look edible.

As I headed out the door, I pulled out my phone and programmed a grocery list into my notes. Then I pulled up a list of restaurants that also provided takeout and made a call.

By the time I returned to her place with real food to keep in her fridge and a delicious chicken parmesan from a local restaurant, Clio had fed Angel and put her back to bed. I found Clio sitting on the couch staring at her laptop.

"What are you doing?" I asked as I unloaded the takeout onto her island.

"Watching Netflix. Need some help?" she asked, putting down her computer to stand and stretch beside the couch.

As she unconsciously showed off that gorgeous body, I forgot for a second what I was supposed to be doing.

"Jack?" she asked, her eyes dancing as she looked at me.

"Oh, yeah. How 'bout you find us some plates or something while I make another trip out to my truck for the rest."

"How much food do you eat?" she demanded with a laugh.

Grinning back at her, I said, "I picked up some stuff we can cook with that garden you're keeping in your fridge."

"What stuff?"

"Meat. Be right back."

Before she could put up a fuss, I was out the door. When I returned to her apartment with my bags of groceries, Clio was making a salad across the island from where she'd set out plates and utensils for dinner.

When I walked back through the door, she eyed my cargo and said, "Looks like you're planning to eat here more than tonight."

"That's exactly my plan. For the record, it was already my plan before I knew about Angel. Discovering her cemented it."

A frown furrowed her lovely forehead. "Jack, what are you saying?"

"I'm saying that I had a plan to date you, show you that we were always meant to be together. I still have that plan even after the stars aligned and proved it for me with us making Angel on our first try."

As I talked, I stowed food in Clio's fridge before joining her at the island. From the look on her face, wheels were spinning at lightning speed in her head, but I needed more time before answering the questions I knew she wanted to ask.

"How much longer will it take you to finish your degree?" I asked as I spooned chicken and pasta out of the container and onto her plate.

"One more year for my undergrad. I had a plan to go on to graduate school to become a nurse practitioner, but now I'm thinking about putting off grad school until I repay the loan I took out to cover my living expenses and what my school insurance didn't cover for Angel's birth."

"Clio." I covered her hand with mine. "I'm in the picture now. Tell me how much you need—"

She interrupted me with a grimace, but I continued. "At least to cover the baby's expenses. After all, I do have a financial obligation to her."

With a sigh, she said, "I'll think about it."

We ate in silence for a few minutes while I tried not to get mad at how stubborn she was about me helping her. About her not trusting me. She changed the subject to the band, and I let her, telling her about how we were on vacation for a month before we returned to the studio to record the new material we'd worked on while we were on tour.

Discovering that the band wrote music while we toured surprised her, and I asked if she'd heard one of our new songs, one we'd recorded on our last tour. When she hedged, I knew she'd heard it. More importantly, I wondered if she knew it was for her.

"I wrote 'Missing You' right after Red Rocks. I've written a couple of other ones about you too. You'll hear them on our new album."

Her brows shot to her forehead, but I pretended not to notice. "Balefire has a well-deserved party band reputation, but Blu, Dakota, and Tron are deadly serious about the music. It's easy to write with them."

We moved back to the couch, and she finished her dessert in thoughtful silence, yet I noticed she nearly licked her dessert bowl clean of the chocolate mousse I'd ordered with dinner. Though she put on a brave face, Clio clearly missed the nice things she'd left behind when she decided to keep our baby and raise her alone. I already admired the hell out of her for her brains and her capacity to give, something I was pretty sure she didn't even notice about herself. Now I added her willingness to put someone else's happiness before her own to the list of her fine qualities. But dammit, she didn't need to be so stubborn. Couldn't she see I wanted to help her? Then she licked chocolate mousse off her plump pink lips, and I forgot our conversation.

I wanted to spend a little time exploring our possibilities before I left her for the night. Taking the bowl from her hand, I said, "I think maybe you need another napkin. Here, let me help you."

Before she could protest, I leaned over and touched my tongue to the side of her mouth, tasting chocolate and Clio. An image of chocolate mousse spread over her gorgeous body and me slowly licking it off slipped into my head, and I grinned against her lips before I pressed a soft kiss to her mouth. She moaned in the back of her throat, and I put my hand on her neck to hold her while I deepened the kiss. Her sweet lips moved so perfectly beneath mine, and she opened them on a sigh when I slid my fingers into her mass of hair and cupped her jaw in my palms.

When our tongues met and started dancing together, I had to shift my position. This woman's kisses had been hardening my cock since the first time I took her mouth at a high school dance. While other women had turned me on occasionally, they always had to work at it. Clio did it with a touch, a sigh, the feel of her skin beneath my fingertips. Tonight, though, was all about seduction. There would be no main event no matter how badly I wanted it. I wasn't so cocky as to believe Clio had let me in. She would be testing me for a while, and I deserved that. Especially since I had yet to tell her about the contract.

As that thought intruded, I pulled away from her. "I want you to know I'm already in love with our daughter. But you're right about keeping her existence quiet, at least for now."

She lifted a brow in question but said nothing.

"I'll be in town for the next month. Since you're not currently taking classes, we can spend time together. What time does Angel usually wake you for the day?"

With a groan, Clio threw herself back into the cushions. "Babies are early risers. Angel, unfortunately, is no exception. We'll be up by six—or maybe sooner if she's not a fan of chicken parm. Why?"

"I was thinking about taking you for a drive up into the mountains, maybe have a picnic."

"That sounds nice." The dreamy expression on her face told me it had been a while since she'd had any fun.

"I'll be by to pick you up around ten. Will that work with Angel's schedule?"

"Sure."

"Good night, Clio." Because I couldn't resist, I kissed her again before I stood and walked to the door. "If Angel doesn't let you sleep much tonight, don't worry. I'll let you sleep in the truck tomorrow."

I smiled at her and let myself out of her apartment. Maybe she didn't trust me quite yet, but she hadn't kicked me out either. For the first time in nearly five years, my life was finally coming together.

CHAPTER FOURTEEN

Jack

OVER THE NEXT two weeks, I took my time and courted Clio properly. We drove up to the mountains and picnicked. I found some bikes and a covered baby car to pull Angel behind us as we rode through the residential areas where all the new homes were going up. With Angel riding in a front pack against my chest, the three of us walked all over Old Town where some enterprising group had set out pianos through the heart of the pedestrian area there. I surprised her by banging out some tunes but stopped horsing around on the pianos whenever other people came by to listen. After all, the point was to be together, not to be an item for social media or the tabloids.

She took me on a campus tour, and we visited her sorority, where she introduced me to Fern, the housemother, who was the only person who lived in the house year-round. However, Clio's friends Stacy and Annabelle were due in town again for some sorority shit Clio and Fern chattered on about that I couldn't follow. Something about rushing around and parties and such. Knowing her friends were coming to town gave me ideas for how I could enlist them to help me with a project I had in mind to surprise Clio.

During this time, I kept my distance physically, limiting myself to kissing her and casually touching her. All right, I couldn't keep my hands off her most of the time, but I didn't try to talk her out of her clothes. Which meant my cock became quite conversant with my right hand when I wasn't spending time under the freezing cold water of the shower in my hotel suite.

I could tell by some of the quizzical looks she threw my way every now and then that she wondered why I hadn't made a move to get her into bed, but she didn't ask. I wanted her to trust that I wasn't ever walking out of her life again, and she wasn't quite there yet.

One day, I showed up a little earlier than usual and let myself into her place. She'd taken to leaving the door unlocked for me in the mornings. I didn't think I was being all that quiet, but I guess I was when I found her lying against the pillows on the bed, nursing our baby, her luscious body completely uncovered. For several minutes, I don't think I even breathed. Never in my life had I witnessed a scene as beautiful as my girl nursing my baby.

It took Clio a few minutes to notice me standing in the doorway staring. She glanced up and smiled a sleepy smile before returning her attention to Angel. Then she startled and reached for the covers to hide all that perfection from me.

"Clio, please don't do that." In two strides, I stood beside her bed with my hand on the blankets to prevent her from covering up. "I've never seen anything so beautiful in all my life."

"You mean it?" she asked, her voice all quivery.

"You have no idea what you're doing to me at this minute."

Peeking up at me from beneath her brows, she patted the bed next to her. I toed off my shoes and joined her on the bed. Unable to help myself, I ran my fingers over the downy soft hair of Angel's head as she nursed and laughed with Clio as our baby snorted and smacked her way through her breakfast.

Clio shifted Angel to her shoulder and rubbed her little back until Baby Girl did me proud by letting loose with a belch that would have made my bandmates, especially Dakota, take notice. We laughed together at the very unladylike way our little lady showed appreciation for her meal.

Clio closed one side of her nightshirt and opened the other, helping Angel to find her nipple before our baby latched on and went back to work. Until I watched her nurse, I had no idea what hard work it was for Angel to get some eats. By the time Clio burped her again, Angel's sweaty baby hair clung to her head, a little red cap from the exertion she put out to nurse.

"No wonder she needs a nap every after time after she eats. I didn't realize sucking on you was such hard work," I teased as Clio handed Angel to me so she could do up the buttons on her shirt.

"When you did it, you weren't trying to have breakfast," Clio scolded as she slipped off the bed. Turning back, she reached for the baby, and reluctantly, I gave her up.

"How long will you be nursing her?" I asked as I slid off the other side of the bed.

"I'll try for a year at least. It'll kind of depend on how things work out with classes and all. The longer I can nurse her, the better it is for her."

"Are you saying I have to wait a whole year to enjoy your tits again?" I pouted.

Clio laughed a nervous little laugh. "I had the impression you weren't as interested in me that way since I'm a mom now."

"Oh, babe, you are so wrong." I put my hands on her hips, careful not to squish Angel between us. "You're even sexier now than you were before. Which is a damn miracle considering how sexy you've always been."

Her eyes widened. "Really?"

I smiled at her and gave her hips a squeeze. "I've been holding off since I did some reading that said a woman should wait at least six weeks after giving birth before going back to playtime in the sack." I blew out a breath. "It's been pure hell being around you without bedding you."

"It'll be six weeks day after tomorrow," she whispered.

"Good to know." I reached between us to adjust myself in my jeans, not bothering to hide my arousal from her this time.

Her eyes darkened as she watched me, and I saw her throat work as she swallowed. Looked like I wasn't the only one who was hot and bothered.

She cleared her throat. "Have you had breakfast yet?"

"Not yet. You?"

"Um, no. Scrambled eggs sound good?" she asked as she put Angel in her little bed before she headed into the kitchen.

Her face pinkened at my admissions, which I liked, and I deliberately put my hand on her ass as she bent over to look in the fridge.

"Scrambled eggs sound great, babe. Maybe add in some of that Italian sausage I bought the other day," I said conversationally as I fondled one sweet, rounded cheek.

"Jack! What do you think you're doing?"

"Helping you decide the breakfast menu."

"With your hand on my ass?"

"Couldn't figure out where else to put it since it's kind of a reach to put it on your tits while you have your head in the fridge." I smirked.

"You are unbelievable!" she huffed as she straightened and faced me with a carton of eggs in her hand.

"And you're beautiful," I said before I leaned in and kissed her softly on the mouth. I had to do something, or I might not be able to wait two more days before making love to her again. It had been almost a year as it was, and between doing without all that time and being around her all day every day for the last two weeks, I'd suffered blue balls long enough already.

When I pulled away from her, she blinked at me and moved

as if in a daze to start breakfast. I understood how she felt: she had that effect on me too.

Her kitchen could only accommodate one cook at a time, so I gave her space, retreating to the other side of the island and seating myself on a barstool to keep her company as she made breakfast. After cooking with her a few times over the past weeks, I understood why her fridge contained only eggs and plants when I looked in it the first time. She pretty much had breakfast down, but outside of sandwiches, any other dish defeated her. On her budget, she couldn't afford to eat out or order in, so her menu consisted of eggs and veggies and fruit.

I thought I'd run the idea of cooking lessons by her friends and see if they thought she'd like that or if it would piss her off. If she wouldn't be up for lessons, I figured I'd have to hire a chef when I inevitably had to be out of town with the band. One way or the other, I had to make sure my woman ate. After two weeks of me feeding her, she looked more like herself, and I wanted her to stay that way.

As I sat there watching her, Clio interrupted my thoughts about her and food. "I had a visitor this morning. That's why I was late feeding Angel."

The eggs sizzled as she poured them into the overheated pan, but she didn't seem to notice as she busied herself popping bread into the toaster.

"Yeah? Who was here already today?" I asked. It was only ten o'clock in the freakin' morning. Then I remembered her friends were due to arrive any day, and I relaxed.

"Clive Carlyle."

She pulled a carton of strawberries from the fridge and rinsed them in the sink then placed them in a bowl and added sliced bananas.

At the sound of that particular last name, I couldn't help it. I fisted my hands and gritted my teeth against my temper. Trying to keep my voice even, I asked, "Any relation to Michael Carlyle?"

"His father. And Harrison's business partner."

She set a glass of orange juice in front of me and went back to stirring the eggs and sausage in the pan.

Michael Carlyle graduated in my class. Shortly after Clio and I began dating, he started sniffing around her. My buddies and I cornered him after school one day, and I'd set his smarmy ass straight about whose girl she was. After I graduated, I heard through the grapevine that he'd tried hard to date her. Still, what could his father want with Clio?

"And?"

Returning to the eggs, she mashed them around in the pan, and as I watched her, I thought again about those cooking lessons. Though she did seem to be getting the hang of putting together an entire meal at once. When the toast popped up, she buttered it and placed it on a plate in front of me before returning to the eggs. Finally, she looked at me.

"He said, and I quote, 'I'm here on behalf of your parents. It's come to their attention that you went through with your pregnancy and gave birth. They are interested in the particulars.' 'Oh, really?' I said. 'So that's why you're here asking after me instead of Harrison or Meredith? Because they're so interested in me?'

"And he said all deliberately, 'Your parents are merely concerned for your welfare. They asked me as a favor to see how you are and to check on the baby.'"

With a nod, I gestured to our breakfast, and she turned off the burner and spooned eggs and sausage onto the plates waiting on the counter.

Setting the plates on the bar, she pulled up a stool and joined me without a break in her narrative. "I called bullshit on that."

"Good girl."

Clio continued as though I hadn't said anything. "I told him I knew he only dropped by to find out if my baby was a boy or a girl." She forked a mouthful of eggs, chewed, swallowed, and added, "Clive is such a suck-up to Harrison. Even his name is pretentious."

"That *is* the name for a guy with a stick up his ass," I said, trying to play along even though breakfast tasted like ash in my mouth and my gut churned at what was coming next.

Clio was on a roll about Clive Carlyle, though, keeping me in suspense for what I feared was the real point of his visit.

Gesturing with her fork, she said, "He affects this posh British accent, which totally cracks me up because I know he was born in Littleton. Michael told me that once at a company Christmas party when he drank a bit too much champagne."

My blood boiled at the thought of my girl attending a party with that asshole, but I kept my thoughts to myself. "Is that why you've been affecting an accent for this little story?" I asked.

"Yeah." She giggled. "Anyway, I told Clive he was still full of shit. The Barneses want to know if I have a son. I told him he could give them this answer: fuck off."

She ate a couple more bites of breakfast and washed it down with a swig of orange juice. I knew she wasn't a saint, but I'd never heard my girl talk like that. Carlyle had riled her up more than she was letting on.

She dabbed her mouth with her napkin. "Clive's mouth dropped right open when I said that."

Bet it did.

"Guess I surprised him."

Bet you did.

"But he recovered pretty fast, telling me I didn't need to curse like that. That my language was common and utterly beneath me. Then he wanted to know what to tell my parents." She gave me a conspiratorial grin. "I told him again to tell them to fuck off. But when he said it in his fancy accent, I was sure it wouldn't sound so common. After that, I closed the door gently, but firmly in his face."

I sipped my orange juice and waited for the shoe to drop.

"Now I'm worried maybe my response to his visit was a bit rash.

I should have found out what Harrison and Meredith truly want before I start closing doors on their messengers."

"What difference does it make if they know the sex of our baby, Clio?"

"Since Angel is a girl, I doubt it makes any difference. She'll be yet another example of what a disappointment I am." She slammed her fork on the counter, and with a glance toward the bedroom where Angel slept, I covered her hand. "But I'll be damned if I let them have any chance at all to hurt her. Little as they are, babies can feel rejection, and my baby will never feel rejected—or invisible—as long as I have control over the situation."

The fierceness in her tone, in her stance, in the way she banged utensils around as she spoke left no doubt in my mind how much Clio loved Angel, how much she would fight for our little girl no matter what. My heart swelled with pride while at the same time I worried about what her father was up to. I could tell she worried about that too.

I gave her hand a squeeze. "Whatever they try, Clio, remember you're not alone. I'm Angel's dad, and I promise, Harrison and Meredith and their minions will have to go through me to get to either of you."

"You'd do that for us?"

"You have to ask?" I didn't mean to growl at her, but seriously? She stood and turned me on my barstool, inserting herself between my legs while she wrapped her arms around my neck. "Thanks, Jack. That makes me feel better about losing my mind and telling Clive to fuck off. As good as it felt to say it at the time, it was probably a dumbass move on my part."

"Actually, I think you standing up for yourself is sexy."

I wrapped my arms around her waist and pulled her closer to me. Because my self-control started disappearing as soon as she said we only had to wait two more days, I leaned in and kissed the hollow of her neck. She whimpered in the back of her throat, and I smiled into her skin. From the way she always responded, I knew she had a thing for my mouth and my hands on her neck. So of course, I took advantage of every opportunity to touch her the way she liked.

Next thing I knew, I had my tongue in her mouth while she sat on my lap with her legs wrapped around my waist. Jesus, I was hard as cement. "Baby," I panted, pulling away from her a little, "as much as it pains me, literally, to say it, we have to wait for what you're asking for right now."

She made a face, and I cracked up.

"I'll make it worth the wait, I promise."

"Okay." She sighed but made no move to disengage herself from me.

"Um, Clio? You need to climb down."

"Fine."

Slowly, so slowly I swear she tortured me on purpose, she lowered her legs from around me and pulled out of my arms. She straightened her shirt, ran her hands down her shorts, and finally moved back around the island to clean up breakfast.

"What?" she asked when she reached across the island for our plates and utensils.

"You're even sexy when you're doing dishes, you know that?"

Softly, she said, "Thanks," as she adorably ducked her head to concentrate on not dropping our plates.

After years on the road and being exposed to every kind of woman imaginable, most of them pushy and loud as they vied for the band's attention, Clio's genuine response to my compliment refreshed the hell out of me. Joining her at the sink, I tucked a stray strand of her silky hair behind her ear and smiled at her. I grabbed the dish towel and went to work helping her clean up.

♪

Clio's friends showed up later that afternoon as the three of us napped together in the close confines of that double bed. Angel lay on one side of my chest, my hand cupping her tiny ass while Clio rested her head on my other shoulder, my arm around her holding her close to my side. When the doorbell chimed through the house, the three of us startled awake together.

Clio left soothing Angel to me as she ran out of the room to open the door.

"I know, Angel. I was dreaming about the three of us together like this every day too. Shhh. Maybe Mommy will send whoever is here away."

Or not.

The loud laughter of a houseful of women echoed through the walls of Clio's miniature apartment. Not only did her place lack size, but it also lacked insulation apparently. Good to know, considering my plans for us for later. If her friends didn't interrupt those plans the way they'd interrupted our peaceful afternoon.

Angel fussed at the noise, and automatically, I began patting a rhythm on her little bum. My rhythmic touch soothed her, so I kept it up, which is how Clio and her posse found us when they trouped into the bedroom, filling it up completely with more estrogen than any one man should be exposed to alone.

"You already know Annabelle, Jack," Clio said.

"Hello, Jack," Annabelle said as she walked around the bed to my side.

"This is my other best friend Stacy Newhouse," Clio added with a grin.

Stacy nodded at me and said hello though she couldn't seem to stop staring. Since people stare at me often when I'm in public, I shouldn't have been surprised by her reaction to meeting me, but in the confines of Clio's suitcase of a bedroom, it was a little freakin' weird.

Turning my attention to Annabelle, I asked, "What gives? That number you gave me for Clio was no longer in service. Was that your idea of a joke?"

"Nice to see you again too, Jack," Annabelle said, liberally lacing her words with sarcasm. "When I gave it to you, I didn't know her parents had disconnected her number when they stopped paying her bills."

"You gave Jack my number? Even though I asked you not to do that?" Clio fisted her hands on her hips and glared at Annabelle.

Still cradling my daughter, I sat up quick. "Whoa! You told her not to give me your number? Why?"

"Maybe we should come back to see the baby later," Stacy suggested as she took a step back toward the living room.

"No, no, stay. Angel's changed so much since you saw her last," Clio said to Stacy. Turning to me, she crossed her arms over her pretty chest, her tone defensive. "Remember what happened that morning?"

"We'll talk about this later," I said. Apparently, I sounded as angry as I felt because the room went silent before Angel let out a yelp.

"Don't scare the baby with your attitude, Jack," Clio warned.

"I don't scare you, do I little one?" I traced Angel's soft skin with my finger. "It's all this other noise that's the problem, yeah?"

Angel looked up at me from her spot on my chest, scrunched up her sweet face, and let out a wail. Clio swooped in and scooped the baby from me, carrying her out into the living room.

While I sat on the bed with my mouth hanging open, Stacy turned tail and followed Clio and Angel.

Annabelle shrugged, smirked at me, and said, "Oops," before leaving me alone in the bedroom.

"Damn it!" I growled. How the hell did my afternoon go from sugar to shit in the space of one second?

I swung my legs over the side of the bed and shoved my feet into my Converse. Striding into the living room, I headed straight for the desk in the corner by the front door where I'd tossed my snapback when I showed up this morning. As I jerked my cap onto my head, I said, "I'll leave you ladies to yourselves. When I come back later, Clio, we have some things to discuss."

I might have slammed the door a little when I walked out.

CHAPTER FIFTEEN

Clio

"WOW, THAT'S JACK Whitehorse," Stacy breathed as Jack banged his way out of my apartment.

"Yeah, that's Jack," I said. I should have been more upset about his threat as he left, but two things preempted me. One, I was unnaturally elated about him being mad about the phone number, and two, Angel wailed in my ear.

"He's even hotter in person." Stacy's sigh bordered on a swoon. "I can't believe he's Angel's father."

Trepidation hammered my heart. "You can't tell anyone. Please."

Angel threatened to crank up again, and I snuggled her close to help us both calm down.

"Why would you want to keep something this cool a secret?" Stacy asked, genuine confusion contorting her face.

"Because Clio knows all about the press, being the daughter of Harrison Barnes and all," Annabelle said so matter-of-factly I might have missed the eye roll if I hadn't been looking at her.

Oblivious to the little drama playing out between Annabelle and me, Stacy plopped down on the couch. "Well, Clio does have a responsibility to keep Angel safe. If the press knew, she'd probably have to drop out of school and hide out. I, for one, would rather not have to run a gauntlet of nosy reporters to see my friend."

Annabelle quirked a brow at Stacy. If any of my friends blabbed about Jack being Angel's father, I had no doubt it would be Annabelle. Not because she needed any money, but because she'd enjoy the ruckus the press would cause and the notoriety she'd gain from her association with me and, in turn, with Balefire.

Angel must have sensed the tension in the room, or the tension radiating through me, because she started crying again.

"Do you need to feed her or something?" Stacy asked, though her question sounded more like a command. Since Angel's birth, Stacy had been reading books on the baby's first year and calling and texting me regularly about Angel's development and what I should be doing with her. Usually, I found her meddling kinda cute, but right now, I wasn't in the mood.

"I changed her diaper and fed her right before the three of us went down for a nap together, which you all interrupted when you laid on the doorbell like you forgot that an infant lives here now," I said grumpily. With a sigh, I changed my tone. "Angel baby, shhh. It's all right. You're all right. Shhh."

I jiggled her up and down and patted her bottom until her cries subsided into cute baby sniffles. When she quieted, Stacy reached for her, and I let my friend hold my daughter. Annabelle seated herself beside them to coo and fuss over my baby. Busying myself in the kitchen with gathering sodas from the fridge and putting out glasses and a bowl of ice cubes, I let my thoughts wander back to my tiff with Jack. He looked so pissed when he found out I'd forbidden Annabelle to give him my number. It made me wonder if that had been the right move.

At the time, I don't think I would have believed him about Dakota's practical jokes. At least it would have been hard to believe him with only his voice on the other end of a phone to go by. Now

I knew him so much better. Our relationship in high school had been so intense that we understood each other exceptionally well. The intervening years hadn't changed that, which was surprising. Still, in the past two weeks I'd come to know him in so many ways that I hadn't before. Annabelle's lack of discretion allowed me to see how my lack of trust had hurt him. Clearly, I'd have to make it up to him somehow.

The woman in question interrupted my thoughts. "What's that secretive smile about?" she asked slyly.

"None of your business, gossip girl." Indicating the spread on my bar, I said, "Sorry I have nothing more drinkable than pop. But at least I have a variety. Come help yourselves."

Annabelle hung back, allowing Stacy to grab a drink before coming around the island to stand near me. "Any chance you can get me invited out with Balefire while the band's in Denver this summer?"

"They'll start rehearsals for their next album in a next couple of weeks. But if Jack invites me to join them, I'm sure I'll need someone to ride with me." I grinned at her, and she winked. "Besides, from what Jack tells me, I owe you a return favor. Though I think you hurt your friend Bailey's feelings when you hooked up with Dakota that night."

"I didn't promise Bailey anything when I accepted those tickets, which were from Jack by the way." She popped the top on a can of pop and expertly poured it over the ice in her glass, a fizzy head forming perfectly at the rim. "Bailey and I were only the go-betweens for Jack to hook up with you." She leaned back against the island and sipped her drink. "How do you know him again?"

I poured a can of cream soda over the ice cubes in my glass, watching to make sure the fizz didn't overwhelm the glass. "We dated when we were in high school. Then he auditioned for a band called Rude Awakening, won the job, and moved on." A sip of creamy, tangy deliciousness soothed the bitterness of the memory. "Until that night at Red Rocks, I hadn't seen Jack in almost five years."

"Obviously, he didn't forget you in all that time. Since you had such a nice reunion." Annabelle smirked. "Not that Angel isn't beautiful and a blessing and all, but maybe you should have listened to me about having condoms in your purse."

"What happened that night is none of your business, Annabelle." I glared at her. "And I wouldn't trade my baby girl for anything. Excuse me."

I walked back over to Stacy who was busy entertaining Angel. Annabelle was a friend, a sister in the house, and someone I truly cared about, but if I talked to her any longer—

The chiming of the doorbell interrupted us.

"You don't make Jack ring the bell, do you, Clio?" Annabelle asked with a laugh.

"Not usually," I said as I stared at the door, perplexed.

"Um, there's only one way to find out who's on the other side," Stacy said when I didn't immediately make a move to answer the door.

The bell chimed again, and a sense of foreboding fell over me.

"Girls, would you mind taking the baby into the bedroom please? Besides you guys and Jack, I don't have visitors, and I'd rather not take any chances where Angel is concerned."

Stacy disappeared into the bedroom with Angel while Annabelle maintained her place casually leaning against the counter in my kitchen. From where she stood, she had a clear view of the front door to my place and whoever I opened it to.

Tugging at my shirt and smoothing my hair, I took four steps to my front door and cracked it open. On the other side stood a man dressed in an expensive charcoal-gray suit over an understated dove-colored dress shirt with a dark purple tie. From his impeccably cut sable hair to his shiny Italian leather dress shoes, he exuded wealth and power. The man who rang my bell looked to be someone used to giving commands that others obeyed.

The once-over he gave me when I opened the door told me he cataloged me just as I'd done him. A barefoot college girl wearing cutoff jean shorts and a sleeveless lemon-yellow button-down shirt, no doubt gave the impression I'd be happy to do whatever this exceptionally well-put-together man demanded.

"May I help you?" I inquired politely. Though I had a sneaking suspicion who, or at least what, he was, I knew better than to antagonize him—at least not right away.

Handing me a business card he retrieved from the inside pocket of his jacket, he said, "You're Clio Barnes, I presume?"

From his tone alone, even without reading his name or the word *Esquire* following it on his card, I knew this man was a lawyer. My breath stuck in my chest before my heart tripped into double time as it tried to climb into the back of my throat.

Practicing a trick I'd learned long ago when dealing with Harrison and Meredith, I inhaled slowly and quietly through my nose, held my breath for second, then let it out before answering. "Harrison Barnes sent you, I presume?" I asked, mimicking the man's tone.

"It has come to his attention that you are perhaps not in a position to take care of an infant to whom you've recently given birth. I'm here to determine if that's true."

He took a step toward me as though he meant to walk right through my door. Over my dead body.

"On what authority?" I asked. My legs started to shake, but I didn't move, requiring him to halt his forward progress or walk right into me.

"Mr. Barnes's business associate came to visit you recently, did he not?"

"So?"

"He gave us to understand that you lack decorum. He also reported a baby cried for nearly the entire time he spoke to you, which shows you to have little understanding of how to take care of an infant since not once did you check on said infant." Glancing past my shoulder, his shrewd eyes took in as much of my apartment as he could see. Which was most of it. "Apparently, your drinking and entertaining are more important than taking care of your infant." I gaped at his ridiculous assumptions, but before I could set him straight, he said, "Mr. Barnes is willing to take in the infant and has the means to ensure its well-being. If you'll allow me, I'll just come in and have you sign the papers. Then we'll send over a nanny to collect the child." Again, he moved to walk into my apartment, but I stood my ground.

"Y-you want me to sign away my baby?" I whispered incredulously.

"Be reasonable, Miss Barnes." The man flashed a patronizing smile. "You're living in a squalid apartment and rearing a child on your own without any means to support it. Surely, even you can see that giving the child to his grandparents is in his best interests. As his mother, you must want what's best for the child."

The man's carefully modulated voice exuded confident reasonableness, like me signing Angel over to him was merely a business transaction—and a foregone conclusion.

Before I could sputter out a response to the smarmy bastard, Annabelle was there shoving herself in front of me like an avenging angel. "I don't know who the fuck you think you are, but you can't barge into my friend's *home*," she emphasized the word, "insult her, and casually demand she give you her child. Her parents"—she spat that word—"kicked her out and disowned her when she told them she was pregnant. Now they want to take her baby?" Her voice rose an octave. "You need to get the fuck out of here before we call the cops and have them drag your sorry ass to jail for harassment. You can't simply show up at someone's house and demand she sign over her child. Where the *fuck* do you get off?"

She jerked the door out of my hand and slammed it hard in the lawyer's face. Then for good measure, she dead-bolted it. Calling through the door, she said, "How's that for decorum? You have five seconds to remove yourself from Clio's doormat before I dial 9-1-1. Five. Four. Three. Two. One."

Annabelle stuck her eye up against the peephole then stepped back and grinned. "Guess he didn't feel like getting arrested today."

My legs went out from under me, and I crumpled to the floor. Annabelle sobered up immediately and knelt beside me. "Clio, are you okay?"

She wrapped her arms around me and hugged me to her.

"They're going to try to take her, Annabelle. Harrison and Meredith are going to try to take Angel away from me. They can't have her. I won't give her up," I said. The dam broke on the emotions I'd been holding back since I opened my door, tears streaming down my face.

"I know you don't want anyone to know who your baby daddy is, but you may not have a choice about making that info public. It might be the only way to keep your parents from taking your baby," Annabelle said into my hair as she held me.

From somewhere behind us, I heard Stacy say, "Jack's a big rock star. He should have some good lawyers. I bet he can make your parents stay away from Angel."

"Wow. After everything you had to do on your own, now they want to barge back into your life? Honestly, when you were telling us what your parents did to you, I had a hard time believing it. Now I see you didn't make that shit up. I'm so sorry, Clio."

The concern in Annabelle's voice tipped me over the edge, and I started sobbing all over again. The lawyer's visit reminded me exactly how little I truly mattered to the people who made me.

My friends let me cry it out for a little while before Annabelle tugged me up to stand. Holding me by the shoulders, she said, "This situation calls for something much more fortifying than Cokes." She walked over to the couch and grabbed her purse. As she unlatched the door, she glanced back over her shoulder. "You clean her up,

Stacy. I'll be back in a few. I'll knock instead of ring the bell. Then you'll know I'm not a snotty lawyer or something."

Understanding what she was trying to do, I sniffed back my tears and smiled weakly at her. Before Harrison's lawyer had shown up at my door, I kind of wanted to smack Annabelle for her attitude. Now I was so grateful to have her as my friend and champion. It took someone with her total disregard for what anyone thought to stand up to people as persistent and coldhearted as Harrison and Meredith Barnes.

When Annabelle left, Stacy helped me to my bedroom, where I changed into a clean pair of white capris and a sky blue camisole. After I changed, I checked on my sleeping baby, unable to stop myself from feathering my fingertips over her precious head, down the side of her face, and over her perfect little body. At my touch, she let out a sigh and stretched, but remained asleep.

"I was always such a good girl, you know?" I began quietly. "Stayed out of their way, never demanded anything, always showed gratitude for everything they gave me. All I wanted was their love, but I guess it was too much to ask."

"They can't take her, you know," Stacy murmured. "They'd need to prove you're an unfit mother, and you're not. You've done everything right with Angel. I would testify in court that you're the best mom ever." She covered the hand I rested on the edge of the bassinet with her own and gave me a squeeze.

"You would stand up for me in court? Because it really might come to that." The tears threatened again, but I swallowed them down. All my life, they'd made me invisible, while I desperately wanted them to see me. To love me. Now I had something they thought they wanted, and all I wanted was for them to leave me alone. More than ever, I needed to hold it together and think through how to fight Harrison and Meredith.

While Stacy and I stood silently together beside Angel's bassinet, we heard sounds outside my front door. My heart tripped at what they might be, but true to her word, Annabelle announced her return a few seconds later with a series of knocks. When I opened the door, she sailed in carrying four four-packs of White Claw. "It's not enough for serious drinking, but enough to give us a little buzz and take away the sound of evil bastard lawyer's voice in our heads," she said as she set the alcohol on the island.

"That guy really worked you up, didn't he?" Stacy asked with a grin as she helped herself to a lemon White Claw.

"Son of a bitch!" Annabelle popped the top off her drink with way more force than the circumstance called for. "Who does he think he is, making unfounded accusations and insisting Clio give up Angel like he's repossessing a car or something?" She paced back and forth in front my couch like the carpet was responsible for every evil lawyer in the world. "He's outrageous! Slamming the door in his face wasn't nearly enough. I hope I'm here when he comes back again." She stopped moving as an evil grin spread over her mouth. "Wonder what his fancy suit would look like with a little extra color, say mustard yellow?"

Stacy's mouth rounded into an astonished O. "Annabelle! You wouldn't!"

"Or maybe grape jelly? That would go nicely with his tie, don't you think, Clio?" Annabelle swigged her drink, her eyes dancing with mischief.

"Somehow I don't think ruining his thousand-dollar suit would help my cause much." I grinned. "But I'm enjoying the visual I have of his face with you shooting jelly all over him." I laughed and tipped my drink in her direction before taking a sip.

"I couldn't help but overhear him mention that you 'lack decorum,'" Stacy said, air-quoting the words. "What did he mean by that? You have the best manners of anyone I've ever met."

"I may or may not have told my father's business partner to fuck off when he came snooping around here the other day." I grimaced.

My friends' collective intake of breath at that revelation was almost comical. Then they started talking over each other.

"You *did?* Oh my God, Clio. You never swear."

"Atta girl, Clio. Show 'em some backbone."

"That visit today is probably because I didn't 'show any decorum.'" I glanced at the four-packs of White Claw resting on my island and sighed.

"Clio, I think you're going to have to ask your boyfriend for some help here," Stacy said as she made herself comfortable on the couch.

"I know." I went to the cupboard to find some chips. "But if we have to involve the band's lawyers, something is going to show up in the press. I don't want to deal with the press. At. All." I tore open the bag and shook the contents into a bowl I set on the coffee table.

We nursed our drinks in silence for several minutes, when a moment in the lawyer's conversation with me came back to me. "Annabelle, you heard the entire conversation with that lawyer, right?"

"Yeah?" She dragged out the word, turning it into a question.

"Did I make this up, or did he keep referring to my baby as 'him?'"

She took a sip from her can, swallowed, and said, "Yeah, he did. He kept calling Angel 'the infant' and 'him.' Why?"

Smiling my first genuine smile all afternoon, I said, "They're fishing. Since I haven't posted anything on social media, and my medical records are private, they don't know the sex of my baby. For whatever reason, probably wishful thinking, they're assuming I had a boy. Once they find out 'the infant' is a she, they'll disappear back into their money and their parties and their life without their embarrassment of a daughter and her failure to even get motherhood right."

"What are you saying, Clio?" Stacy asked, a horrified look flaring over her face.

"My parents wanted a son. They had me instead. When I turned out kind of smart"—my friends rolled their eyes at each other and at me—"they decided I might have some value. But I disappointed them again by not following my father to business school and a seat at his corporate table." I sat heavily on the couch. "They want their grandson to be Harrison's protégé and heir apparent in his business. Only there is no grandson. When they find out, they'll go away again." The thought both elated and depressed me.

"How can your parents be so sexist?" Annabelle asked.

"They have old-fashioned values, I guess." I toyed with a chip, snapping it into crumbs. "They were older when I came along, and Meredith couldn't have any more children. Harrison was well on his way to building his financial empire by then, and he wanted it to be a dynastic enterprise carrying the Barnes name into eternity."

"No megalomania there at all." Disgust dripped from Stacy's words.

"But Clio, even if you'd been a boy, there was no guarantee you would have followed in your dad's footsteps or even been very good at finance," Annabelle pointed out.

I waved my hand at her. "I doubt that would have been a consideration. Anyway"—I gathered chip crumbs into my palm and stood to put my mess in the trash—"it doesn't matter now. Though I do have to admit to being surprised they're coming after my baby after denouncing me the way they did back in October."

What I truly wondered was what was going on in Harrison and Meredith's lives that made them decide they wanted something—anything—from me.

CHAPTER SIXTEEN

Jack

AFTER SPENDING THE better part of the afternoon shopping for furniture for the condo I'd leased for Clio and me—her bed needed replacing in the worst way—I returned to her apartment in a better mood than when I left it. My better mood didn't change that we needed to discuss why she wouldn't let me have her number after Red Rocks, though. That move had cost us way too much time apart after all the years we'd already lost because I didn't read the fine print on a contract. Once.

When I arrived, I found Clio cleaning up her kitchen. Judging from the empty White Claw cans she dropped in the trash, the girls had had a little party while I was out.

"You enjoy your afternoon?" I asked as I tossed my snapback onto the desk by the front door.

"Um, mostly."

Her voice and her body language were off. And she'd changed her clothes since I left. Something was up.

I stepped right into her space, interrupting her cleaning. "What happened? Is Angel okay?"

Clio puffed out a breath. "Angel's great. She's sleeping off a rather big meal at the moment." She barely glanced at me. "Apparently, she enjoys a White Claw every once in a while, just like her mom." Her lame smile made her attempt at humor less than convincing.

"What happened?" I steadied her with my hands on her shoulders. "You and your friends have a fight or something? You mad at Annabelle for giving me your number?"

"She shouldn't have done that, but it didn't matter in the end, did it?"

"It did. That night after we played Red Rocks was the best night of my life, Clio." Lifting my hand, I toyed with a stray strand of her fiery hair. "I'd wanted to reconnect with you for a long time, and when I finally did, you totally rocked my world." I ducked my head to capture her eyes. "Then you disappeared from it. That's not what I wanted at all."

"We didn't talk much that night, so when I heard that message on your phone, I thought, well"—she looked away from me—"I thought I'd interrupted your real life. I didn't want to stick around and be in the way."

I pulled her into my arms and held her close to my chest. "You're my real life, Clio." I rested my chin on the top of her head. "You and now Angel." Pulling back a bit, I recaptured her eyes with mine. "Promise me you won't close me out again."

She slid her troubled gaze to my chest and nodded. "Okay."

That was too easy. It made me uncomfortable. "Okay? Just like that? After you spent nearly all of the last year avoiding me, keeping me from you and the family we've started?" I ducked my head again to see into her eyes. "What happened this afternoon?"

She squeezed her eyes shut and tightened her arms around me.

"That bad? What is it Clio? You're scaring me."

"Harrison sent his lawyer over here this afternoon."

I tightened my arms around my girl. "What the fuck?"

"Not long after you left. He arrived with papers for me to sign Angel over to Harrison and Meredith."

My entire body stiffened. "He did *what?*"

"Whatever Clive Carlyle told them about me after I sent him away with my fuck-off message was evidence enough for them to determine me an unfit mother to a child they wanted to make go away in the first place."

With her face buried so deep in my chest, she had to feel my heart kick into overdrive at her words. "You didn't sign those papers, though, right?"

"Of course not." She sniffed into my T-shirt. "But I'll have to take out another loan for a lawyer to fight them. At least until they discover I have a daughter."

"What are you talking about? A loan? Where did you miss the fact that I'm loaded? Plus, the band has a stable of lawyers on retainer. We aren't giving our daughter to anyone, Clio."

As tightly as she held me, I wouldn't have thought she could snuggle in any closer, but at my words, she tried to burrow herself into me. Though I didn't appreciate the circumstances, even a little bit, I'd be lying if I didn't admit to enjoying the consequences. Aside from that one glorious night when she'd let me inside her, I'd never been so close to her, physically or emotionally. I could have stood there with her like that all day in her saucepan of a kitchen.

Something else she'd said intruded on the moment, and I pulled away enough to look down into troubled gray eyes. "You haven't told them anything? They don't even know the sex of their only grandchild?"

"Why would I tell them anything? Why would I even think they'd want to know?" She pushed away from me and wandered over to the couch. "You weren't there the day I told them I was pregnant, Jack." She sat down, dropping her face into her hands. "You didn't see the expressions of utter horror on their faces, hear the disappointment morph into disgust and disdain in their voices as they kicked me out of their lives," she whispered.

The hitch in her voice tore at my gut. As hard as she tried to remain indifferent to her parents' cruelty, she couldn't deny how they'd hurt her. She never admitted it in words, but her voice, her eyes gave her away whenever the subject of her parents came up. If they'd been present in the room with us, I doubt I could have restrained myself from taking swings at both of them.

Joining her on the couch, I pulled her into my side and ran my hand over the silk of her hair, soothing her and myself. "You think they'll reject Angel once they find out she's a girl?"

"I know they will."

"Because of how they treated you." It wasn't a question.

"That and because the lawyer who showed up today kept refer-ring to *the infant* as *he*. Once Harrison and Meredith know I have a daughter, they'll reject her and—"

Her voice caught, and she didn't finish the thought. She didn't need to. Clio held back the information her parents demanded because she couldn't face being rejected—again—herself. I squeezed her tighter to me. It was either that or punch a hole in the wall.

"Babe, you and Angel are the best parts of my life. I admit, dis-covering I was a father threw me at first." She stiffened in my arms, and I hurried on. "But now, I can't imagine my life without Angel in it. I already know what my life is like without you in it, and I don't want to go back there." I kissed the side of her head. "We'll fight your parents."

"Harrison and Meredith," she corrected me.

I nodded. "We'll fight Harrison and Meredith, and when we're done, they'll be sorry they ever worried you or made you think for one second that you aren't up to parenting our baby. You're an amaz-ing mom, and our little girl is lucky you're hers."

I felt her smile against my shirt and pulled away enough to see it.

"You do know I come from a family of six sons, right?"

Clio blinked. "I forgot about that."

"Yeah, after she had my older brother, my mom wanted a daughter. If I'd been a girl, I think they might've even stopped having kids. Instead, I was a boy, and then they had four more boys. A basketball team plus a sixth man," I said with a laugh as I remembered the standing family joke whenever we had a holiday dinner with the grandparents. "When Mom had my youngest brother, she finally gave in. She told my dad she'd have daughters eventually. Six of them. She hoped he could live with that." I laughed at the memory. "When my parents meet you and Angel, Mom is going to be over the moon."

"You're going to introduce me to your family?" she asked, wide-eyed.

"What the fuck, Clio? Hell yes, I'm introducing you to my family. You're not my dirty little secret."

Jesus, what had her parents said to her when they'd tossed her from their lives? Not only did they not want her, but no one else would either? Harrison Barnes had a lot to answer for whenever I had the misfortune of seeing that bastard again. He didn't want me to have her, but she wasn't good enough for his family either. What kind of sick situation was that?

We sat in silence for a few minutes. Clio's stomach growled, and I had to laugh. "You spent the afternoon drinking and not eating, I take it."

"After that nasty lawyer left, Annabelle decided we needed to buzz him out of our heads. Food might have impeded the plan."

I laughed. "She's a piece of work, that Annabelle."

"If it hadn't been for her, I don't know if I could have stopped that lawyer from barging right into my place. Annabelle stood up for me. Aaaand she also told the guy to fuck off. More than once." Worry clouded her face. "So now Harrison and Meredith will probably add another black mark that my friends are a bad influence on *the infant*, another indication of my inability to parent *him* properly." She sighed.

"Like I said, babe, I have access to some of the best lawyers in the country. In fact, I'm going to give one of them a call right now, make this go away before it even begins." I reluctantly set Clio away from me so I could fish my phone from my pocket.

"Won't involving your lawyers mean the press will find out about us, about Angel?"

I shrugged. "It could happen." Outside her front window, a flock of bluebirds landed in the treetop beyond her tiny deck. "Our guys will do their best to keep everything discreet, but like I said before, I'm not ashamed of either of you. If the press finds out, the press finds out."

Crossing her arms over her chest, she leaned back into the too-soft cushions of her couch. "Easy for you to say. You're used to the celebrity. Maybe you even like it. But that's not me." She stood and went back to the kitchen to finish cleaning up. "I'm perfectly happy to remain out of the spotlight, and I don't want to have to worry about Angel every second I can't be with her when I'm finishing up my classes." Her stance as she leaned against her tiny island, like she was prepared for battle, made her meaning even more clear than her words did.

"Babe, I'll keep us as quiet as I can, but I play in the hottest rock band in the country, so word is going to get out. We were going to need to make plans for that before Harrison sicced his people on you." I stood and walked around the island. "When I talk to my lawyer, though, I'll ask for some advice on restraining orders and how we can keep the press away from you and especially away from Angel. Okay?"

I tilted her chin up with my knuckle. Because I couldn't help myself, I slipped my fingers along her jaw and cupped her face in my hand. When I leaned in and kissed her, I meant for it to be a light brush, a little reassurance. Yeah, right. The second our lips touched, I had to have more.

Tugging her close, I increased the pressure, and she sighed into my mouth, opening for me like a flower. Hers was an invitation I could never refuse. When I slid my tongue into her mouth, my body caught fire. Before I could even think, I had her back in my arms, her sweet ass backed up against the counter, my thighs pressing into hers.

The whimpering sound she made in the back of her throat as I deepened the kiss drove me wild and made my cock pound against the fly of my jeans. My response to her should have been no surprise, but the need to make love to her finally overpowered me. I tore my mouth away from hers and panted. "If you aren't ready for me yet, I need to know right now. 'Cause Clio, baby, I'm about to explode. I want you that much."

She smiled at me. "I'm so glad I'm not in this alone, Jack."

I spun her around toward the bedroom so fast we both almost lost our balance. She laughed a breathy little sound, but I was too focused on my goal to appreciate the humor of the situation.

As I righted us and backed her toward the bedroom, I asked, "How quiet do we have to be?" and flinched at how the hoarseness of my voice made me sound as desperate as I felt. In all my life, I couldn't remember wanting anything as badly as I wanted inside Clio Barnes in that moment.

"I don't know. Angel sleeps through everything else, so hopefully the two of us making love won't wake her. There's only one way to find out though." The look on her face and the tone of her voice dared me to finish what I'd started.

Oh, hell yeah. I took that dare.

Before she had a chance to think, I had her sprawled out on her bed, my hands busy palming her tits through her thin camisole and bra. She rewarded me with hard nipples and moans of pleasure as I kneaded and plucked her beautiful full breasts. Nursing Angel had definitely made her bigger in the chest, a circumstance I whole-heartedly approved. Not that I thought she'd lacked there, but the additional volume was a bonus.

Kissing the column of her neck, I tasted her sweetness, savored her pulse racing beneath my lips. Her breathy moans echoed through me, firing me up. Her neck was so sensitive, something I remembered from when we first dated, something that hadn't changed.

Her responses to my touch had my cock straining painfully to escape the fly of my jeans. When she arched up into my hands and my mouth, I groaned against her skin. She captured my lips with hers while she reached for me, unbuttoning my fly and easing the pressure there. Then she slipped her hand down my boxers and palmed my length, and I surged into her grasp.

"Jesus, Clio. I'm already on fire for you, and then you go and do that."

Sliding my hand under her top, I smoothed my way along the silky skin of her belly, dragging her camisole up. When I reached her bra, I slipped my fingers beneath it too until she picked up the hint and lifted her shoulders off the bed so I could finish undressing her upper body.

Staring down at her full ripe breasts, I smiled. "I've never seen anything in my entire life prettier than your tits. I want my mouth on you right now." Out of the corner of my eye, I caught the edge of the bassinet and remembered Angel. "Can I do that? Can I lick and kiss your gorgeous breasts?"

She smiled up at me and arched her back, giving me an even more impressive view. "I want your mouth on me so much. But be prepared for a little something extra."

Bending to her nipple, I kissed and licked her until I couldn't stand it and had to suck her completely into my mouth. I sucked hard, and Clio cried out and shoved her hands in my hair, holding me to her. The little drops of her milk I pulled from her tasted sweet and sort of rich. Nothing like what I expected. She rubbed her hips against me, and I couldn't think about anything other than getting us both out of our pants.

I rolled away from her, sat on the edge of the bed, and pulled my T-shirt over my head, flinging it to the floor as I simultaneously shucked my Converse. My jeans and boxers followed fast. Snagging a condom from my wallet, I lay back on the bed and discovered Clio naked beside me.

Focusing on arousing her completely, I stroked her from her shoulder, across her nipple—still wet from my mouth—and down her smooth belly to the apex of her thighs. The tangle of curls there pulled my fingers down farther, and I slipped them over her swollen clit, rubbing the pad of my finger over her.

Clio moaned and opened her legs for me, giving me the access I silently insisted on. When I slipped a finger into her folds, I pleasured her hot, wet channel and gazed into her eyes, smiling at her. I used my teeth to tear open the condom packet one-handed, smoothed the condom over my dick and rolled over, inserting my body between her legs while bracing myself over her with my forearms on either side of her head.

"This first time we need to go slow, Jack," she whispered as she dragged her hands over the skin of my chest and down the length of my torso until she grasped my cock. Lifting her hips to me, she guided me to her entrance, her words and actions so at odds I didn't know what to do.

But my body did. I lowered myself into her, her wetness making it easy for me, the tightness of her pussy reminding me she hadn't done this in a long time. Gritting my teeth, I sank into her as slowly as I could, but, sweet Jesus, she felt so perfect. It was all I could do to stop from pounding into her from the first thrust.

"Oh, Jack," she said on a sigh as she ran her hands up and down the length of my back. And that was it.

All the months of being without her, all the weeks of being with her and not having her came together in that sigh. Her response gave me a bigger rush than playing any stadium show in front of thousands of screaming fans. Everything I ever wanted lay in this bed with me, and I couldn't have stopped myself from claiming her if a firing squad encircled us.

"Clio!" I shouted as I pounded into her, all good intentions of taking it slow forgotten as she wrapped her arms and legs around me and tightened her pussy, pulling me so deep inside her I didn't know where I ended and she began.

The pressure inside me built and built as I gave and gave and gave her everything I had to give. She arched against me and screamed my name. The orgasm gathering at the base of my spine exploded, and I thrust hard into her again and again, joining her as I blasted us into space.

Afterward, my arms gave way, and I fell onto her chest. She tightened her arms around me and sighed into my skin in the curve where my shoulder met my neck. It wasn't until I came back down that I noticed the rough soreness in my throat, so I knew I'd been shouting. It was all I could do to pick up my head and look over at the baby's bassinet to see if I'd awakened her. Mercifully, my perfectly named little angel had slept through her parents' rather loud reconnection.

Dropping my head back down to the pillow, I groaned. "Babe, you are going to be the death of me, but I'm going to die a very happy man."

"Jack, I'm so glad you're persistent."

"You have no idea how persistent I can be, Clio."

"I hope you're going to show me. In fact, I'm counting on it," she said, her smile warm on my skin.

At last, I found the strength to roll off her, but not wanting to end our connection, I pulled her half over me. She snuggled contentedly on my chest, her hand tracing lightly over my pecs and abs. After a few minutes, she pushed up onto her elbow to check out my ink.

"What's this?" she asked as she traced the stylized C I'd had inked over my left pec after I'd attended her high school graduation.

"What does it look like?" I teased.

"Is . . . is that for me?" she asked, wonder in her tone.

"Yeah, babe, it is," I answered truthfully and held my breath.

"How long have you had it?"

"Four years."

Her eyes flew to mine. "But we weren't even talking to each other then. I was about a minute out of high school."

"Even though I was touring and trying to make it as a musician, you were never far from my thoughts"—I glanced down where her finger traced over my skin—"or my heart."

Her smile lit me up like the sun. I should have told her everything then, but we were so happy, so connected in the postcoital afterglow, that I didn't want to ruin things. No doubt her dad was a first-class asshole, but I hadn't been entirely innocent in the deal either.

At least Clio let me off the hook.

"These other ones on your shoulder and down your arm? From a distance, they look like something tribal, but up close, I can see they're flames." Her finger tracing my ink soothed me. "They're so intricate. What are they for?"

"I got that ink on my one-year anniversary after joining Balefire."

"The band is important to you." Her tone took on a sadness I had to deflect.

"The guys in the band are my other family. When you spend as much time together as we do, either you become brothers, or you want to kill each other. Tron, Blu, and Dakota are my brothers. I wanted something to honor us as a band. My tats are all about the connections in my life, the people who matter most to me."

She laid her head back down on my chest and wrapped her arm around my body, holding me close to her. "Your ink fascinated me before. Now I think it's super sexy," she whispered.

When she said that, she let me breathe again. But in the back of my mind, I knew I had to tell her about the deal I'd made with the devil in the guise of her father. And I had to tell her soon.

CHAPTER SEVENTEEN

Clio

WHEN JACK MADE love to me the first time after Angel's birth, he made the whole world disappear. Afterward, I awoke from my post-lovemaking nap to Angel's fussing and the low sounds of Jack talking to someone. From the lulls in his conversation, I could tell he was on the phone. I rolled out of bed, grabbed my short bathrobe from the back of the chair, and wrapped it around me. I scooped Angel out of her bassinet and walked out into the living room where late afternoon light slanted over the floor in front of Jack. He sat on the couch wearing nothing but his boxers. From the animated way he spoke, he was obviously working hard to keep his temper in check.

I stood quietly by the arm of the couch and cuddled Angel close to me. Jack looked up, the scowl on his face briefly replaced with half a smile as he patted the spot next to him.

"For fuck's sake, Tucker, I don't need a paternity test to prove the baby is mine. What I need is a restraining order against Clio's parents and anyone associated with them. They've harassed my girls for the last time." He sat forward, his hand gesturing to drive home his point even though the person on the other end couldn't see it. "And I want you to make it clear to Garrett that my being a father is *not* a publicity stunt, so it doesn't need to be splashed across social media and the press."

He listened for a few seconds before saying, "I know that Tucker. But the longer we can wait to share the news, the better I'm going to feel about the safety of my family. I have to consider them now too."

When I heard Jack say that, I shivered. Even with his focus on his conversation, he noticed and slipped his arm around me and pulled me in close to his side. In early July in Fort Collins, the weather was not the cause of the chill ghosting over me. Unfortunately, even cuddled up to the furnace that was Jack Whitehorse at the moment, cold still passed over my skin. Cold dread of being in any kind of spotlight. Cold dread of Angel's pictures available for anyone to see. Cold dread my little girl could be in danger purely because her daddy played drums for a famous rock band. Most of all, cold dread Harrison and Meredith Barnes could come anywhere near Angel, could hurt her the way they'd hurt me. The coldness of my thoughts left my skin goose-bumped and clammy.

Jack's sigh pulled me out of my morose reverie. "Thanks Tucker. The restraining order is the most important thing right now. I'll call Garrett and the band today, let them know what's going on."

He clicked off and tossed his phone onto the coffee table.

My thoughts must have crossed my face, and he tried to put my mind at ease. "Clio, baby, I told you I'd take care of you and I meant it. I wasn't here for the most important day in all three of our lives . . ." When my upturned brow prompted him, he clarified, "The day you gave birth to Angel."

I smiled. That day truly was the most important day of my life.

"But I'm going to be here from now on. Your parents need to know that. Right now, they think you're on your own with no support since they jerked theirs right out from under you, but you have some great friends, and most importantly"—he wrapped his arm tighter around me—"you have me. I'm not going anywhere."

With his free hand, he held my face for a kiss that might have gone places had Angel not chosen that moment to remind me I had other obligations.

"Shhh, little one. I'll fix it." Turning to Jack, I said, "She needs a change and a snack. Back in a few."

In the bedroom, I lay Angel on my bed to change her. Before I could even turn around to retrieve a clean diaper and the wipes, Jack was there with them in hand. "I got this, Clio." He smiled.

Ever since I'd introduced Jack to Angel, he'd shown me time and time again he meant to be a hands-on dad. But what did that mean with his career? With the band?

"Um, Jack? I take it the person on the other end of your call was your lawyer?"

"Yeah," he said as he efficiently stripped off Angel's soiled diaper and tossed it into the Diaper Genie.

"You said something about telling the band. What are you going to tell them?"

"That they can stop calling me the monk since I'm a dad now." He glanced away from his task long enough to grin at me. "And Garrett won't be booking more concerts far from home over Christmas since I'll have somewhere more important to be."

The tone of his voice when he made that comment told me there was a story behind it, but that wasn't important at the moment.

"You're not quitting the band?"

Though he'd been in the middle of changing Angel's diaper, his hands stilled. "Do you want me to?"

"Of course not. You're a musician." I forced a smile. "The band is probably part of your DNA. I could never ask you to stop being who you are. I wouldn't want you to be anyone else."

He let out a breath and finished changing Angel.

As he lifted her up onto his shoulder, he gazed over her at me.

"Being in the band means I'm still going to be in the studio, and I'm still going to tour. But my home base has changed. Now it's going to be wherever you and Angel are." Angel seemed on board with that idea judging from the cooing sounds she made as Jack absently rubbed his hand over her back. "I know how much you want to finish your degree and be a nurse, so when you finish school and decide where you want to work, we'll set up our home there."

"That sounds pretty permanent."

He stared at me like I'd suddenly grown another head. "We have a kid together, Clio," he said, his voice low and rumbly. "We have a history together." Then a smile like sunshine broke over his face. "Besides, I'm crazy about you, which means I'm gonna be with you whenever I can."

He leaned down and kissed me softly. A slight brush of his lips over mine, but it felt like a promise.

Again, Angel interrupted.

"You know, little girl, as the daughter of a drummer, your timing sucks. We need to work on that," Jack teased before he handed our baby to me. "Guess it's snack time."

I smiled at him over Angel's head and walked back out to the living room. We returned to the couch where I opened my bathrobe and put our little girl to my breast while Jack busied himself with taking out the trash I'd been working on when he arrived home earlier.

Home. Maybe my place lacked in size and style, but it was mine. Now, it seemed, it was ours.

♪

Later that afternoon, Jack disappeared for a couple hours. When he returned to my place, he carried two rather large duffel bags. He dropped one in the corner of the living room before taking the other into the bedroom. After a few minutes, he came back out to the living room and proceeded to unload a drum kit from the bag.

I watched in amazement as he set up an entire trap set made up of pads and wires. As he went to work connecting all the parts, he looked at me and smiled.

"I carry this with me everywhere. I can set it up in a hotel room or in your apartment, bang away on my drums, and not bother anyone. Pretty fucking cool, huh?" The little boy grin on his face made me laugh.

"You'll have to show me."

"In a few minutes. I need to grab something else from my truck."

He walked back into my place a few minutes later carrying a guitar case.

"You play the guitar too? How did I not know this about you?"

He laughed and set his guitar in the corner of the room beside my desk. "I don't play much in public—wouldn't want to hurt Dakota's feelings by showing him up." The wicked grin on his face emphasized some of what he'd told me about his little rivalry with Balefire's lead guitarist. Patting the top of the case, he said, "Sometimes when I'm writing, it's easier to work out a lyric on a guitar than behind my traps."

When he headed back into the bedroom, I followed behind him. He stopped in front of the single-door hole-in-the wall masquerading as my closet, a space I'd stuffed to the point of bursting. A look of consternation furrowed his brow.

"Got any room for a few T-shirts and jeans in your dresser?"

"I'll make some space," I said with a chuckle before a thought struck me. "Wait. You're moving in with me? For real?"

"Clio, baby. I'm here all day and all night already. Keeping my clothes here is common sense."

He traced his finger across my forehead, down my temple, and over my cheek before bouncing it off the end of my nose. "Right?"

I rolled my eyes at him and fought a smile. Turning to my dresser, I consolidated my panties and bras into one drawer and made room for his things.

♪

Our days fell into a routine of waking up to Angel's demands for breakfast followed by slow lovemaking while she took her morning nap. The afternoons found us on some sort of adventure—long walks along the river, poking around in Old Town, a picnic in the mountains. In the early evening, we'd return home for Angel's nap. Most days, Jack would use that time to work out at a nearby gym, which solved another mystery—he rocked his cut abs, heavily muscled shoulders, and strong sculpted legs because he kept himself in shape. He said he needed to stay in shape to play the way he did. After watching him play live at Red Rocks, I believed him.

Along the way, he casually suggested cooking lessons.

"What the heck, Jack? I can cook," I said, even as heat climbed from my chest and up my neck to fill my face at his suggestion.

"Babe. You can't live on scrambled eggs and salad."

I crossed my arms over my chest. "It's been working okay so far."

He put his big hands on my shoulders and smiled into my eyes. "We both know you eat half your weight of the chicken parm and the Hawaiian pizza and the steak and potatoes deliveries I order."

I snorted. "A gentleman wouldn't comment on that. Besides, I'm feeding two, you know."

With a laugh, he gave my shoulders an affectionate squeeze. "I do know. Honestly, I love how much you enjoy your food. It's why I thought maybe you could use a little help learning how to make the good stuff." He ducked his head and waggled his brows. "Bet Angel will like it too."

"That's low, Jack." But I was laughing.

When I gave in and admitted I needed some help in the kitchen, our adventures included cooking lessons with a chef friend of Jack's. After a couple of afternoons with Chef Jeff, we discovered to our mutual delight that I had a knack for cooking. I only needed some basics and direction.

Following our afternoon adventures, we'd return home to order in dinner, or later, after I started my lessons, to let me practice making dinner. Sometimes we'd watch a movie. Sometimes I read ahead for the start of my next semester while Jack wrote music. Usually his songwriting distracted me, and science texts took a backseat to listening to him as he worked through a some notes on his guitar or practiced his drums. Even though the drum kit only sounded like drums in his headphones, sometimes he'd share his headphones with me, his rhythms affecting me almost as powerfully in their subdued state as they did when his drums were all miked up.

Two nights a week I went into the dorm for my desk clerk shift.

The second time I went to work after he came back into my life, Jack asked to come with Angel and me.

"Seriously, Jack?"

He nodded.

I blew out an exasperated breath. "Think about it. You play in Balefire. How long do you think it will take for it to get out that you're on campus? And how will I explain why you're with me?"

"But—"

Pulling out the big gun, I asked, "How will we keep Angel safe if people make the connection?" When he opened up his mouth to speak again, I put up my hand. "It will take a hot minute for anyone with eyes to connect her to you if someone sees the two of you together." He pulled a face. "It's your eyes, Jack."

He laid his drumsticks on his tom-toms and ran his fingers through his hair. "Clio, you don't even need this job."

I planted my hands on my hips. "How do you figure?"

"You know I'll help you. I can pick up your rent, cover your groceries and whatever you need for the baby."

In two steps, I stood beside him. He turned on his stool and tugged me between his legs. Resting my hands on his shoulders, I said, "When Harrison and Meredith kicked me out, I thought my world was imploding. But after living on my own, learning how to take care of myself and Angel, I'm discovering that I kind of like it."

He squeezed my hips. "I'm proud of you, babe. I am. But we're a team now. You don't need to do everything on your own."

"Thank you," I whispered against his lips as I brushed a soft kiss over them. "But here's the thing, Jack. I kind of like the independence that comes with making my own money."

He huffed out a breath.

"Besides, I'm going to need something to do at night after you head back out on the road."

He tugged me closer to him. "You're not giving in on this, are you?"

Suppressing a grin, I said, "Nope."

"Just please promise me that you'll tell me if you need something. I need"—he swallowed—"I want to take care of my girls."

Some days, he would disappear for a couple of mysterious hours in the morning or afternoon. When I asked him about it, he grinned and told me I'd love the surprise if I didn't ruin it first with badgering him about it. So I shut up, but I'd have been lying if I said his absences didn't cause me some worry.

After we put Angel to bed at night, he'd make everything all better. Occasionally, our lovemaking went on and on until it was time for Angel's 2:00 a.m. feeding. Other times, we only made love once before dropping into satisfied exhaustion. But after that first time back together, a day didn't go by that we didn't start and end our days by using our bodies to show each other our feelings.

A couple of blissful weeks passed, time in which I hadn't thought about Harrison and Meredith Barnes even once. Then one morning, my world collapsed around me in the aftermath of the earthquake that was Harrison Barnes at my door.

I was still smiling after we'd made love and Jack had headed into the bathroom to shower when the doorbell chimed through my apartment. My smile froze into some grotesque grimace I'm sure when I opened the door to find Harrison standing on the other side of it.

"Hello, Clio. Are you often in the habit of opening your door in such"—he looked me up and down—"dishabille? No wonder I've received such grave reports concerning you recently."

Pulling my bathrobe more tightly around me, a defensive gesture for which I immediately despised myself, I straightened my spine and mimicked his imperious tone. "I don't recall inviting you or your minions to my home. Since I'm twenty-two and no longer dependent upon you in any way for anything, I cannot imagine what you're doing here."

Harrison glanced behind me, and his eyes narrowed. "Are you the father of my grandchild?"

"Babe, you want me to answer that question?"

I sensed Jack's heat as he stood close behind me and settled his hands protectively on my shoulders.

"Yes, Harrison, Jack is my baby's father."

"That, young man, puts you in breach of our contract."

Contract? What was Harrison talking about? I turned my head to ask Jack, and cold dread shivered through me at the stone set of his jaw as he regarded my father through hostile eyes.

"That contract ran out four years ago, Barnes, and you know it. There's nothing to stop me from being with Clio now."

"Just the part that applies directly to you. There were other considerations."

Behind me, Jack's body stiffened.

"What are you two talking about?" I demanded as I rubbed my hands over my arms, trying to stave off the chill stealing over me, a chill that defied the summer heat radiating through the morning air.

"We'll talk about it later, Clio," Jack said.

"Something happened between you two that clearly involved me, so I think you should start talking now." I didn't know which one of them I addressed, but the sudden sick weight in my stomach told me it didn't matter. I wasn't going to like what I heard regardless of who told me.

"When given the chance, your boyfriend here chose his music over you. When forced to choose, he chose his family over you. Mr. Whitehorse has proven his selfish nature, and there is nothing in his actions to indicate he will make different choices in the future." Harrison moved to step through my door, but I didn't budge. He huffed out an impatient breath and continued. "If you give me access to the child, I can help you when he leaves you again to follow his dream, which never included you."

The satisfaction sneering across Harrison's face as he wrecked my world seared my heart almost as much as his words. I'm not sure where I dredged up the strength, but the steadiness I heard in my voice surprised me considering my insides felt like Jell-O. Apparently, Harrison heard the conviction in my voice too because he paled when I said, "I don't need anything from you. It's been nearly a year since I've seen or heard from you. I've taken care of myself and my baby without your help since you disowned me." I straightened my spine and delivered the blow. "However, for the record, I have a daughter, not the son you've punished me my whole life for not being. And I'm never giving you the chance to hurt my little girl for not being the boy you want to inherit your business empire."

"We're done here Barnes. I believe my lawyers made that perfectly clear when they served you with the restraining order. There's nothing ambiguous in it. Right down to the fine print," Jack added.

There was something going on between them, something I could sense involved me, but I couldn't take the tense way Jack's hands dug into my shoulders or the cold expression on Harrison's face any longer. I closed the door slowly in his face, but I didn't turn around to face Jack. I couldn't.

A lifetime passed in the silence that settled over my tiny apartment with the snick of the catch on the front door. Time in which my entire world collapsed into rubble.

At last I turned from the door and walked back toward my bedroom. Jack reached for me, but the touch of his calloused hand on my arm only reminded me who he really was.

"I can explain, Clio. Let me explain." His voice, low and harsh, ripped through me, making my insides churn.

I kept walking to my bedroom where I gathered up his clothes. Meeting him at the door to my bedroom, I shoved his clothes into his chest. "You need to go now, Jack."

"Clio. Let's talk about this."

"This is my house, so I get to decide."

"Not before you let me explain."

"There's nothing to explain. You didn't trust me enough to tell me the truth." His eyes flinched, but otherwise, he stayed silent. "I always knew your whole world revolved around your music. Even when we were in high school, that was obvious. It's what makes you who you are," I said sadly. "But I grew up in a house where my parents' passions didn't include me. Until I gave birth to Angel, I didn't come first in anyone's life. She's not growing up invisible like I did." I stared down at my daughter, innocently sleeping in her bassinet.

"Go out and be a rock star, Jack. That's your dream. You have no choice but to be who you were meant to be."

He took a step toward me. "Clio, I'd give it all up for you."

The anguish in his voice, the pain on his face tore at me, but I had to let him go. "And do what? Be miserable because you can't play anymore? How long would we last before you started resenting me, resenting Angel?"

I sucked air in through my nose and clamped my teeth together to hold back the sobs burning the back of my throat. When Jack tried to reach for me again, I sidestepped him, giving myself time to control my voice. "Whenever you want to see Angel, we'll work something out."

Somehow, I'd made it to the door and stood there holding it open for him. I squeezed my eyes shut and wrapped my free arm around myself, trying to hold in the agony threatening to erupt out of me.

"You don't trust me. Jesus, Clio. After everything we've done together these last weeks, how can you not trust me?"

His phone sounded in the pocket of his jeans, interrupting him, the ringtone a heavy metal riff I recognized as the one he'd set for Blu.

"You better answer that," I croaked around the lump in my throat.

Jack stared at me with tortured eyes, but he fished his phone out of his jeans pocket and finger punched the screen. "What do you want, Blu?" He listened for a second. "Now? I thought we agreed to meet at noon."

I opened the door wider.

"Fine. I'm in Fort Collins. I can be there in about an hour."

He shoved his phone back in his pocket and dropped his Converse to the floor before he dragged his T-shirt down over his chest. Then he threw himself into the chair by the door and shoved his feet into his shoes.

"Our conversation isn't over, Clio. Just postponed is all. I'll be back this evening to continue it," Jack said.

Before he brushed past me and out my door, he clamped his hands on my shoulders. "We're not done, baby." His brutal kiss tasted of fear and desperation before it gentled into regret. Then he was gone.

I closed the door behind him and sagged against it. "I'm afraid we are," I whispered to the empty apartment that echoed around me in the silence of Jack's absence.

CHAPTER EIGHTEEN

Clio

JACK DIDN'T RETURN to my apartment that night. He told me a couple of days before he left that the band was gearing up to go back into the studio to record their new album. When he talked about the songs he'd been working on for it, his body glowed from head to toe with happiness and excitement. Every time he talked about playing or the band or touring, it was obvious that Jack Whitehorse was placed on this planet to share his music.

He warned me that sometimes recording sessions could go on literally for days when the band was in the zone. Once he headed to Denver to record with the other guys, there could be days on end when the most I could expect from him might be a short phone call in the middle of the night. He said he'd work hard to avoid doing that to me with the baby and all, but he also said he didn't want to go a full twenty-four hours without hearing my voice for at least a minute or two.

But that conversation had taken place before Harrison Barnes darkened my door.

When Jack hadn't called by the time I'd bathed Angel, fed her, and put her to bed, I knew the band had started its most recent recording session in the zone. After the way things had gone this morning with Harrison and him, it didn't surprise me not to hear from Jack all day. Still, he'd said we'd talk about it when he returned tonight. So I didn't slide the chain over the door when I went to bed. Nor did I sleep during the four hours between when I put Angel to bed and when she awoke for her 2:00 a.m. feeding.

After I put her back to bed, I drank a cup of warm milk and turned off my phone. When I went to bed the second time, exhaustion combined with the nightcap helped to shut my brain off enough to fall asleep. In the early morning after Angel woke me to start the day, I discovered I hadn't needed to bother turning off my phone. No one had tried to call or text me at all.

♪

Midafternoon the day following Harrison's visit, my doorbell chimed through my apartment again. "I'm really starting to hate that sound," I muttered as I walked over to answer the door.

Leaving the chain in place, I cracked the door open to find my friends smiling at me on the other side.

"Hi Clio! We're here! Sorry it took so long," Stacy said, her grin nearly swallowing her face.

"Why is your chain on? Were you expecting someone else too?" Annabelle asked, suspicion clouding her pretty features. "Come on, Clio, open the door."

I closed the door enough to release the chain and stepped aside to let my friends into my apartment.

"Hey, where are the boxes?" Stacy asked as she looked around my living room.

"You don't look like you've even started packing. We're here to help, but come on, sister, you needed to start *some* of it without us at least," Annabelle said in her don't-mess-with-me tone.

Stacy studied my face. "Um, I don't think Clio has a clue what we're doing here."

"That's the first thing either of you has said that's made any sense at all. Why would I be packing? I'm not going anywhere."

"Oh-oh. I sense trouble in paradise. Didn't Jack tell you? By the way, where is he? He doesn't think we're moving the heavy stuff without him, does he?" Annabelle asked, her hands planted firmly on her hips as she shot a glare toward my bedroom.

"Tell me what? What was Jack supposed to have told me?"

First Harrison. Now my friends? Maybe Jack's absence had more to do with what I didn't know about him than about any new recording.

"Your condo, silly." Pure delight danced across Stacy's features.

"My condo?" I repeated stupidly.

"He didn't tell you, did he?" Stacy said. "Jack leased you a giant condo on the other side of campus. It's got a monster kitchen, a sunken living room, and a master bedroom and bath suite that's bigger than your whole apartment." She spread her arms wide. "And the sweetest nursery for Angel. He asked us to help him set it up so it would be exactly right for you. The plan is to move you into it today."

Sitting down hard on the couch, I grabbed a throw pillow and hugged it to my chest. "It must have slipped Jack's mind after Harrison stopped by yesterday to tell me that he and Jack had some kind of contract. Something that concerned Jack's music, his family, and me."

Annabelle knit her brow. "You don't know?"

"I couldn't follow the particulars, but that's the gist of it. Then Blu Connolly called Jack, and he left. The band returned to the studio yesterday to record their new album, which means Jack's and my summer fling is over." I gripped the pillow tighter as I worked to contain my emotions.

"But the condo—" Stacy began.

"Since Jack never mentioned it to me, I think it may have been nothing more than a diversion. Jack playing house." I squeezed my eyes shut, gathered myself, and continued. "Now that the band is off hiatus and back to work, his real love has taken him back. To be honest, I've always known I'll never be as important to him as his music." I struggled to keep the sadness out of my voice. "Girls, I'm sorry you came all this way for nothing."

Annabelle took my hand and gave it a tiny squeeze. "You didn't see him as he set it up. He bought all the furniture, had it delivered, asked us to take a look at it, make sure it fit your taste." Her voice trailed away as I stared at her, knowing my expression conveyed my disbelief loud and clear.

Stacy rushed in to back Annabelle—and maybe even Jack. "He invited us to go with him when he went shopping for the nursery. That was so much fun." She smiled as she took my other hand. "Jack wore dark glasses and a snapback pulled low over his forehead. The sales lady kept looking at him funny as he asked questions about the safety and durability of the furniture. I think she wondered why he never took off his glasses inside the store."

"He was so excited for you to see it, but even more excited to move you into it—with him," Annabelle said.

I pulled my hands back, wrapping my arms around the pillow, my life preserver in the sea of emotion threatening to swallow me. "Yeah, so excited that he didn't say a word about it to me. He left yesterday morning, and I haven't heard from him since. Not that I expected to." I was trying to hold it together, but from the looks on their faces, I was failing spectacularly. So I stopped trying to hide it. "Girls, there will be no moving party today or anytime in the foreseeable future."

"What happened, Clio? Did the two of you break up?" Stacy asked as she slid closer beside me. "Why?"

"Harrison stopped by yesterday."

"Yeah, you mentioned that. What was he doing here?" Annabelle wanted to know. "I thought you said Jack had a restraining order taken out against him."

"Apparently, such petty items as restraining orders are beneath Harrison's notice." I sniffed back a sob. "From the little I could follow of their conversation, Jack and Harrison had some kind of contract. One involving Jack's career and me. Jack chose his career."

"That can't be true, Clio. We've seen the way Jack looks at you. Plus, he's an awesome dad to Angel," Stacy said as she went into mothering mode, smoothing her hand over my hair.

"Be reasonable, Clio. He has a job to do. You knew that about him from the beginning. He's not cheating on you. He hasn't left you. He's gone back to work for a while," Annabelle said, her tone brooking no argument. "Now what did Harrison do?"

Her explanation for Jack's behavior and her indignation at my father's behavior cheered me up a bit. "He turned tail when I informed him his coveted grandson is, in fact, a granddaughter."

"Well, that's something. Now maybe he'll leave you alone," Annabelle said with a satisfied smirk.

We were silent for a few minutes when Annabelle determined our course of action. "Since we're not moving you out today, but we're all here, I have a great idea. Let's drive into Loveland and go shopping. Classes start in a couple of weeks, which means more new men on campus. I need to find some sexy things to pique their interest." She slid off the back of the couch where she'd perched when Stacy had sat me down and headed toward the door.

"Like you need any help there," Stacy said, laughing as she stood and joined Annabelle. "But I'm in. I need to find some accessories for my costume for rush next week. When we planned rush, I didn't realize we didn't have everything for a jungle theme tucked away in the costumes closet at the house. Come on, Clio. We'll stop at the baby store and pick up something adorable for Angel."

"I don't know, guys. I'm not sure I'll be very good company today," I hedged. The truth was, I wanted to be home in case Jack came back.

As if she read my mind, Annabelle said, "He has your number,

Clio. If Jack finishes up early today, he can call you. It's not good for you to sit around here by yourself and brood. Grab the little angel, and let's go."

She crossed her arms over her chest and tapped her foot like I was making her late for a date or something. The mock stern expression on her face cracked me up, and before I knew it, I had Angel in my arms and her diaper bag tossed over my shoulder. I locked up my apartment before we headed out for an afternoon of shopping. I didn't know how much I'd needed my friends until they'd shown up unannounced at my door.

♪

Four days passed before I finally heard from Jack. Then he only texted me: *Session began in the zone. We still need to talk.*

A second text followed a short time later: *I'm crazy about you, Clio. Please don't give up on us, babe.*

It felt like an afterthought. Like I was an afterthought.

Annabelle's talk had made sense at the time. It still did. It was only that I'd spent my entire life as an afterthought—whenever my parents didn't treat me as plain invisible. Being an afterthought for Jack hurt even more, so much more since for a short time he'd shown me what it felt like to be the center of his universe. Even when he practiced his drums or wrote a song on his guitar, he was aware of me in the room. He'd stop often to talk to me or smile at me or see what I was doing. Four days of silence followed by a couple of texts drove home what I already knew: Jack Whitehorse would always put his music first. And I needed more than that. I needed to be first.

No matter how unreasonable someone else might find my feelings, twenty-two years of invisibility with intermittent moments of attention had left me craving love and affection, left me craving the experience of being the true center of another person's world. For the first month of her life, I was the center of Angel's universe, and it was enough. It was more than enough. Then Jack Whitehorse blew back into my life, showed me what a real relationship could be, showed me the kind of family we could create together, and more than anything I knew that's what I wanted, what I needed. But like a summer storm, Jack blew back out of my life as completely as he blew into it.

The kicker? I didn't want him to change. I didn't want him to be anything else but himself. His music defined him, made him so dynamic and attractive and powerful. It drew me in the first time I heard him play, two years before he ever asked me out. I think I fell in love with his music before I fell in love with him. So even *I* couldn't give up his music. How could I ask him to give it up?

Sitting on my couch, I hugged my knees to my chest and thought about Jack and me. Outside, the long summer twilight finally faded into night, plunging my apartment into full darkness. I'd resolved nothing when I turned in for another night in my now very lonely bed.

♪

Two more weeks passed before I heard from Jack again.

"I'm sorry I've been out of touch," he began without even a hello when I picked up my phone. "Clio, baby, I warned you I could be MIA when the band went into the studio to record."

"Did I say anything?"

"No, but I can hear you thinking it."

"I get it, Jack. When you're in the zone, nothing else matters. You made that clear when you disappeared from my life the first time back in high school."

It sounded like he growled.

Then silence.

"Listen, we're on a break to do some interviews, so right now I can't explain what happened back then. But you have to believe me when I tell you it's not what you think. Harrison made me out to be the bad guy, but that wasn't how it went down at all."

"You didn't choose music over me? Over us? You didn't erase me from your life and disappear from mine? I dreamed all that?" The loose thread I'd been picking at on my couch pulled free, alerting me I'd put a hole in the cushion.

"Clio, that's not fair."

"No, it's the truth."

I tried to keep the bitterness out of my tone, but it snuck in anyway.

"I didn't call you so we could fight."

I heard someone in the background calling for him. "They want you, Jack. You better go."

"Are you all right? Is Angel doing okay? Do you need anything?"

You.

Jack sounded a little desperate at the other end of the connection. Or maybe that was wishful thinking.

"We're fine. Everything's—fine."

On the other end of the call, I heard another voice call for Jack.

"It sounds like you need to be somewhere right now. We'll talk when you're not so busy. Goodbye, Jack."

"Clio. Baby."

I waited. What did he want me to say?

"I'll talk to you as soon as I can. Maybe later tonight. Clio. Please don't give up on us."

Another week passed with only intermittent texts from him, mostly checking on Angel. Looking at Jack's things scattered throughout my apartment depressed me, so I washed his clothes and packed them into his duffel bag. After that, I carefully disassembled his electric drum set and repacked it in the other bag. I placed all his things between the desk and the wall near the front door where I didn't have to look at them so much and found my eyes straying there all the time.

The next week classes began. The way my schedule worked out, I only had to take Angel to the campus daycare for one class a week since the girls' schedules worked around mine, which meant they took turns watching her while I was in class. Between taking care of Angel, going to class, studying, and working, I could keep my thoughts from straying to Jack Whitehorse to only twenty or thirty times a day.

Then came the phone call that stole my breath.

"We're headed out on tour, Clio."

"When?"

"We leave tomorrow. We have several dates in Europe during September and October before returning to the States for some stadium shows in November and early December. But I'll be home for Christmas, I promise."

"Sure," I said, my voice hollow.

"Clio, I was eighteen with stars in my eyes."

"They're still there, Jack."

"Babe, please. Don't be like this."

"Like what? I know you need to fly, Jack. Go out on your tour. Blow the world away—again."

"We'll talk. FaceTime, text, Instagram. Please."

The pleading in his voice nearly undid me because I knew he meant every word. I also understood he'd be far away from us in every way that mattered.

"Sure, Jack."

CHAPTER NINETEEN

Clio

SEEING HARRISON BARNES in my baby's daycare center talking to one of the assistants as she held Angel in her arms sent all thoughts of the organic chemistry test I'd just finished flying from my head.

"Excuse me," I said, taking my daughter into my arms but my eyes were focused on my bio donor. "I have a restraining order against this man. He is not to come within a thousand feet of my daughter or me. I'll bring the papers with me the next time I have to leave her here."

My pronouncement, and my arctic tone, sent the assistant into a frenzy of apologies. She scooted off to find a supervisor while I stared Harrison down.

"Your daughter is beautiful. She looks exactly like you as a baby," he said quietly.

I couldn't read his face or his tone, so I said nothing.

He seemed to find himself then, and he continued in his usual condescending fashion. "I had to know, Clio. You see, it wouldn't have surprised me if you'd misinformed me of the sex of your child."

"You always assume that I'm like you. But you never tried to know me, not even a little. Which means you don't understand that more than anything, I do not ever want to be like you or Meredith." I put Angel over my shoulder so Harrison couldn't stare at her face. "Therefore, I told you the truth. In the end, it was an easy truth to tell since I knew a girl child was of no use to you."

For a second, I thought he might have flinched before his usual haughty expression stole back over his face.

"However, you are in violation of a court order, so I suggest you leave here and do not return. Not that you would return now that you have the information you wanted so much." Somehow, I must have channeled Meredith. Deep inside, the nastiness of my tone surprised me. But I didn't break.

"You're wrong about the value of your daughter. I understand your boyfriend is out of the country on some tour for his music. Perhaps you need to rethink the restraining order and give us a chance to get to know your little girl."

My blood turned to ice. Involuntarily, I squeezed Angel tighter in my arms, and she let out a yelp in protest.

Still, I managed to ask, "Are you threatening me, Harrison?"

"No, but I'd like an opportunity to know my only grandchild." Way too easy. "Why?"

"Because I have only one."

"Not good enough. What do you really want?"

"Maybe we made some mistakes with you, Clio. Maybe we could try again, get it right with our granddaughter," he said, his voice more subdued than I'd ever heard it.

The arrival of the daycare supervisor interrupted our conversation. "Is there a problem here, Miss Barnes?" she asked, giving Harrison the once-over.

Because I'd seen the way Harrison wielded his power, my fear for my daughter made me bold. When I thought about it later, I could devise no other explanation for my response.

"I have a restraining order against this man. I'll provide a copy for you tomorrow," I said to her. I faced Harrison again. "In some ways, I guess I am your daughter. When it comes to my child, I will always get my way. Please do abide by the terms of the court order. It won't look good in the press if you choose not to do so."

Turning away from him, I headed toward the infant room to retrieve Angel's diaper bag. When I took once last glance over my shoulder, he completely perplexed me with the brief look of pure pain that crossed his face before he composed himself and walked away.

Once I had Angel out of his line of sight, I hugged her close and whispered fiercely, "I don't know what he wants, sweetheart, but whatever it is, he will never ever hurt you. No one will ever be allowed to make you feel invisible or unloved. No one." A picture of Jack Whitehorse flashed across my mind, and I realized there were lots of ways someone could make another feel invisible. And one way wouldn't be any less painful than another.

♪

My stress level approached the stratosphere between adding hours at my desk clerk job and taking midterms in all my classes. I certainly didn't need the threat of Harrison Barnes again. Then there was Jack.

We'd shared a few brief phone calls during which he talked about the European capitals they played and the wild crowds and how much he missed me. Usually in that order. I talked about Angel, how she'd learned to roll over and could push up on her tiny hands and hold her head up. I talked about her increasing curiosity with the world and her decreasing hairline.

One day I told him about Harrison's visit to the daycare. A few days later, I received a certified letter from Jack's lawyers, a copy of the terms of the restraining order and the reminder they'd sent to Harrison and Meredith. It should have made me feel better.

It didn't.

That was it.

We never talked about the future, and we didn't really talk about us. He always asked me not to give up on us, but after everything that did—and didn't happen—since the day Jack returned to Bale-fire, our life together was more dream than reality.

After a month of looking at Jack's packed duffel bags and his guitar case, I'd had enough and shoved the whole works under my bed. Weirdly, though, I slept better with his things lying directly beneath me. Or maybe I slept better after I gave in to wearing one of his T-shirts to bed. Since I'd washed all his clothes, it didn't smell like him, but knowing it was his seemed to be enough to make me feel close to him anyway.

The semester flew by, and it was Thanksgiving again. Like déjà vu, I found myself riding with Stacy back to her parents' place in northwest Wyoming. So much had changed over the past year, and yet it seemed I hadn't moved forward at all.

On Thanksgiving morning, I overheard Stacy and Chase when they came downstairs to breakfast and didn't see me nursing Angel in the rocker in the living room.

"Doesn't matter to me that she has a kid. Clio is one hot woman. I can ask her out now that I'm in college too," Chase said.

"She's in a relationship with Angel's father, dumbass. I'm trying to spare you the embarrassment of being shot down."

"If she's in a relationship with Angel's father, how come she's spending Thanksgiving with us? Can't be too serious."

"Trust me, it is."

Stacy's words knifed through me and sent a stabbing pain through my stomach that left me gasping for breath. I'd done such a great job of pretending that my best friends honestly believed I had something with Jack. Truth was, I didn't even know what country he was in since I hadn't heard from him in over a week.

Trying to convince myself he was being considerate because of his crazy schedule and the differences in time zones had stopped working long ago. None of those things meant he couldn't shoot me a text once in a while at least. As though I'd conjured one, my phone pinged an incoming text. I finished nursing Angel and checked my messages as I rubbed her back over my shoulder.

We're playing the halftime show of the Dallas game. It would mean everything to me to know you're watching.

So, Balefire was back in the US. "How 'bout that, Angel baby? Your daddy is back in this country, and this is the first we've heard from him," I whispered. I was trying hard not to be bitter, but it had been so long, and I was tired of needing Jack and never being able to connect with him even when we did talk.

Apparently, my comment to my daughter alerted Stacy and Chase to my presence.

"Oh, hey, Clio. We didn't know you were up already," Stacy said, color staining her cheeks.

"Angel is a great kid. I didn't hear her make a peep all night, and my room is right next door to the guest room," Chase added.

"I think the drive yesterday wore her out. But I'm glad she didn't wake you this morning. She was kind of vocal about breakfast today." I smiled at my daughter.

"So, Clio, I was wondering—"

Stacy elbowed her brother. "Chase, we talked about this."

"Um, I overheard," I said.

"Well, then. What do you say, Clio? We can go out tomorrow night, see a movie or something. Stacy won't mind babysitting, will you Stace?" His enthusiasm made my next words difficult.

"I'm not sure where my relationship is with Angel's father, but until we figure it out, I'm not dating anyone else. Thanks for the compliment though, Chase."

Unfortunately, he didn't want to go down without a fight. "It's pretty obvious you don't have much of a relationship with Angel's dad since you're spending Thanksgiving with us again this year. How 'bout a sure thing? 'Cause I'm definitely interested."

Stacy smacked her brother's arm.

"Ouch! Why'd you do that?"

"Clio was trying to let you down easy, and you're making it awkward." She groaned. "Maybe you should tell him who Angel's dad is, Clio. He might get it then."

"What do you mean? Do I know the guy?" A perplexed look crossed Chase's face.

"Not personally, no." Turning to Stacy, I added, "No, I don't think I should tell Chase who Angel's dad is. Dealing with my own parents over him is enough without the additional possibility of the press if word gets out."

"Angel's dad is somebody famous?" Chase's eyes rounded. "Oh wow. No wonder you have a complicated relationship. Still, I'm right here, and your famous guy isn't, so what do you say?" The smile on his face was equal parts cocky and hopeful. If nothing else, he gave my ego a massive boost.

"Chase!" Stacy smacked him upside the head. "Have you no class at all? Who keeps trying to move in on someone who's in a relationship? Are we even related?"

"It's okay, Stacy," I soothed. "Chase, you're cute and all, but even though my situation with Angel's dad is complicated, I'm not interested in dating anyone else."

"Oh." Chase's shoulders slumped, and I felt like I'd kicked one of the Newhouse family's dogs. Then he rallied. "If your famous guy is stupid enough to walk away, you know where to find me."

"In the kitchen making my breakfast like a good little brother," Stacy said with a smirk.

Chase rolled his eyes before he grinned back at her and ambled off to the kitchen.

"You're so lucky, Stacy. I envy you your relationship with your brother. I wish I had a sibling to tease and love."

"You have the next best thing," she said. At my quizzical look, she was quick to clarify her comment. "A houseful of sisters who would do anything for you."

"You're right. I've been sitting here wallowing in self-pity about what I'm missing when I have so much to be thankful for. Beginning with Angel and my Chi Phi family and your parents who have so generously shared their holidays with me. Most especially, you. You're the best, Stace."

I hauled Angel and myself out of the rocker and gave Stacy a fierce one-armed hug. "Let's go supervise Chase. I'm sure after my cooking lessons, I can give him a few pointers." We were still giggling about that when we entered the kitchen.

♪

The usual Newhouse Thanksgiving ensued with an afternoon spent eating and watching football. As halftime of the Dallas game neared, my tension levels practically left me visibly vibrating. No one in the Newhouse residence knew about the halftime show or Jack's text, yet I felt exposed. Angel, the little traitor, had dropped into a food coma shortly after dinner, so I couldn't even play with her to distract myself.

When the announcer trumpeted Balefire's name over the airwaves, Chase almost injured himself as he raced to a chair after snagging some leftovers from the kitchen. From the corner of my eye, I caught Stacy's concern, but I ignored her, my full attention trained on the screen in front of me as the band launched into a shortened version of their current number one song.

The segue into the next song included Blu Connolly's running narration as he strutted from one end of the stage to the other. "We arrived home from Europe yesterday. Man, it's good to be back in the USA!" Applause nearly drowned out the instrumentation backing him, but like a magnet, Jack's rhythms drew me in, and I focused on finding him despite the camera's love affair with Blu. Blu continued,

"Happy Thanksgiving! Since we're so thankful for all y'all here in big D, we'd like to try out a new tune on you. What do you say?"

Again, the roar of the crowd in the sold-out stadium virtually obliterated the band's sound before Jack's rhythms changed, a driving beat that at first quieted the crowd before fomenting it into a frenzy. Tron joined him with some heavy bass riffs before Dakota and Blu jumped in together, Dakota with a blistering lead guitar arpeggio and Blu with a primal scream. The whole combination simultaneously raised the hairs on the back of my neck and forced my body to move to the beat.

Once the instrumentation had everyone on the edge of crazy, the music suddenly stopped. Then Blu began to sing:

I spend my days dreaming
You and me and our baby
Walking together, laughing together
Playing out our lives forever.

The instrumentation rejoined Blu's vocals with an intensity that haunted me while it mesmerized the live crowd.

But night falls
And I'm somewhere alone again
Living without you, lonely without you
Wondering what the f*ck I think I'm doing without you.

So far away.
Wish I weren't so
Far away.
And I want you more
And I need you more
Every day.

I spend my days dreaming

You and me and our baby
Walking together, laughing together
Playing out our lives forever.

Jack ratcheted up the drums, the tom-toms calling to me on a visceral level while the live crowd lost its collective mind.

Wake up!
I keep telling myself to
Wake up!
You need me now.
I need you now.
My dreams won't come true
Until I can dream them with you.

So far away.
Wish I weren't so
Far away.
And I want you more
And I need you more
Every day.

Once again, the instrumentation abruptly ended, leaving Blu to solo the last lines:

I dream you more
Every day.

The crashing drum solo leading to the bridge reverberated through me, and by the time Blu reached the second chorus, silent tears streamed down my face. When I finally came back to myself, the halftime concert was over, and Stacy sat beside me, lightly rubbing my back and looking concerned.

Chase interrupted the moment. "Why are you crying? Wait. Is Blu Connolly Angel's dad? He the famous guy who's complicating your life?"

"N-no." I sniffed. "But Angel's dad is in the band," I admitted before I gasped at the explosive slip I'd made. "Oh please, Chase. You can't tell anyone. Promise you won't tell anyone," I pleaded.

"I can't tell what I don't know. Since there are three other choices, I can only guess. And I guess you're not even going to hint at which one he might be," Chase said.

I smiled through my tears at his quick understanding. "Excuse me." With Stacy hot on my heels, I left the room, gathered up my coat and boots at the back door, and let myself outside. After Jack's public display on national television, I needed some air.

For the remainder of the weekend, the rest of the Newhouse family kept giving me speculative looks, which I studiously ignored. Stacy, my stalwart friend, didn't cave and reveal Angel's paternity to her brother or her parents, even though I overheard them pressuring her a couple of times when they forgot I might be around. Still, I didn't relax even after we returned to Colorado to finish up the last few weeks of the semester.

When Stacy suggested I join her and her family for Christmas, I politely declined.

Chapter Twenty

Clio

FINALS CONCLUDED THE week before Christmas. Even with all the distractions—fearing the press discovering Angel and me after my Thanksgiving slip at the Newhouses, Harrison's persistent attempts to reconnect with me, and Jack's continued absence as the band wound up the first leg of its US tour—I aced all my tests. Which left me feeling rather good about that part of my life.

Weirdly, Harrison and Meredith invited Angel and me to spend Christmas with them, an invitation that played serious head games with me. In the end, I did the only thing I could—I turned them down. Since Harrison extended the invitation in person, I watched what looked like genuine disappointment mar the smooth construction of his face before he recovered himself and wished me well. For days afterward, I couldn't decide if he'd meant it, or if I'd once again disappointed him when he'd planned on having me available to show off to his friends and colleagues—or to make it easy for some lawyer to steal Angel away from me.

When Harrison and Meredith sent a gift to Baby Barnes care of

Clio Barnes—by courier of course—I didn't even bother to check the origin of the expensive store from which it came before I declined to sign for it. They couldn't buy me through my daughter, and seeing what a personal shopper thought a seven-month-old couldn't live without didn't especially interest me.

A day after I turned away the gift, another courier arrived bearing a letter on Harrison's distinctive stationery. Anticipating a dressing-down for declining their invitation and their gift, I accepted the letter all the same. As Angel batted happily at her floor gym on the rug in front of the couch, I sat down and read.

> *Dear Clio,*
>
> *You are right to question us. As you have learned growing up in our home, there is usually a hidden agenda. I am putting this in writing so you have proof of our intentions.*
>
> *You surprised us, first by becoming pregnant without benefit of marriage or appropriate timing for a decent career and second by following through with the pregnancy and choosing to rear your child yourself.*
>
> *You showed us resiliency we should have seen in you earlier and did not. Your mother and I know now that there were mistakes made in your upbringing. You see, we had so many plans for our child that didn't conform to our reality. Instead of adjusting our plans, we tried to adjust our reality. Along the way, we made your happiness a casualty of our disappointed hopes. More damning, we tried to dictate the circumstances and even the person you would love. We should have understood the impossibility of success in this particular endeavor. In every way, you thwarted our intentions, and we punished you for it. Yet seeing your fierce love for your daughter made me realize what an amazing young woman your mother and I reared.*
>
> *We would like a chance to start over, come to know you and your*

daughter. To that end, we will no longer attempt to contact you in any way—courier, intermediary, lawyer, social media, or in person ourselves. Instead, we promise to wait for you to reach out to us if that is your decision. We sincerely hope you decide to give us a second chance.

We have not been very good at showing it, but your mother and I do love you.

Your father,

Harrison Barnes

Over the years, I'd received lavish presents from my parents—designer clothes, porcelain dolls, state-of-the-art electronics, a brand-new SUV—but never had they given me anything from their hearts. Until now. Tears flowed freely down my face, and I dashed them away with the heel of my hand as I tried to reread the letter. After I finally managed a second read, I placed it carefully on the coffee table and scooped Angel up into my arms, hugging her tightly to my chest.

"You're the best thing that's ever happened to me, baby girl. Maybe someday, you'll be the best thing to happen to your grandparents too," I whispered against her precious head as I kissed her.

As though she understood her mom completely, Angel lifted one chubby baby hand to my face, holding it against my cheek as she stared intently into my eyes. That one move proved her to be her father's daughter. Even though for the first time in my life my parents had noticed me, reached out to me, that one small touch from my daughter overshadowed the magnitude of my parents' overture. More than anything, in that moment I missed Jack.

♪

Now that I'd opted not to spend the holidays with the Newhouses, I looked forward to spending Christmas with my daughter without sharing her with anyone else. I wanted to make Angel's first Christmas special and to start our own traditions.

My limited budget meant I couldn't give her much in the way of material things, which suited me fine. Building my own tiny family meant I could break away from the emphasis on spending money on items whose real value lay only in showing them off to others. Instead of buying lavish gifts, I could concentrate on emphasizing the spirit of the season with her.

On Christmas Eve, I bundled her into the snowsuit my sorority sisters gave her for Christmas, loaded her into her car seat, and drove the two of us to church. I'd never been to church on Christmas Eve, but I remembered that Jack's family went to church, so I thought it might be nice to share that tradition with Angel.

As I pulled away from my parking space outside my apartment, I noticed a car roll in behind me. It followed me all the way to the church. But Harrison's letter said they'd wait for me to come to them. I shook off my suspicions. Probably, someone else in my apartment complex attended this church too.

Having seen church services as part of traditional holiday movies, I had an idea of what to expect. Of course, those experiences didn't prepare me for Jack's appearance at my side as I stood in the last pew holding Angel during the singing of the first carol. His gorgeous tenor voice carried as he effortlessly harmonized with the voices around us.

When she heard him, little traitor that she was, Angel turned her head to Jack and reached for him. Not wanting to make a scene in a congregation of total strangers, I gave her up without a fuss. The smile lighting up Jack's face at Angel's response to him alternately swelled and broke my heart . . .

As did seeing him in person again.

He'd let his hair grow, so now it brushed the collar of his leather jacket. Beneath his jacket, he wore a button-down shirt. The top two buttons of his shirt he'd left undone, exposing the thick column of his neck. His throat working as he sang mesmerized me. A few days growth of beard stubble couldn't hide his strong jaw, a jaw I longed to feather with kisses. When he caught me staring, his smile tore me in two.

Between his packed schedule and my preparation for final exams, we'd hardly spoken since the televised concert he'd asked me to watch on Thanksgiving. When we did have a few minutes on the phone together, the conversation centered on Angel, so I didn't trust that Jack and I were still even a thing. Yet here he was, standing beside me in church.

The service went by in a blur, and before I knew it, Jack had followed me outside. We didn't speak until we reached my car. With the weather cooperating for a regular white Christmas, I didn't waste time chatting while holding my baby in the crisp December air. After I seated her securely in her car seat, I closed the door and turned to Jack.

"How did you know we were here?"

"I was pulling up to your place when I saw you back out of your driveway. So I followed you. It was nice to spend Christmas Eve in a church for once. I can't remember the last time I could do that." A wistful smile crossed his face. "Hello, Clio."

"Hello, Jack."

For a few minutes, we stood in awkward silence, snow falling silently around us. At last I said, "I need to get Angel home where it's warm."

"I'll follow you."

"Why?"

He gifted me with a *duh!* expression. "So I can spend Christmas with my girls."

I sighed and said, "Fine," before I walked around to the driver's side and climbed into my car.

When we arrived back at my apartment, I carried Angel inside, not bothering to wait for Jack. Instead of flipping on the lights as usual, I walked in and set Angel on the rug in front of the Charlie Brown-style Christmas tree I'd decorated with one strand of lights and some Christmas balls I'd bought on clearance. Even though it wasn't much, when I plugged in the tree, the cheery twinkle of the multicolored lights bathed the room in soft light and revealed the few presents I had for my girl. Though I couldn't afford much, all the presents beside the tree were for her. At her age, she wouldn't care, but she would have the photos of her first Christmas when she was older.

As I removed my coat and tossed it on the couch, Jack walked in and stepped directly in front of the tree where he started unloading gifts from the Santa-sized bag he carried. I freed Angel from her snowsuit and pulled her onto my lap on the floor in front of the tree.

"Looks like your dad decided to spoil you, little one," I said.

Jack's presence still rattled me, but he had a right to spend time with his daughter.

"It's Christmas, Clio," he said drily.

Ignoring his comment, I asked, "Which one do you want to open first, Angel baby?"

In answer, she reached out for Jack, who sat down beside us on the floor.

Reluctantly, I passed her to him.

Grabbing a medium-sized package I'd wrapped in shiny paper, I extended it to her. "How 'bout we start with this one?" My voice sounded insincere and bright to my own ears, and Jack shot me a look over Angel's head, which I pointedly ignored.

The silver wrapping paper of the package I handed to Angel sparkled with the light reflected from the tree. She gazed at me curiously, so I started to tear the wrapping paper from the gift. In response, Angel slapped her tiny hands against the box, making sweet cooing baby noises. I helped her open my gift to her, a plush puppy she could easily wave around with her seven-month-old hands.

Jack snagged a present from his stash, a Balefire T-shirt in Angel's size.

On it went until we opened all the presents. A frilly velvet-and-lace Christmas dress from me. A baby-sized tom-tom and sticks from Jack. A soccer ball from me. A beautiful French doll from Jack. Wrappers and boxes littered the floor, and Angel started fussing for her bedtime feeding.

"Go ahead. I'll clean up here," Jack said.

Over the course of our gift-giving to our daughter, Jack and I had reached some sort of truce or understanding or comfort zone. We weren't where we'd been before that terrible morning when Harrison showed up at my door and blew my world to hell, but at least we could smile at each other. The photos would show Angel that her first Christmas had been fun.

"She go down okay?" he asked when I returned to my now tidy living room.

"All that excitement must have worn her out. She barely finished nursing before she fell asleep."

I crossed my arms over my chest, unsure of what to do now that we were alone.

"I found this when I was cleaning up." He handed me a box about the size of a bag of bagels.

"Angel can open it Christmas morning."

"Um, it doesn't have Angel's name on it."

My hand trembled when I took the box from him. Beneath the bow a sticker read, "To Clio, From Jack." I held the box in front of me. A barrier? A shield? I didn't know. I only knew Jack stood too close, stealing the air from my lungs with his sexy broad-shouldered, deep-chested nearness.

"Why?"

"Why what?" he asked, a smile in his eyes.

"Why did you buy me a present?"

"It's Christmas, Clio."

Like any of this was normal.

"But—"

"Maybe before you open this, I need to explain some things to you. If you're finally ready to listen that is."

I gripped the box, snagged a deep breath, and nodded. Whatever he had to say was going to hurt—a lot. Might as well rip the Band-Aid off cleanly. The slow peel of the last four months hadn't made the wounds he and Harrison had given me hurt any less.

He sat on the couch and patted the cushion beside him. "When we were in high school, I was one cocky sonuvabitch. If you'd asked me then, I'd 'a told you I had balls of solid brass."

Seating myself in the corner of the couch, I smiled a little at that. "There's a visual."

Jack grinned back.

"Yeah. Anyway, your dad—Harrison," he amended, "had that all figured out about me. What I didn't realize was that he also understood how naïve I was, how clueless. He seemed to give me an opportunity to have it all—a music career and a chance with you. All I had to do was agree not to date you until you graduated high school."

With a gasp, I sat up straight, anger coursing through me. "He bribed you not to date me?"

"He offered me a chance to join an up-and-coming band if I didn't come around to see you." He ran a hand through his hair. "Of course, I thought I could sidestep him. After all, there are other ways to date."

I raised my eyebrow in question, and he continued. "I figured we could hang in there for two years with phone calls, texts, Instagram. After all, I'd be on the road for most of that time, so seeing you in person was gonna be tough anyway."

In fascination, I watched as he balled his hands into fists in his lap.

"Harrison intended for us to be done, though. After I signed the contract, he casually pointed out the fine print where it spelled out the terms in terrible detail." The tortured expression in his gorgeous seafoam-green eyes made my stomach flop. "From the minute I crossed the *t* and dotted the *i* in Whitehorse, I could have no contact of any kind with you. I couldn't even talk to you one last time to explain."

"He made you erase me," I whispered.

Jack nodded. "That wasn't all. He threatened my dad's construction business. He was still threatening it that day he showed up here."

My hands flew to my mouth. "Oh my God, Jack. He wanted to take everything from you."

Jack's expression was bleak. "He succeeded. He took you."

By now we faced each other on the couch. Jack reached out and took my hand in his. Rubbing his calloused thumb across the smooth skin of the back of my hand, he continued. "For two long years, I toured with Rude Awakening even though I figured out in the first six months with them that the music took a backseat to the rock 'n' roll lifestyle. The day you graduated, I came back to Denver for the ceremony. I stood in the back of the auditorium and listened as my girl delivered a kick-ass valedictory speech."

I smiled at him. "You were there for my speech. Wow."

He squeezed my hand. "In your speech, you said, 'When people we love hurt us, we have to acknowledge the hurt, but we can never let those hurts make us bitter.' It felt like you were speaking directly to me, and more than anything, I had to see you, had to explain." He cleared his throat. "But your parents saw me before you did. They hustled you out of the graduation reception so fast, the Town Car you all rode in nearly laid rubber. It took me three more years to find you, to reconnect with you."

His explanations soothed some of the hurt, but not all of it. "Why didn't you come back, at least for an afternoon, before you went out on tour?" I swallowed down the lump trying to form in my throat. "You walked away that day Harrison shot my world to hell, and we haven't had a meaningful conversation since."

"This conversation couldn't take place on the phone. Clio, I've been touring and playing music almost nonstop for nearly five years. I didn't know how to work it out properly with you." He ran a hand through his hair. "And the band didn't give me an afternoon before we went out on tour."

I arched an eyebrow and remained silent.

"We've since had some conversations about that. After they all meet Angel and you, I think they'll finally get it."

I pulled a face, but Jack preempted what I was going to say.

"Babe, you deserve so much better than I've given you so far. I know that. The time away from you showed me how much I needed to step up. To grow up." He inched closer to me. "After Christmas, I'm moving you and Angel into the condo I leased for us, and I've already lined up a studio here in Fort Collins so the band can practice here while you're still in school. Plus, I had Tucker put it in my contract that I have at least two days alone with you and Angel before we go out on the road from now on." He pushed my knee down and caged me in with his thigh along mine, his arm over the couch behind me. "Unless you're going out on tour with us."

My eyes rounded.

"You're my world, Clio. I need you. After I was even more of a monk than usual on this last tour, the other guys in the band figured that out too. That song we played in Dallas on Thanksgiving? I wrote that for you." He stared deep into my eyes. "And I meant every word."

"You never gave up on us," I whispered in wonder, my voice barely audible as I spoke over the tears in my throat.

"Clio, I fell in love with you the first time I kissed you on the dance floor on our first date." He lifted my hand to his mouth and brushed a kiss over my knuckles. "I fell in love with you the second time when you appeared like a princess in the foyer of your parents' house when I picked you up for my senior prom." Slowly, he dragged one calloused finger down my arm. "I fell completely in love with you the third time when the magnitude of what I'd signed away with that contract hit me in Harrison's office." He pushed my hair behind my ear and cupped my face.

"The fourth time I fell in love with you was when I saw you staring at me from the front row of the amphitheater at Red Rocks the night we made Angel." His voice caught for a moment even as a smile ghosted over his lips. "The fifth time I fell in love with you was when you gifted me with your virginity. You were waiting for me all that time, weren't you?"

The cockiness of his tone should have irritated me, but all I could hear was how much he loved me. Which meant I could only nod the truth when he asked.

Pulling me closer to him, he continued. "The sixth time I fell in love with you was the day you introduced me to our baby." He slipped his hand beneath my hair to hold the back of my neck. "The seventh time I fell in love with you was the first time I watched you nurse Angel." My nipples tightened when his eyes flicked to my chest before they caught mine again. "The eighth time I fell in love with you was when we made love again here in your apartment." His other hand smoothed down my thigh. "The ninth time I fell in love with you was when you took our daughter to church tonight for Christmas Eve."

All the while Jack spoke, he slowly weaved his spell over me. His big hand on the back of my neck dropped behind me, snuggling me next to him until our faces were so close I had nowhere to look but deep into his beautiful eyes. "What I've discovered over the last five years is that I'm never going to stop falling in love with you, Clio. No matter who tries to stop me, no matter how great the distances between us, no matter how long I have to be apart from you, there is no obstacle big enough to keep me from loving you."

He cupped my cheek in the way that always got to me, holding me still as he lowered his lips to mine. The kiss was slow, tender, and so thorough that when he finally ended it, I gasped for air as a torrent of silent tears cascaded down my face.

"You're everything to me Clio." He sucked in a breath. "I was afraid of how much I'd hurt you to trust you enough to tell you everything when I should have. I'm sorry for that, but I've learned my lesson."

"You're the only person who's ever seen me, made me feel like I mattered. I should have trusted that, trusted you. I'm sorry too, Jack."

With his thumbs, he gently brushed the tears from my face before he leaned in and kissed me again. This kiss, however, was hungry, his tongue sliding inside my mouth to demand a dance with mine, claiming me, ratcheting up my desire for him to stratospheric levels in the space of an inhale. The hand on my face slipped down to my neck, sending shivers through me before it dropped lower to cup my breast, driving me from zero to sixty in one heartbeat.

Passion drove me as I climbed onto his lap, straddling him while I removed my sweater and bra. After all this time apart, my need, my only want was to feel his body pressed to mine, to show him with my whole self how much I trusted him. How much I loved him.

Our kisses grew frantic, and after a few brief minutes, Jack unbuttoned his shirt and shrugged out of it. Rubbing my naked breasts against his naked chest, I reveled in the friction that hardened my aching nipples into hypersensitive peaks. He groaned into my neck where he licked and kissed me in the perfect way only he could do, making me squirm against him, struggling for more.

His hands were at the fly of my jeans, and I slid off his lap to help him remove them. In short order, his jeans joined mine on the floor beside the couch. Before I knew it, I was on my back with Jack on top of me, his erection hard against my pubic bone. Reaching down beside the couch, he rummaged in his jeans to retrieve a condom.

"Looks like someone is still cocky," I teased.

"Hopeful, babe. Hopeful."

"I hope you arrived here really hopeful," I said as I lifted my hips and bumped my body into his before I opened my legs, letting my slickness show him exactly what I meant.

"I got a whole box of hopeful in my duffel bag," Jack said, a smile dancing in his eyes as he sheathed his cock. "But I need you to pay attention to right now."

He took his cock in his hand and guided himself into my wet waiting heat. As I lifted my hips to meet him, we stared deep into each other's eyes at the incredible sensation of Jack's shaft sliding home inside me.

He rode me hard and fast that first time we were back together, neither of us able to deny our need for each other. I clenched my pussy tightly around him, my body bowing up into his as a shower of green stars burst behind my closed eyelids. Jack pumped into me two more times after I started to come, and with a shout he joined me, our bodies seeming to melt into one.

When the first storm of our lovemaking passed, Jack rolled over between the back of the couch and me, spooning me close, my back to his front. He pushed up onto one elbow, supporting his head in the palm of his hand as he smoothed his other hand over my skin. After a few minutes in the afterglow, he said, "I think now is good time for you to open your present, Clio."

Turning my head, I glanced up to find him smiling at me. After I grabbed the present from where it had fallen to the floor, I rolled onto my back to open it. Giving it a little shake, I noticed how light the box was for its size, and I couldn't imagine what it might contain. Shaking it gave nothing away, so I tore off the fancy red and green wrapping paper and opened one end of the box to discover layers of tissue paper. When I tugged on the paper, a small velvet box came out with it. My heart thundered in my chest as I stared at the box then at Jack's face.

Looking more serious than I'd ever seen him, he reached out and took the velvet box from me, opening it to reveal a perfect solitaire diamond in a thick platinum band.

"Clio, I knew you were the one after our first date. It's been a long hard road for us, but we're finally here together. I love you. Please say you'll be mine for the rest of our lives."

Cupping his handsome face in my hands, I said, "I've been yours since you first noticed me. I love you." I tilted my face to his and kissed him, a lingering joining of lips, tongues, breath.

Finally, he pulled away long enough to lift the ring from the box and slide it over my finger before he laced his fingers through mine and pulled our hands to our hearts. We smiled into each other's eyes and breathed each other in.

"From now on, we're a team, Clio. A family."

My heart felt like it might swell out of my chest. "The best family."

I glanced down at his erection pushed into the space between us.

"Definitely hopeful," I said, laughing.

"You have no idea, but you're about to find out," he said with a grin.

He let go of my hand to feather his fingers up my rib cage, lightly tickling me and making me arch into him. We were both laughing when he wrapped his arm around me and hauled me up on top of him. "Your turn to lead this time."

"So that's how the game is going to be played," I deadpanned.

He nodded sagely, a dare I couldn't resist. Without giving him a warning, I pushed up and back on my knees to straddle his legs before I dropped down to take his length in my mouth as much as I could handle. Jack cried out and buried his hands in my hair as I hollowed my cheeks and pulled slowly on his cock until I reached the head, where I lavished all the attention of my lips and tongue, kissing and licking and sucking. I savored the smooth texture of his shaft and the kissable resilience of the head. Bobbing my head to my own rhythm, I worked his length, licking my way down, hollowing my cheeks on my way slowly back up before sliding up and down fast until I could feel the barely leashed tension in his legs beneath my own and in his abs beneath my hand.

"Clio," he gritted through clenched teeth, "I'm really close. Jesus, babe."

That was all the encouragement I needed. Massaging his balls with one hand and jacking the base of his cock with the other, I licked and sucked and kissed and sucked as much of his cock as I could take in my mouth until his body stiffened beneath me, his cries of ecstasy filling my apartment as his come filled my mouth.

I swallowed him down then let him go and pitched forward to rest my cheek on his taut stomach. Idly, he ran his hands through my hair, his breath sawing in and out of his lungs while I discerned his taste. Salty, kind of primal like the sea, like nothing I'd ever tasted. Jack tasted delicious.

When he had himself under control enough to speak, he said, "You never did that even once when we were together last summer. Why now?"

"Because you dared me to."

"I did? Please tell me how I dared you so I can dare you again," he said with a chuckle before he sobered up. "Seriously, Clio. That was amazing. Incredible." He cleared his throat. "Maybe I don't want to know the answer to this question, but I'm going to ask it anyway."

"How did I know how to give you a blow job?"

"Yeah. Especially one as fucking awesome as that one."

I grinned impishly up at him. "I lived in a sorority for over two years. Women talk."

"About giving blow jobs?" Jack's voice rose on the question until he nearly squeaked.

His comical response cracked me up. "Some of them even gave demonstrations. I learned so much living there." I peeked up at him from beneath my lashes, gifting him a saucy grin.

"Your sorority friends are something else, I'll give you that. I think I'm really glad you lived there for a while." He smirked. "Come here."

He tugged on my upper arms and pulled me up his body to lie on top of him. I rested my cheek on his chest, my hands on his shoulders as he ran his hands up and down my back and over my ass like he wanted to create a tactile memory of my body in his hands.

As we lay there in the quiet, I gazed at the twinkling lights of my miniature Christmas tree and knew I'd experienced the best Christmas of my life. Jack must have been reading my mind as much as he read my body because he said, "When I flew out of Atlanta after the concert last night, I worried I wouldn't make it home for Christmas. Now that I'm here, I can't remember any Christmas in my life as good as this one."

The soft rumble of his voice in his chest beneath my cheek made me want to snuggle in even tighter to him. I was so focused on the sensations that I almost missed what he said next. "It's going to be even better tomorrow when I introduce you to my family. My mom is going to freak. I can hardly wait to see that."

Jerking my head from his chest, I stared in shock at the playful smile on his handsome face.

"What did you say?"

"I can't wait to see my mom's face when she meets you and Angel. You two are going to be the best Christmas presents in my parents' house tomorrow morning." His grin grew even wider. "I'm going to be the favorite son for the whole fucking day. It's going to be awesome."

"W-we're going to your parents' house for Christmas?" I stammered. Quite honestly, the idea of meeting his family scared the hell out of me and stole away some of the lovely afterglow of the amazing sex we'd shared.

"We're a family, now, Clio. The way I was raised, that means we spend time with the rest of the family on holidays. Unless you had plans with someone else?"

He looked at me strangely, like the idea had just occurred to him.

"No, no plans," I said. "Although, Angel and I were invited to Harrison and Meredith's for the day," I added offhandedly.

"*What?*" Jack sat up, rolling me up with him to sit across his lap. "Tell me about this," he demanded. "They haven't tried to take Angel again, have they?"

"No. They've backed off from the threats. But I turned them down for Christmas and returned the gift they sent Angel without opening it. A few days later, I received a letter from Harrison." His raised brow told me what he thought about that, so I hurried on. "I'll let you read it. We haven't fixed anything, but they've opened a door to working on our relationship."

"How do you feel about that?" Jack asked in a careful tone.

"I'm thinking about it."

"You have no plans for Christmas Day?"

"I had this idea of creating my own traditions with Angel."

He slanted me a look.

"But that was before you showed up beside us in church tonight and followed us home afterward. Jack, what if . . ." I swallowed. The idea of his family scared the hell out of me. "What if your family doesn't like me as much as you think they will?"

Hugging me close to him, he whispered against my skin, "Clio, they're going to fucking love you. Maybe not as much as I do. I don't think anyone can love you as much as I do. But they're going to love you. Especially since you come as a package deal with Angel."

"I hope you're right."

"Oh, I'm so right. In every way."

His laughter rippled over the skin on my neck before he started nibbling there. In short order, his hands were all over me, his mouth on my neck creating lovely sensations that shot straight to my core.

"You've been saving up, I think," I managed to say as his cock hardened beneath my ass.

"Did I mention I brought a whole box of condoms with me? I have a plan for every single one of them."

He waggled his eyebrows at me when I looked at him in mock horror. "Tonight? You plan to go through a whole box tonight?"

"Depends on your stamina," he said, trying to keep a straight face.

Abruptly, he lifted me off his lap, stood up, and scooped me up high in his arms. As he carried me toward the bedroom, I shrieked in surprise and delight.

"Shhh! You're going to wake the baby, Clio," Jack teasingly admonished me.

I answered with a giggle. In my bedroom, he laid me out on the bed and climbed on top of me. We didn't use the entire box of condoms on Christmas Eve, but we definitely tested each other's stamina. Neither of us wanted to open our eyes when Angel woke us on Christmas morning.

EPILOGUE

Jack

I N GREEK MYTHOLOGY, Clio is the muse of music. My Clio was the muse of my life. Marrying her, making her mine, was the only option.

I would have settled for a fifteen-minute ceremony at the court-house the day after Christmas, but Clio wanted to have a proper wedding. That's how I found myself dressed in a tux, holding Angel in my arms while standing beside my older brother Colin and my Balefire bandmates in front of our family and friends one June after-noon. Standing in my parents' backyard, I admit, I couldn't wait for Clio to emerge from their house.

We decided to get married after Clio finished her nursing degree. As a present to my mother, she asked Mom to host our wedding. Though she'd made a tenuous reconciliation with her own parents, Clio wanted our big day to take place in "a real family home" as she described my parents' place.

In a concession to her parents' sensibilities, we hired a string quartet to play the prewedding and the wedding ceremony music. It was going to be fun to see her parents' reaction to the special song the guys insisted on including in the ceremony before I slipped Clio's wedding band on her finger. The justice of the peace knew about it, but it didn't make it into the wedding rehearsal. The thought of Harrison and Meredith Barnes's reaction to our rock band antics put a smirk on my face.

Catching my smile, Angel leaned across my chest to stick her little mug right in my face, a new habit she'd developed. Placing her chubby baby hands on both of my cheeks, she stared solemnly into my eyes before tipping forward to give me a big open-mouthed baby kiss on the lips.

"Hey, Angel baby, I love you too. Now let's watch for Mommy," I whispered to her.

The music changed from the classical strings of Vivaldi to Pachelbel's *Canon*, and I held my breath for my bride. She stepped through the back door and locked eyes with me. If the world caught fire in that moment, I wouldn't have noticed. In her tight strapless lace dress, Clio stole all my thoughts as she walked slowly and purposefully to me. The smile on her face eclipsed the summer sun. I'd never seen anything more beautiful in my life than my gorgeous bride walking toward me on her way to becoming my wife.

When she reached me, she whispered, "I love you, Jack, so much."

Angel let out a squeal, making the assembled crowd laugh before Clio took her from me. She gave our baby a kiss before handing her off to my mom, who sniffed back her tears as she smiled at us before she carried Angel back to the front row of chairs to sit with her and Dad and my four younger brothers.

Clio smiled at me as she slipped her hand in mine, and together, we faced the JP, who began the ceremony. When the time came for her to slide the wide platinum band on my finger, I knew I'd never felt anything so right as that physical symbol tying me to her forever. Maybe I should have been manlier, but I didn't care as my voice thickened over my vows when I added the diamond-studded band to the giant solitaire I'd already placed on her finger. That was the cue for my bandmates to grab their axes from where they'd discreetly placed them behind the JP. They launched into a raucous acoustic version of "Far Away" that had all our guests on their feet and cheering as Clio laughed with me, her eyes shining with love.

Of course, I couldn't let the ceremony end and our life together officially begin without some of my own theatrics. I play drums in a rock band after all. At the JP's invitation to kiss my bride, I pulled Clio close and dipped her as I fused my lips to hers and slid my tongue in her mouth.

What started as a very public claiming on my part, Clio changed into something far more intimate as she wrapped her arms around my neck and tangled her tongue with mine, kissing me back fiercely before she changed the angle of her mouth into something seductive and wild. A long time later from a far distant place, I heard the applause of our guests and at last tipped her back up onto her feet. She smiled at me with a flushed face and mischief in her eyes before we turned to greet our cheering audience. No stadium full of crazy loyal fans could compare to the heartfelt response of our family and friends to our marriage. That moment began the real rock 'n' roll party that would be our life together. Greatest tour I've ever been on. And the best part? It was never going to end.

Play For Me playlist:

"Love Isn't Always Fair"—Black Veil Brides

"Untraveled Road"—Thousand Foot Krutch

"Save Today"—Seether

"If You Only Knew"—Shinedown

"Don't Wake Me"—Skillet

"It's Not Over"—Daughtry

"Here Without You"—3 Doors Down

"Turn the Page"—Metallica

"Torn to Pieces"—Pop Evil

"Every Time You Leave"—I Prevail (feat. Delaney Jane)

"Second Chance"—Shinedown

"Happens All the Time"—Cold

Thank you for reading *Play For Me*.

Turn the page for an excerpt from *Sing For Me*, Book Two in the Balefire Series coming in August 2021.

CHAPTER ONE

One year ago
Blu

ITH A TALL pretty blonde tucked under my left arm and a gorgeous bronze-skinned brunette under my right, my fingers loosely holding the neck of a bottle of beer, I surveyed the action. Music pounded a decibel-ripping beat. A rainbow of lights pulsed across the ceiling and along the walls of the ballroom. Raucous laughter punctuated loud conversation. Buffet tables groaning beneath a feast of regional food lined one wall while bars flowing alcohol lined two others. People gyrated on the dance floor in the middle of the room, and something resembling a mosh pit writhed in front of the dais where a local band thumped furiously to impress the crowd. Oh yeah, this after-party was ending the Australian leg of our tour in epic style.

Spotting the monk, I carried my half-empty bottle of Australia's finest beer with me while I walked the girls over to where he sat in front of one of the bars.

"Hey Jack. Look what I've got." I grinned. "You know I like to party with multiple ladies at once, but I'm up for sharing if you're interested. Blond or brunette, which do you prefer?"

Jack Whitehorse, Balefire's drummer, saluted me with his beer, took a pull, and said, "Wouldn't want to horn in on your fun, Blu my man. You enjoy yourself." He smirked at me before turning his attention to the ladies in my arms. "I have no doubt you two beauties will enjoy yourselves."

He took another swig of beer and gave me a pointed look to shove off. I stared back at him for a long moment, daring him with a smirk to do something.

Jack joined Balefire a couple of years back when our old drummer decided he couldn't stay sober and tour with us. Though it drove our lead guitarist Dakota Perri nuts, Jack preferred to keep to himself, and not once had I ever seen him wander off with a woman while we were on tour. One time, Jack overheard Dakota and me talking about his preferences, and he burst out laughing, so I guess he likes girls after all. You wouldn't know one way or the other from his behavior.

I leaned in and spoke directly into his ear. "It's the last night of our Asian tour, Jackie-boy. You haven't indulged in any of the first-class exotic pussy on offer anywhere we've been. You're worrying me, man."

Jack pulled a face and sat back. "We discussed this on the jet, Blu. I've got someone special waiting for me back home." Addressing the girls, he added, "Thanks for the offer."

Dakota and Adam Tron, our bassist, said Jack hooked up with a hottie last summer after we played a show back home at Red Rocks, but I think they might have been jerking my chain. From where I stood, Jack had earned his nickname "the monk."

When I'd offered him one of the girls with me, I already knew his answer. The standing joke between us involved me offering whatever candy I scored during or after a show and Jack politely declining. Dakota liked to steal his phone and program it with a wake-up call featuring a prerecorded come-on from whichever girl he took to his room after a show. The joke had worn pretty thin with Jack these days. The two of them had almost come to blows over it more than once, so I might have been walking on thin ice making my offer tonight.

Still, with it being our last night on tour for a while and all, I thought Jack could use a good time. The two pretty sheilas I had my arms around could be exactly what he needed to pull him out of the dark mood he'd crawled into since last fall. Couldn't say his refusal surprised me though.

I poked the bear anyway. "If you change your mind, buddy, here's the spare key card to my room." I let go of blondie long enough to fish the card from my back pocket and hand it to him. "Don't bother to knock. Just let yourself in. We'll welcome you right into the party, won't we girls?"

"Sure, Blu. Anything you say."

"Whatever you want, Blu. We just want to be with you tonight."

Jack laughed and took the card. "Ain't gonna happen. But thanks again for the offer. You all have a nice time."

"I'm sure we will."

I noticed he pocketed the card before taking another pull off his beer. Interesting.

Dakota and I often shared girls when we were on tour. Sex, drugs—in our case booze—and rock 'n' roll were big draws when we started Balefire back in high school. Tron had never been into sharing women, and apparently, Jack favored Tron in that department. Unlike Jack though, Tron did entertain his fair share of the ladies whenever we hit the road on tour.

After ten years together, Dakota, Tron, and I remained best friends and committed to the life. Changing drummers three years ago, though, amped up the music, and none of us could deny how much our new drummer improved our sound. Not only was Jack Whitehorse a virtuoso drummer, he was also a damned fine song-writer. On this tour alone we'd written like ten or twenty new songs.

As much as I enjoyed touring, I couldn't wait to go home, relax my vocal cords a bit, and hit the studio to record our new material.

The giggling of the girls pasted to my sides brought me out of my reverie, and I smiled at each of them in turn. "Looks like you're going to have me to yourselves tonight, ladies. You do know how to share, don't you?"

More giggling answered my question.

I walked the girls down the bar and signaled the bartender. "Hey buddy. Snag me a couple of bottles of champagne, would ya? And three glasses."

Speaking to each girl in turn, I asked, "Champagne all right with you?"

"We love champagne," brunette said.

"Whatever you want, Blu," blondie added.

Something about the girls' unconditional willingness to do whatever I suggested irritated the back of my conscience, but I finished off my beer, set the empty on the bar, and pushed the nebulous thought from my mind before it crystallized into something I had to deal with. I grabbed the bottles of champagne the bartender set in front of us and gestured to the girls to snag the champagne flutes before I escorted them from the after-party to a different kind of party up in my suite.

Ashleigh

"I swear I have never seen a young person who loved her flowers as much as you do, Ashleigh Baker," Diane Connolly commented from her side of the fence separating our yards. "You're renting your place, aren't you, darlin'?"

I leaned back on my heels from my hands-and-knees position in front of the roses I was planting. "Diane, I moved into this place because my landlady said she'd subtract some rent if I indulged my hobby. Win-win." I grinned.

The last Saturday in May found me in my favorite place—my backyard garden. My part-time job as a substitute teacher surprisingly limited the time I had to spend in my garden since finding my rental earlier in the spring. I wanted to complete my long list of tasks while I still had the time. Plus, the weather in Denver cooperated so beautifully with my gardening plans that nothing could have kept me indoors.

"Are you at a point in your planting that you could take a break and join me on my patio for lunch?"

"Is it lunchtime?"

A quick glance at the sun high overhead and a rather embarrassing rumble from my stomach confirmed I'd lost myself in my yard again.

Diane laughed. "Why don't you ditch your gardening gloves and come over for a bite to eat? I made chicken and avocado sandwiches and a lovely fruit salad with strawberries and feta cheese. And I have a gallon of fresh-brewed sun tea to wash it all down. It's on my table waiting for us."

I stood and brushed dirt and mulch off my bare knees. "You're absolutely the nicest neighbor anyone could ever have. Let me go inside and wash my hands, and I'll be right over."

"See you in a few," she said with a smile.

After living in a tiny apartment for years while I finished college, I'd become claustrophobic. All the noise and lack of privacy and space wore on me, something I mentioned one day at one of the schools where I worked. One thing led to another, and a teacher friend suggested I check out a sweet little house she'd heard had come up for rent. Something with a yard. Next thing I knew, I was living next door to Diane Connolly.

Yes, *that* Diane Connolly, mother of Blu Connolly, lead singer of my all-time favorite band Balefire. I'd skipped lattes for a month to save money for a ticket to their show at Red Rocks last summer. It was worth every penny I'd paid and more. I'd fallen half in love with Blu Connolly merely listening to his voice on the Balefire station on my music streaming app. Seeing him perform in person with all that raw energy radiating excitement and fun and sex—did I mention the guy's moves as he projected his stadium-sized voice to the world?—completely blew my mind.

Almost as much as discovering I'd moved next door to his childhood home, the home where his mom still lived. The amazing part? Diane turned out to be the most normal, down-to-earth, open, and sweet person I'd ever met. She also seemed lonely. Ever since I'd moved in, whenever she invited me to lunch most Saturdays or the occasional Sunday, I accepted.

Ancient elm and willow trees shaded her backyard and patio, a welcome respite from the blazing sun I'd worked under all morning. I seated myself at her table and downed a cooling swallow of iced tea.

"This looks delicious. You must have spent the whole morning cooking, Diane," I gushed as I surveyed the feast in front of me—a feast she served on fine china with cloth napkins and fancy silver flatware. The woman knew how to entertain, even if the only person I knew she entertained was me. It seemed no one else ever came to her door.

"It's nothing, really," she demurred. "I saw this recipe for California chicken sandwiches on one of the cooking shows I enjoy and thought I'd give it a try. Go on, dig in."

With her avidly watching me, obviously eager for my response to her offering, I cut my sandwich in half and took a bite. Closing my eyes, I groaned in pure ecstasy as a symphony of flavors reverberated over my palate. Smooth, rich avocado, spicy chicken, something sweet yet tangy—the dressing maybe?—and the full-bodied flavor of sun-ripened tomatoes flowed over my taste buds, all bookended with warm buttery homemade bread.

Opening my eyes, I said, "Diane, are you married? 'Cause if you're not, I might ask you to marry me." I savored another bite.

"I've never had the pleasure of enjoying a gourmet sandwich before, but I think I could get used to it if given the chance."

At the mention of marriage, a cloud briefly passed over her face before she banished it with a smile. "I'm so glad you like it. Honestly, I wasn't sure about the dressing. It's sometimes a challenge deciding whether certain flavors will work together, like Dijon mustard, fennel, and poppy seed."

"Ah. That's the secret dressing." I grinned and took another bite of sandwich heaven.

"There are one or two additional ingredients, but putting those three together worried me a little. I'm so glad you like it." At last, she cut into her sandwich and took a delicate bite.

"Like it? It's borderline orgasmic." I licked sauce from the corner of my mouth before being polite and using my napkin. After watching Diane with her sandwich, I tried for a more ladylike bite. "I need to eat this slowly, savor it, but it's so good, I'm not sure I'm disciplined enough to slow down."

She beamed and took another dainty bite of her sandwich.

For a few minutes, we ate quietly, enjoying the food and the lovely early summer day.

Diane broke the silence. "What are your plans when school finishes this week? Do you have a summer job lined up?"

"I've been hitting the local bars on the weekends to listen to the bands playing them and writing reviews for a couple of online newspapers and a blog. The writing doesn't pay much, but it keeps my name and, more importantly, my work in front of editors." Setting my sandwich down, I sipped some tea and continued. "I'm hoping someone at one of those venues will give me the chance to write for them full-time. After all, that's what I went to college for."

"Well, I've read some of your reviews in the local paper, and I think you're a very talented writer. As you can probably guess, I enjoy my son's music, but one of your reviews of some bluegrass band had me tapping my feet as I read it and thinking I might catch that band the next time they're in the area."

"You're sweet to say that. Thanks."

"Speaking of bands, Blu's Asian tour wrapped up yesterday. I expect him home early next week. If you don't have any plans, I'd like to have you over for a meal, introduce you to my son."

She extended the invitation so casually, so matter-of-factly. Like she didn't have a clue about her son's fame. Of course she had no clue about my private love affair with his incredible voice. Good thing we were eating alfresco since I splattered the sip of tea I'd taken all over her patio.

"Ashleigh! Are you all right?"

I choked and coughed for another minute before trying ineffectually to wipe up tea from the patio's flagstones.

"Fine, Diane. Really." I cleared my throat. "Sorry about that." My face felt like it was trying to mimic the color of the tomatoes on my sandwich.

She laughed so hard that tears ran down her pretty face. The woman damn sure didn't look old enough to have a son who was nearing thirty. Her good humor at my expense was infectious, and before long I found myself laughing with her.

"If you could have seen your face when I told you Blu will be in town next week," she gasped.

I sobered up at last. "You do realize that normal people don't just drop that sort of information into a casual conversation, right?"

"He's my son, Ashleigh. I brought him into the world and changed his diapers and listened to his teachers love his charm and despair of his wildness. That was something I despaired of even more than they did. Forgive me for forgetting for a minute how famous he is."

The visual of Diane changing Blu Connolly's diapers momentarily sidetracked me as I tried to get a handle on it. "I guess I have a hard time thinking about the guy I saw strutting all over the stage at Red Rocks last summer as someone's little boy. Especially *your* little boy."

At the look she shot me, I hastily added, "Only because he has a reputation as a wild man and you're so sweet and normal. You live in a modest house on a quiet street in the suburbs of Denver. You don't drive a fancy car or flaunt a lot of money." She cocked a brow, and I rushed on. "Plus, with your trim figure and smooth skin and that thick blond braid you favor, you look more like Blu's older sister than his mom. How old were you when you had him? Seven?"

"You're a sweetheart, Ashleigh," Diane said, and there was genuine warmth in her voice. "I can't wait for you to meet my son. I think you two are going to hit it off so well."

ACKNOWLEDGEMENTS

It takes a team to bring a book to readers. Thanks to Angela Forester for reading an early, early draft of this book, giving me valuable constructive criticism, and encouraging me to finish it. Thanks to Bri Weigel who's been there for every book both in the Talisman Series and now in the Balefire Series. Your beta reads and comments help me produce better stories. Special thanks goes to my hubs, Grady Jackson, who read an early draft of this one and told me all the things I did right and gave me specific examples of what and where I could improve. The book is better for you having read it, babe.

To my critique group—LindaRae Sande, K.J. Gillenwater, Sara Vinduska, and Jacque Coburn—thanks for catching things I miss. And thanks a ton for our bi-monthly dinners where you educate me on all things book marketing and production. Having you as friends and colleagues has helped me grow exponentially.

As always, thank you, thank you, thank you to my team—my editor Nikki Busch who keeps me on schedule and polishes my words to a fine shine; my cover designer Maria at Steamy Designs who creates such gorgeous covers for my words; Chrissy at Damonza for the interior designs that make my words look so pretty; and

Levi Meyer at *www.wyosites.com* for building and maintaining my beautiful website. You make me look good, and I truly appreciate it.

Most importantly, thank you, readers, for giving this book a read. You are the reason I write. Your opinions matter, and indie authors need your reviews. If you found this story entertaining, please leave a review at your favorite bookseller or on your favorite review site. Thanks so much!

Follow me at *www.tamderudderjackson.com* and on Instagram @tamstales32, on BookBub, and on Facebook at Tam DeRudder Jackson.

ABOUT THE AUTHOR

Tam DeRudder Jackson is the author of the paranormal romance Talisman Series and the contemporary romance Balefire Series. Her favorite "room" in her house is her back patio where she dreams up stories of romance and risk. When she's not writing her latest paranormal or contemporary romance, depending on the season you can find her driving with the top down in her convertible or carving turns on the slopes of the local ski hill. The mom of two grown sons, Tam likes to travel, attend rock concerts, watch football and soccer, and visit old car shows with her husband. She lives in the mountains of northwest Wyoming where she spends most of her free time trying to read all the books. Her TBR piles are threatening to take over her office, and she's fine with that.